To: Barbara!

Dan

Evanston
8/1/2004

*Other Books in The Vintage Library
of Contemporary World Literature*

THE QUESTIONNAIRE

THE QUESTIONNAIRE

or prayer for
a town & a friend

JIŘÍ GRUŠA

Translated from the Czech
by Peter Kussi

AVENTURA

The Vintage Library of Contemporary World Literature

VINTAGE BOOKS   A DIVISION OF RANDOM HOUSE   NEW YORK

First Aventura Books Edition, September 1983
English translation copyright © 1982 by Farrar, Straus and Giroux, Inc.
All rights reserved under International and Pan-American
Copyright Conventions. Published in the United States by
Random House, Inc., New York, and simultaneously in
Canada by Random House of Canada Limited, Toronto.
Originally published in Czech under the title *Dotazník aneb
modlitba zd jedno mesto a prítele* by Sixty-Eight Publishers
Corp. in August 1978. Published in the United States by
Farrar Straus and Giroux, Inc. in 1982.
Library of Congress Cataloging in Publication Data
Gruša, Jiří.
The questionnaire, or Prayer for a town & a friend.
Translation of: Dotazník.
I. Title.
II. Title: Prayer for town & a friend.
PG5039117.R87D613 1983   891.8′635   83-6849
ISBN 0-394-72212-4
Manufactured in the United States of America

CONTENTS

Those who love know how to forgive others.

PLUTARCH

SULTAN: *But I ask you whence you come
and whither you are going. I address you
in Turkish.*
JESTER: *And I will answer in plain Czech.
Where do I come from? From behind me.
Where am I going? Straight ahead.*

MATĚJ KOPECKÝ
(celebrated Czech puppeteer)

ZNAK MĚSTA
CHLUMCE

UMEC ·

LEGEND:
1 Moran   12 Soccer Field
2 Church of St. Barb.   13 Railroad Station
3 Cepin   14 Meetinghouse
4 Pleasure Park   15 Svetlice (Light-Crest)
5 Deanery   16 High School
6 Town Hall   17 Cepin Station
7 Monastery   18 Brewery
8 Gate   19 Ceremonial Hall
9 Yard   20 Old Execution Gr.
10 Cemetery   21 Newer Execution Gr.
11 Chocolate Factory   22 Rabbit Hutch

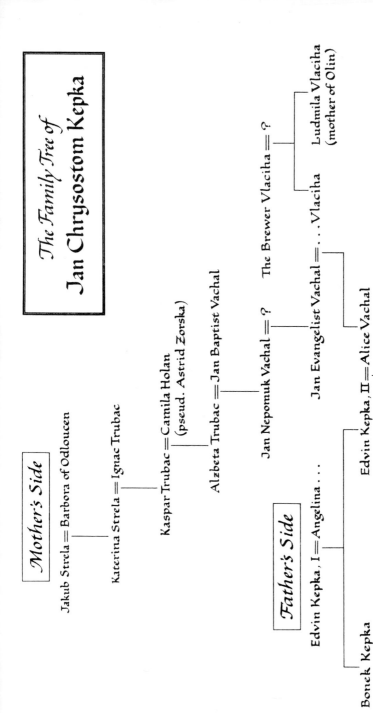

The Family Tree of Jan Chrysostom Kepka

Mother's Side

Jakub Strela = Barbora of Odloucen

Katerina Strela = Ignac Trubac

Kaspar Trubac = Camila Holan
(pseud. Astrid Zorska)

Alzbeta Trubac = Jan Baptist Vachal

Jan Nepomuk Vachal = ?   The Brewer Vlaciha = ?

Jan Evangelist Vachal = . . . Vlaciha   Ludmila Vlaciha
(mother of Olin)

Father's Side

Edvin Kepka, I = Angelina . . .

Edvin Kepka, II = Alice Vachal

Bonek Kepka

Jan Chrysostom Kepka

THE QUESTIONNAIRE

1. GRANIT 01

On September 19, 197—, in the city of Prague (i.e., right here, not in the town of Chlumec), I visited the enterprise GRANIT, the sixteenth organization I had contacted over the past two years, and I received my sixteenth *Questionnaire* (in room 102, second floor), from the hand of Comr. Pavlenda (Comr. = Comrade; i.e., friend, mate, companion, fellow member of a Communist society).

In contrast to those previous questionnaires, this one was marked in the upper-right-hand corner, in blue pencil, most probably by Comr. Pavlenda himself: DO NOT CROSS OUT!—an exhortation I considered highly significant, since nothing like it had appeared on any of the previous forms. In fact, I considered this bit of information extremely encouraging. When I first spotted the form in Comr. Pavlenda's hand, my heart sank, but now I decided without hesitation to complete it.

After all, this was a message, an omen. None of the Comrs. (Comrades) with whom I had dealt before felt any need to elaborate on the bare questions or prescribe any particular method for filling out the form. They merely asked that I hand it in. In return, they generally sent me a curt notice two or three weeks later, that my application had been rejected.

True, in those previous questionnaires I had indulged in quite a bit of crossing out; e.g., in Question 19 (*Public Functions*) I always deleted "Lay Judge" as a function for which I had neither inclination nor opportunity. I also crossed out Question 27 (*Names of Relatives Living Abroad*). There were a few additional items I had been deleting because they referred to activities in a period when I had not yet been born or I had been too young to have possibly participated in the events in question. I had always filled out all the questionnaires with a perfectly clear conscience, solemnly declaring each time that the information given was complete and correct to the best of my knowledge and belief, as attested by my handwritten signature.

This last questionnaire, however, was a challenge. An invitation.

The way that fellow Pavlenda kept looking at me with his blue-green eyes, the way he adjusted the cushion under his behind, the way he leaned toward me as I sat facing him in my chair (only on one other occasion had I ever been asked to sit down), the way he slid the questionnaire across the marble-top table (Form 01-240-0, Printed in Pilsen—I had grown so familiar with these forms I practically knew them by heart), the way Comr. Pavlenda breathed almost in my face as he smiled—all this seemed extremely promising.

A woman came in from the hall carrying a folder with letters for signature, and as she opened the door the questionnaire, which had already been within reach of my fingertips, suddenly took off and with a looping glide landed on the office rug.

We rose to our feet, Comr. Pavlenda and I, and bowed deeply before the woman because the questionnaire was lying at her feet, but Comr. Pavlenda was quicker than I and reached for the form before I did. In the course of this effort his necktie flopped out and his hair lost its neat part. I examined him in this dis-officialed state and saw before me a flushed albinoid man more or less my own age. But a Comrade. That was promising, too.

He smiled a second time.

I accepted the smile along with the questionnaire.

Then I stepped past the lady with the folder and descended the granite steps of Granit—to have a dream, or vision, or premonition, as is my wont.

The lady with the folder, or rather: a lady whose face remained hidden but who undoubtedly was the same person as the woman who had caused a gust of air to blow upon me in Comr. Pavlenda's office—this lady was waiting for me on the first landing, where she told me to enter the elevator, even though Granit occupied only a small two-story rococo building. We rode the elevator high up, and as we stepped out of the cage we found ourselves in a pharmacy full of bottles and glasses. The bottles had labels in Latin and Greek, yet for all their high-flown names they were quite common drugs, at least according to the woman (still faceless), busily pouring and decanting, until at last she reached for a green fluorescent vial full of deep-green liquid labeled *Pharmakon athanasias*. But as she was about to pour me some of this elixir of immortality I shouted and begged her to stop, because inside the vial there was another me, in the shape of a homunculus. But the woman continued to drain me of fluid until I felt myself gasping like a fish, suffocating.

And so I went to see Olin, who is my cousin but old enough to be my uncle, to ask him to explain this vision. For he also serves as interpreter of my dreams, diviner of my intuitions, and general prognosticator. This time, however, he turned me down and derisively suggested that for the sake of sounder sleep I learn to stand on my head. I let it pass and asked him whether he agreed that things looked promising.

"Sure," he nodded, "you're turning into a nut."

"True. You know what occurred to me? That I've been filling out those forms all wrong. For instance, the part about Lay Judge."

"What's that?"

"Lay Judge. You know—a judge picked from the

people. I always crossed it out. But that hurt my chances, you understand?"

I glanced at Olin, and strangely enough, this time he seemed unable to follow my thought.

"They always took it to mean that I didn't want to serve as a Lay Judge; in other words, that I was rejecting the honor. Otherwise, why did they keep the question-naire if they had no intention of hiring me?"

"Because you're not entitled," replied Olin.

(*Not entitled*, in Olinian terminology: an expression denoting the ultimate degree of inadmissibility.)

"On the other hand," said Olin, "if they take one questionnaire after another and note the trend of your X-ation, they will have to admit that you're improving."

"In other words, that document is really a message," I said. "They're actually hinting . . ."

"Go to sleep," interrupted Olin. "Enough of this non-sense!"

I went to sleep with my dream still unclarified, I went to bed drunk and befuddled as always happens when Olin starts to drink and to sing . . . and to interpret dreams, especially his own, which are so totally different from mine. In his dreams there is always a river or a light or a woman who's got one and knows what it's for and lets Olin enjoy it. In my dreams there is always some kind of disk or wheel (anything circular) and it keeps turning.

Perhaps I should have mentioned that in the question-naire. Or at least in my *curriculum vitae*. But I always attached my c.v.'s to the questionnaires quite mechani-cally, in the form of carbon copies, without the slightest change. I should have mentioned the dream with the circle, about the way it turns and about the faceless women and the women whose faces are made of layers of pink petals which I keep peeling off to get at the likeness underneath but the layers are without end and the petals circle as they spiral to the ground. Good Lord, this dream makes me dizzy, but I'd rather feel drunk than dead-tired. Though sometimes I even seem to die in this dream.

.   .   .

Item: I have determined not to cross out anything.

Not even those autumn leaves in Jiven when Pluto was about to enter Leo and a new moon was dawning, those leaves in Jiven (not far from Chlumec), on Thursday the 20th of October. My progenitor Edvin (ah, that name!) was circumspect at first and had no intention of creating me. Ever the cautious one, at least in comparison with Mother . . . even at this moment, he was hesitating.

Not that he didn't feel like doing it—he was a soldier, a corporal, his army coat was slung over his left arm, never mind the chilly weather, his right arm was supporting Alice, my mother, in my fore-memory there is a clear image of the autumnal puff of mist rising from her mouth as she smiled and gaily bantered with that same Edvin who was leading her into the leaves between Jiven and Vrat, actually leading her into lawlessness, for both of them were fugitives: Edvin had deserted the army and Alice her foster-mother, Aunt Vlaciha. Once Aunt V. had caused Edvin to be arrested by the gendarmes, and so this time our runaways were meeting halfway. Edvin set out from Hradek and Mother from Chlumec; in Jiven their trains crossed and vanished as if they had swallowed one another, and in this suddenly vacated space stood Alice and Edvin cheek to cheek; then, clasping each other tight, they crossed the track. I heard Mother's purse slapping against her legs, I felt the fluttering of her skirt, but I was not the least bit cold. In the pocket of Edvin's overcoat there was a copy of the *Czech Daily*, folded but with the date visible—that's why I remember the date so clearly. Beyond Jiven, far out of sight of anyone, Edvin hesitated for the last time. "What if your aunt is on to us again?" But Alice said: "Who cares!"

Thus she decided on me for eternity.

I kept silent for the time being, but I observed everything carefully and I can now provide a detailed report. For example, Comr. Pavlenda, when that overcoat was spread on the ground, the newspaper fell out and I noticed an item dealing with your Party: they had just outlawed it. Edvin had scanned the headline in the station and idly passed the article by (he was never politically conscious; *viz.*, Questions 7 and 23); i.e., he calmly proceeded on his way, quietly rose from the bench, walked to the exit, and along the way stuck the paper in his coat pocket, from where it fell out at the very moment of my procreation.

I was engendered joyfully and rather incidentally; i.e., not deliberately, because as far as Alice & Edvin were concerned, I was not the raison d'être of it all; which is as it should be. Mother's hair was full of burdock burrs which grasped her loosened, coppery tresses as she strained for the most wide-open position possible, and her head slipped off father's coat.

The burdocks clung tenaciously and could not be combed out. Not even that evening, when Alice (Miss Vachal) had her face slapped by Aunt Ludmila—on account of those very burrs. That blow shook me up. I heard Aunt berating Mother, but I was in no position to really listen or look around the house; I had enough to do to try to keep the blow from dislodging me. That was already the second threat to my life, and within such a short span of time, too; a month earlier I might have fallen in battle together with Edvin if the war had not shifted elsewhere and I had not been ensconced so deep in Bohemia. Fortunately, however, the jolt of Aunt's slap did not prevent me from *hearing* that tree-lined alley, from *hearing* the yellowing leaves crunching underfoot. I also heard Edvin piling the leaves under his military greatcoat to cushion mother and raise her up, I heard the crackling of the leaves resound from the spot where they were doing it, i.e., right next to me, so that this sound etched itself into my memory; it is there to this day and I love the end of October and the beginning of November; I amble through the foliage in the parks and I remember that shout which compelled Edvin—about to pull back—to stick tight and pound home, to rescue me from limbo and plant me in that womb, where I took hold and stuck like the burdock spears in Alice's hair, unuprootable and unoutslappable.

Edvin, too, once he saw that *it had to be*, did not let any needless constraint deprive him of the thrilling gush, but pressed against Mother's pelvis to the very bone (she was as wide open as could be); he felt her insides writhing and loosening, he felt the soft, breathing, juicy essence which later dries on the fingers, the blessed burning stuff which always—dear God—inflames me to rapture. Senseless rapture, of course, at least that's how Edvin thought of it after it had evaporated, and he begged the good Lord to forgive his enjoyment of it.

He was a Catholic, and it bothered his conscience that he let the Lord's name pass his lips in the middle of screwing. He therefore prayed to the Lord for pardon. And the Lord probably pardoned him, for after all what was He to do with Edvin, after He had endowed him most generously with the gifts of beauty, tenderness, and an appetite for this very thing? This Edvinian tenderness was surely what Mother loved best about him. He would lie with his head resting in the hollow of her collarbone, drained but still clutching at the last undulation down below, and Mother's eyes would fill with tears as he called her his little Alka, after the arctic bird about which Edvin knew nothing except its melodious, mysterious name.

Alka stroked Edvin's hair, and because his name resisted transformation into a loving nickname, she simply addressed him as *you*. But that pronoun also included me, creature of the leaves, seed of seeds.

I was passing from one state into another, into a creature of the leaves, no mere fuckling but a love-child. Alice was seventeen, it was ruining her life, she would now have to sit among schoolmates of the Chlumec high school with me growing in her belly . . . and, except for love, Edvin was able to do little to help her.

My subsequent fate—more precisely, my participation in the nation's domestic resistance movement (I didn't take any direct part in military actions abroad)—consisted of the following events:

As already mentioned above, I resisted Ludmila Vlaciha on the occasion of her slapping my mother, which gave me a severe jolt, and furthermore I also prevailed over my aunt in the dispute about my abolition. She feared scandal more than my mother did. She sought out Blanka, the midwife, and tried to talk her into turning abortionist. Aunt V. also advised Alice to shake me loose by vigorous hopping and by carrying heavy burdens, but Mother said she would not let them take me away (at that time she actually referred to me as an object, i.e., take *it* away) and Auntie capitulated. She, too, had no stomach for seeing me killed willy-nilly, for no good reason, but she had promised her sister (my departed grandma) that she would look after Alice, and now it appeared as if she hadn't been doing a very good job; Alice was a pregnant orphan and everything was topsy-turvy. And afterwards (*directly* afterwards) I had trouble with the Gestapo (secret police, German variety). On the 4th of April, officials of the Gestapo came to the chocolate factory where Dad worked as foreman, not to arrest him, but just to ask him some questions. We were living (there were already three of us, i.e., Alice + Edvin

+ me) in Draper Street, in quarters belonging to the Hatus plant. It was the only modern building in the old part of town and those Gestapo agents needed decent quarters in Chlumec. They came as if this was what they wanted to discuss with Dad, but in reality they were just squeezing him a bit, finally letting him go with ruffled feathers.

In this disheveled state he returned home to Mother and to me-inside-her. We were sitting at the table in the dining corner of the room, my head directly opposite the open drawer where Mother was straightening out some polished silverware (Note: *Personal Property* actually belongs in a later category, Question 10), the knives glistening after having been cleaned with cotton and cigarette ash, (cigarettes were still plentiful in those days), when Edvin entered and said: "They're after us!"

"Who?" asked Mother, looking up at him with her Jewish eyes.

"The Germans," he answered, and I—most probably roused by the quiver in Father's voice—braced my legs against the wall of my abode, jumped up, Mother's belly banged against that open drawer, slammed it shut, and Edvin collapsed.

These two sounds connected with my resistance activity are precisely recorded in my memory. The first was a metallic crash, the vibrations of which trembled through the room even after the drawer had slammed shut. The second was a hollow dull thump.

Edvin, I didn't mean it! Honestly, I am awfully sorry!

Mother, too, was terrified. She reached for me and pushed me back, so that I was once again afloat inside her body on a voyage far more complicated than any of my later journeys. She heaved a sigh, thinking what a sensitive organ the uterus was, nestled me in my original place and propped me up with her hands so that I wouldn't weigh her down so much as she knelt beside

Edvin. She lifted up her belly, kissed Father on his high forehead, and with her kisses tried to resurrect him like Sleeping Beauty . . . no, like my mother! For any other housewife would have run for a glass of water or smelling salts, whereas she kissed and cuddled until Edvin stirred, opened his eyes, and uttered the classic question of waking princes: "Ah, where am I?"

And mother replied: "In Chlumec, with me, in the Hatus place. Actually, it's time we moved out of here."

"Right," said Edvin. "We'll move to Little Hollow Street, opposite the soccer field. They have an apartment for rent there."

"Yes," Alice said, "that's a good idea," for she knew there were times for agreeing and times for disagreeing, she knew how to distinguish them precisely, and then it occurred to her again what a sensitive organ the uterus was, because Edvin had already lifted his lips to her Adam's apple. I guess I should let him, she thought.

And she did. Right there on the floor where he had been sprawled out a moment earlier, even though I was furious, even though I thrashed about. But they gave me something to drink to mollify me. They got me drunk on rose-hip wine and on something called Vignac Tonic, manufactured by the Chlumec pharmacy, Goda & Sons.

I heard them toasting each other, but by that time I was almost asleep. I stopped squirming and kicking.

They, too, were asleep, hugging each other in dreams as they did in reality.

"It is not impossible," it occurred to me, "that inebriation may be an antidote against that arch-enemy of newborn infants, prematurity."

I slept, hummed to myself, felt no pain.

Seventy-seven days more and I shall be.

2. ANADYOMENE

In the course of those seventy-seven days Olin was to run away (Olin = Olin Vlaciha, son of Aunt Ludmila), so that I would never lay eyes on him before the age of six. But he was destined to have a vision in the Libyan desert.

You too, Comr. Pavlenda, better hurry and fix yourself up with a mother, so that you can trail me in the zodiac as Scorpio.

I was already walking around town, or rather I was being walked. Contrary to Aunt Ludmila's apprehensions, I was causing no scandal, people had their own worries and paid no attention to anyone's belly. The only humiliation that happened to us during those seventy-seven days was a grade of D from Kuruc. He got even with us for Mom's beautiful pregnant shape. Kuruc was her French teacher. He scowled at her, raised himself on tiptoe and rocked on his heels, snorted and pouted, kept examining her on the *passé composé* of irregular verbs, made her tell and retell passages from *La Noce au Village*, a proper wedding in which the bride enters the church *au bras de son père* (i.e., neither knocked up nor an orphan), until Alice got fed up one day, grabbed Kuruc by the chain dangling from his belt, and gave it a good yank. This chain was similar to a watch fob but carried a medallion of Krakonos, patron of the Giant Mountains, because Kuruc (nicknamed Shorty) was a skier whose ability was no match for his enthusiasm and his sporty knickers. And that fob tinkled in front of Shorty as a substitute for his own member (i.e., tail) because the latter was so insignificant that Shorty thought it wise to hang out a pendant, lest one fine winter day on the slopes his real, pitiful piddler go into reverse and vanish inside his body.

Mother grabbed this fellow Kuruc by the lapels of the frock coat in which he was performing his calling, shook him so hard his face flushed, and then she gelded his pendant. It all happened in a flash. She was conjugating *se laver* and got as far as *nous nous étions lavés* when without warning she reached for the teacher's lapels and down he went, his face turning red and then the color of his frock, i.e., blue, and with a graceful quick motion she reached out for the middle of his body. It was a shamanistic gesture which clearly showed that this beautiful knocked-up girl knew perfectly well what she would be reaching for had someone like Edvin been standing there (and in that event Edvin would be *standing*, all right), and that she knew *perfectly* well how to be tender had she chosen tenderness rather than castration. There! At one swoop she pulled off Shorty's shorty and he fainted.

As it struck the ground, Kuruc turned livid and slumped beside the lectern. The belly of my mother, Alka, loomed above him. She stepped over his body like a majestic elephant cow and returned to her seat in the second bench by the window (right side). Other students ran for the principal, while A. Vachal, immediately upon sitting down, broke into tears. Her crying made me pitch and toss, so I did a few breaststrokes as a reminder; she cupped her hands over me and tried to calm me; actually, we tried to calm each other, because we didn't want to ruin our anatomic position, for fear of complications.

No, good Lord! I couldn't do that to Mother! She had heard so many stories from midwives, she would be very upset if I stupidly slipped into some awkward posture. And so she cupped her hands over the areas protruding farthest, where my rear end pressed against the placenta, and that's the spot which she patted. She thought that what was sticking out was my head, she was convinced that she was, so to speak, stroking my hair and cuddling me like a lover. In reality, she was talking to my rear end as she quieted me with a finger over her lips: Hush!

But my position was perfectly normal, my head was directed downward, pointing straight to the exit . . . Its rounded crown was situated most conveniently; in short, I was prepared to slip out with a slight twist, a quick slide—without any undue delay. The position of the stars was not bad, either (at least according to Olin's subsequent calculations; *viz.*, attached chronoscope); the moon was about to enter Virgo. Mother went to Cepin. It borders on Chlumec, yet it is a separate locality, consisting of a ruined castle and at the bottom of the hill a brewery with two smokestacks, a farm, a few dwellings, the Silver Poplar tavern, and Aunt Ludmila's gabled house, where Alice received that smack in the face.

It was getting dark when Aunt saw Mother climbing the path from the railroad station, past the Klahn house, and in the evening twilight Mother's belly glistened like that of the Virgin Mary in the illustrations out of *Ways to Heaven.* In those pictures, too, rays of light radiated from a swelling womb, while the Divine Mother, with slightly outstretched arms extending the curve of her womb, smilingly contemplated the light emanating from her body. Alice learned it from Her; she was walking up from the station to the Vlaciha house and from a distance she was respectfully greeted by Mr. Vostarek, the local brewer, and by Mr. Klahn with his pretty wife, who at once started longing for the same kind of belly, and at last Mother was spotted by Aunt Ludmila, who was shaken by remorse, appalled by the idea that she had ever considered my death, now that she could see me palpably alive. She begged the midwife's pardon and asked her to be my godmother, to wipe the slate clean, to make her forget what she had requested earlier. Blanka, the midwife, agreed to be my godmother, and I was glad. She was Dr. Brazda's best assistant, she was sure to see to it that I didn't cause Mother any needless pain.

I accompanied Mother to pick up our report card. We did poorly in Moral Attitudes and in French. But Alice and I took it all as a joke.

On the day of the Visitation of Our Lady I visited for the first time the Church of St. Barbora in Chlumec. At first there was some hesitation—Mother was not very keen on going there with me in my present guise—and only after Edvin had agreed to walk resolutely by the side of that belly as its unabashed author did we enter the church and pray.

Aunt Ludmila's behavior was downright sinful. She offered me to the Virgin Mary, imploring the intercession of St. Barbora, and as if she knew beforehand that I would turn out to be of the priestly sex, she pledged my future to a career as priest of the Virgin. I was angry. Why didn't she ask me first? Why did she so openly ignore me? God would punish her by rejecting her plea and permitting me to serve him as Chrysostom, the golden-mouthed one. He would put gold in my mouth but raise me no higher. I was still indignant when we got home, my third home (if I count as my first home the Cepin apartment, where we received that famous slap). I fidgeted so much that Alice sat down at the piano, in the room with windows facing the street (Little Hollow St., No. 1278—date of the ill-fated battle of Marchfeld), and played a minuet for me. It was one of the three piano pieces Mother knew. I listened and my anger melted away.

Or Mother and I would moonbathe—that's what I called our sunbathing in moonlight. Mother would go out into the garden (i.e., a plot of ground bounded by apple trees, gooseberry bushes, and lilacs, and a rabbit hutch in the back). It was impossible to sleep in that heat, anyway; Allie covered herself with nothing but a sheet, and when the rumpled sheet slid to the floor and Mother despaired of counting any more sheep, she wrapped a long robe around her naked body and stepped out into the garden. The robe was Japanese, of the type popular when Aunt Ludmila was heavy with Olin Vlaciha; a peacock preened himself on the back of it. Mother would sit down on a bench, her legs spread slightly apart—on account of the belly—her arms hanging loosely by her sides. The robe parted to admit the light, the rain of light, for that's how Mother thought of the cool moonlight flowing over her belly.

As the moon waxed, the light increased, and Edvin, on waking and seeing Mother once again out in the garden, would call out to her to stop the nonsense and go to sleep, and she would always answer yes, I'm coming, but she would continue to sit there, listening to the trees and the grass and the flowers, mooning herself on and on, but one night a sudden stab of pain made her clutch the small of her back. She sighed, straightened up, but I felt pressure in the same spot, i.e., the place where I didn't have my head but my rear end. Of course, I still did not take the summons seriously. I did not want to leave my snug harbor, I became panicky, pressed my chin against my arms, and burrowed deeper. No, I did not like that summer, with the moon in Virgo, and if it had not been for the smile on Alice's face, I might have burst into tears of dejection.

Alice called out to Edvin, and he ran across the street to Mr. Draksi's garage to borrow a van. We then drove to the hospital, with Edvin clutching Mother and me with his arm free (to keep us from shaking loose).

.　　.　　.

It is not true that Alice felt much pain. I was resolved to do my utmost to slide through without a hitch. In the end I realized that I had no way out except hair-first. I had a head of fine black hair, Comr. Pavlenda, while you probably had nothing but whitish fuzz, with the help of which you became an albino. Anyway, I pushed in that direction, and all the waters in which I was floating, my pillow-waters, swirled toward that exit, which opened somewhat, and I *felt* a light shining on the back of my head, the light was coming from the room and God knows where else, and this illumination of theirs was so foreign to me that even with my eyes closed and veiled by curtain-waters I sensed this foreignness and as I raised my left arm to my eyes to protect myself I caused a snag in spite of my resolve. This hurt Mother and she cried out and moaned. Up till now she had been quiet except for an occasional gasp, gnawing the palm of her hand so that she looked as if she were suppressing a smile rather than grimacing with pain. During that last moan I made my final decisive salvo, slid down with my left arm leading the way, and suddenly I found myself flat on my face, eyes shut tight (closed tight as a fist by fear). I snuggled my forehead and nose and mouth against that lovely velvety cuddly smoothness some fool had dubbed by the ugly word "membrane." I kept on sliding and twisting and I kept saying to myself: my God, why is my head so big, and I closed my eyes even tighter, tighter, I felt ever more keenly how Mother's innermost flesh was sliding past me, I felt how I was freeing myself, how my cheeks pushed upward against my very eyeballs, the flesh of my face was pressed into a mass of wrinkles and twists and folds, and then I got snagged again, for the second (and last) time. I wanted to stop myself, I sud-

denly realized what I was about to fall into—Chlumec,
Bohemia—I wanted time-out to think things over, to re-
consider, and if that was not possible, at least a pause,
to wait until the stars shifted into a more favorable configuration so that I wouldn't be stuck with the Sun in
house No. 8 (*Mors!*). But then I suddenly *stopped hearing* Mother's breathing, it seemed to me as if she were
fainting, as if I was hurting her, tormenting her by my
procrastination, and so I stretched my body in the direction of my left arm, and when Alice once again took a
deep breath (thank God), I resigned myself to the impending new locus of my activity (see Question 4: *Tem-
porary Domicile*); I obeyed Mother as in fact I have
always done in matters of importance . . . She suddenly
bore down, I clenched my muscles and flew along with
such speed that neither Dr. Brazda nor Obst. Asst. Blanka
Jenistova (the one who was especially well-disposed toward me) was able to catch me and I plopped into the
porcelain vessel routinely placed under women in child-
birth. It was obvious to me that I was drowning, and
that's why I cried for dear life.

Mother took her toothmarked hand from her mouth
and asked (in a very subdued voice) whether it was all
over.

"You bet," answered Dr. Brazda, and fished me out.

"Of course," said the midwife. "Our doctor has golden
hands."

And at that moment his hands really did have that
color. He bathed me and brought me to mother.

She put me down on her breast, and I was so tiny that
my whole chest fitted into that much-bitten hand of hers.

I went on screaming, but in a softer register.

The time was 15:41, the 20th of July 1939, Uranus
and Neptune were in trine, Saturn and Mars in quadrate,
and the Sun in the eighth house, the house of death.

.   .   .

CHRONOSCOPE

Jan Chrystostomos

8/20/1939 ARMC 11:28 a.m.

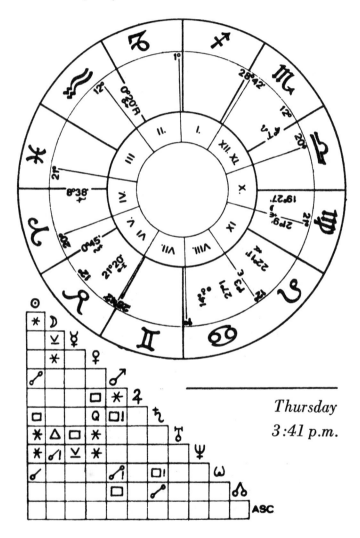

Thursday

3:41 p.m.

The Sun was supposedly in that same house on Friday, the 28th day of July, as St. Barbora's father aimed his curved sword at his daughter's slender neck. He held her by her long, fair hair, she was kneeling and praying with clasped hands, her eyes lovingly fixed in the upward gaze of death or ecstasy, alongside a tower topped by peacock feathers (as on that Japanese robe), a chalice with the Host, and of course Luna, the Moon, in the light of which I had been bathing.

"St. Barbora!" my mother called out to the saint in the painting on the church wall. She could not cross herself because she was carrying me in a blanket for purposes of baptism. "Let his name be Chrysostom if that's how they want it, the main thing is that he is here. Intercede for him!"

Alice did not like my baptismal name; it sounded to her like a brand of toothpaste, and she thought it out of keeping with the simple Janism of the Vachals. In the Vachal family she came from, all the sons had the name Jan; for example, Alice's father was Jan Evangelist, others in the family had names like Jan Nepomuk, etc., one after another in a straight line, until I came along to knot things up by being born to Alice on the distaff side of the family. Mother came into the world an heiress, as her father was just leaving, dying without male descendants of a disease contracted in the First World War. They passed each other so fleetingly there was barely time for a mutual nod.

Of course, Alice did not realize that I was named Jan Chrysostom not only because all the common combinations of Jan had been used up but also because this was Aunt Ludmila's way of dedicating me to the priesthood and to Monsignor Rosin, the Dean of Chlumec, whose baptismal name was Chrysostom. I was to be his namesake, and to aspire to the same title of Msgr.!

Efeta! she said, and before I had a chance to express

myself on the matter, Blanka, the midwife, exorcised the evil spirits on my behalf. Then the Dean breathed on me (still in the sacristy), Mother lifted me up, and everyone in the procession went inside, into the nave, beneath the picture of St. Barbora, where they prayed over me without disturbing the quiet. Then I bathed! That Friday, afternoon rays of light resembling moonlight shone through the stained-glass windows, my blanket turned bluish-red; I was moonbathing once again.

Now we reached the pulpit, next to the three-legged, tin baptismal font decorated with lions with golden rings in their mouths. The Dean sprinkled water on my head and placed a white veil over me while Blanka Jenistova accepted a tall candle from his hand. As we turned back, the candle dripped on the sepulcher inscribed

The Boddy of
MASTER JOST OF CHLUMEC
who departed this Life A°.Dom.1562
lyeth buried in this Monument
where it expects the Resurrection of the Just

Or was it my Uncle Bonek who let his candle drip? Alas, I was not paying attention to this uncle or to his candle! A mistake. I did see—for a second or two—his lips, and they were twitching. He may have been praying, though I've never caught him doing anything of the kind since.

Alice handed me to Edvin, Edvin to my aunt, etc.; I traveled from arm to arm.

3. FORTRESS IN THE DESERT

On my left shoulder they painted the number 9 in indelible ink, a number which in your questionnaire, Comr. Pavlenda, designates the category *Original Occupation* but in *The Booke of Dreams and Ghosts* designates OXE, BULL, OF THE MALE GENDER.

As soon as Alice looked it up in the dream book, she ran to tell it to Edvin and they had a good laugh, but I, Jan Chrysostom, did not laugh, for it was too serious a time. Besides, I was jealous because Alice had left me lying there, all uncovered; she had stopped paying attention to me and cuddling me and instead was spending her time with Edvin, so that her hair no longer lay fragrant on my face—a closeness I loved and, after all, had every right to expect.

But, all in all, the number 9 is truly a lucky one. It is 3 times 3. It transcends the loneliness and isolation of one, the polarity of two, in order to bring out *genesis*, which is the real significance of the number 3. A triple 3 denotes this world as well as that other, maternal one whence I had come and whither I am going to seek refuge. Of course, it also signifies a *pyramid*, converging toward my initial calling, my original occupation as Jan Chrysostom. I should have mentioned that number on my shoulder in Question 9.

The number slowly faded into the pulse of that year (nineteen-hundred thirty nine; also a pyramid, Comr. Pavlenda, the last digit being triple the preceding one), a stifling year, with war aborted again and again. It was coming closer, certainly, but because it had repeatedly failed to break out, it seemed that once again some post-

ponement would occur. But I knew the precise date on
which it would begin; the date was foretold by the Sun
permanently captured in the eighth house. Its light was
clearly a dying light. My Uncle Olin Vlaciha perceived
it that way, too. Facing the sun and sand, he laughed
as he recalled that back home this was the day of Our
Lady of the Snows. He was sitting by the fire, in the
middle of the desert near El Arish. Soldiers were picking
up the glowing embers, passing them to the man who
was heating up the little stone oven. It was time to eat,
meat gravy was handed out together with flat bread pancakes, which the soldiers kneaded in their fingers to
double as spoons. The sun was rising on the left. Olin
looked up at it and that long sandy stretch of yellow
began to undulate like a wheat field, and at the point
where the sun's disk was burning, a girl's tresses burst
into flame. The girl was walking through the wheat,
which parted, bowing to her. And even though the blaze
made it impossible to see the girl's face, her radiance
proclaimed: behold a lovely nude. Her right hand
shielded her breast, her left grasped the longest of her
burning tresses to cover her loins in the most defenseless
of girlish gestures. Olin knew that gesture intimately,
that's why he addressed the girl without hesitation. She
smiled, and as she did so, the nearest wheat stalks bil-
lowed out, swelled, and burst into flame, the grain crackling and frying, blazing with heat which was becoming
unbearable, the whole wheat field exploded, there was no
way out . . . Oh, die, then! So be it! Olin commanded
himself, and prepared to burn up like those stalks of
wheat. He closed his eyes to keep out the horror, and
the place of the smile turned into a snoutful of fangs
which grasped Olin by the neck, lifted him high in the
air, and carried him over the burning field. Olin hung on
like a kitten in its mother's mouth, those teeth could
have killed him but they did not bite, they were safe.

Olin shook his legs, one of his boots came loose and fell into the fire. Strange: the fiery surface broke into a series of circles like concentric rings spreading out over water; Olin hung suspended over this bull's-eye and asked the teeth: Who are you? But he was deposited barefoot on a well-scrubbed floor, and the sulphurous yellow which had burnt all around him now gleamed from the fur of a rusty-yellow cat.

The cat said: "My name is Ma Fille. It is I who brought you here."

Olin understood, she spoke French and he was in El Arish as a member of the Foreign Legion. "It's clear now: *there will be war*," he said to the people around the fire.

And the bandleader from the village named Zdar (his band had broken up in Holland, whereupon he joined the Legion) said: "I can't wait!" He stretched out toward the oven, and from under his legs crept the rust-yellow dream cat. Olin stared at her in such disbelief that they all burst into laughter.

"Haven't you ever seen a cat before?"

He answered: "On the contrary. It's *because* I have just seen her . . . it's because I've seen too many of them all at once."

And the cat took off toward the barracks and they called after her: "Fatima!"

Whereupon: Olin got up, turned around, the sun thus swung over to his right, and he hurried after the cat to ask her whether that was truly her name. The cat shook her head.

"You are Mafille, aren't you?"

She nodded in agreement.

That's why he started looking after her. At least he tried to do so, as much as he could under the limitations of life in the fortress, with those long exhausting marches into the desert. And under the limitations of the work

Capt. Mauger (pronounced Moh-jay) assigned to his Czech legionnaires. He was very concerned lest they pine away for their so-called homeland, whose place in their hearts had now been taken by the Legion.

"Fatima!" Olin called to the cat, but when she came he addressed her as Mafille, stroked her, ran his finger over her raspy little tongue to remind himself of his flight over the burning wheat field. "Mafille, my little girl, there will be war," but when he heard his own voice (both inner voice and outer) he shuddered, for it sounded pleased. "Then let war come. And you, yellow cat, see to it that among those who die there be at least a few of those who deserved it."

Then he remembered Captain Mauger, who had said (in French, as desert commander) that nowadays it was no longer possible to repeat the bloodbaths of twenty years back.

"Ah, my good cat," said Olin, "forgive him his mistake, for the bloodbath will be boundless."

Item: The captain appeared and asked Olin whether he had nothing better to do than fondle the cat.

With the help of a smile, Olin answered that questions posed in such a tone were not popular in the Kingdom of Bohemia (*Royaume de Bohéme*), though of course now in Africa the situation was somewhat different.

Fatima expressed similar sentiments, by clawing at the floor and stretching.

To which Olin added (in Czech):

> *Oh, cat seraphic, cat mysterious*
> *Oh, cat subtle and harmonious . . .*

"*Qu'est-ce que c'est?*"

"Baudelaire."

"I see," said the captain. "I'll have you locked up!" Perhaps, Comr. Pavlenda, he added: "till your ass rots off," but in view of my linguistic limitations (*viz.*, Question 13) I cannot render his remarks adequately.

They put Olin in the stockade, but by morning war had broken out. It was Sunday morning and my uncle skipped off in tight French parade step to meet the bandleader coming to announce that the prison sentence was canceled.

"I accept the pardon," he said, "but only on condition that it also applies to the cat."

"The cat is kaput," replied the bandleader. "Either it croaked or somebody killed it."

"She lives," Olin maintained. "Cats are extremely resourceful."

"She was a Moslem, anyway," said the bandleader to cheer Olin up. Whereupon: they departed. Olin was determined to come out victorious, with other members of his battalion. They could now form a battalion of their own, they no longer needed to be dependent on the Legion, but in other ways they continued to be plagued by bad luck. I passed my anal phase more or less successfully; by Christmas I had just about learned to control my bowels (rewarded by Alice's praise), and by May I was completely *free of problems*. Unfortunately, no such statement could be made in regard to France, which failed to rally even after Olin *invaded* the region near Montigny . . . or at least he thought this was what he was doing. He believed that he was part of an army capable of attack, but by evening he found out that the ammunition provided to his outfit was barely sufficient for mounting guard duty. This made Olin very nervous, and face to face with the enemy he kept trying to swallow his nonexistent saliva.

It also seemed strange to him that they were marching toward the front while other units were marching in the opposite direction. It poured, the terrain was blanketed by fog, and they assumed that somewhere in the rain and haze and darkness they would find a system of fortifications. But then the weather cleared and not a single defensive position was in sight, not as much as a trench. Bridges across the Marne were intact.

And so Olin dug trenches, barricaded approaches to the village, and counted shells, but then a lieutenant arrived on a bicycle and instead of ammunition brought orders to retreat.

Until that time, they had all been under the impression that they were on the verge of going into action.

Precisely at 2200 hours, as ordered, Olin retreated to a certain village near Vibert-Rozoy en Brie. As they approached, a barrage perked him up. A Senegalese platoon was lying in the grass, shooting in all directions. The corporal in charge fixed a grenade launcher to his rifle, loaded, and lobbed a shell at the church steeple. They were all yelling that German parachutists were in the area.

Olin told his soldiers to fan out, and they advanced cautiously to the edge of the village, where they found an Arab standing under a tree, shooting at a crow.

After each shot the bird seemed to shrivel and to cling even tighter to the branch. He was probably terrified, or felt safer among the leaves than in a sky full of shells . . . or perhaps he was already stone-dead and merely stuck to the tree.

A short distance away, a French officer sat on a white lawn chair which for some unknown reason had ended up in the fields, and watched the proceedings.

Olin said to him: "How could you permit such a circus to go on?"

But it was the Arab, not the Frenchman, who replied: "*C'est la guerre, mon lieutenant.*"

And once again he took aim at the crow, but this time he knocked it down, demolished this black parachutist, blew it to pieces. Leaves and splinters and black feathers rained down on the village, on the river Grand Marrain, while the Frenchman continued to sit in the lawn chair, gazing at the river without answering my uncle. He merely shrugged his shoulders; he was drunk.

Item: Olin withdrew behind the Seine, retreating until evening of the following day. In the meantime people were busily dying all over the countryside, German airmen were at work plowing up the ground, a headless woman lay next to a bomb crater, near some horses, swollen stiff and bloody, stinking and full of flies, all around lay soldiers, lifeless uniformed bodies, while other bodies in the same uniforms marched, retreated, fled. Pursuit planes kept swooping down on clusters of Frenchmen, killing them with zest.

It was morning. Everyone was retreating, individually or in small, coherent groups, preferably without arms. But with *bidons*, the Frenchmen's field canteens filled with wine, which they zealously guarded and saved. Olin saw a soldier pushing a baby carriage full of those canteens. The carriage was a high one, with huge wheels— obsolete compared with mine, Comr. Pavlenda—but its cargo rattled and tinkled. They passed one another, the soldier and the lieutenant carrying orders to retreat.

"Where to now?" asked Uncle.

The Frenchman answered: "Nowhere, because France is negotiating surrender."

Olin felt like bawling, for the moment he could not think of anything to say, 2,450 Czech soldiers were silent too, they had their dead and wounded, a part of their train had been left behind the Loire, they were overcome by sorrow, it engulfed them—at first it had not been their sorrow, but now it felt all the heavier.

"Does that mean," said Olin, "that Germany has won the war?"

But the question was already addressed to a backside

rubbing against the bicycle seat and disappearing toward the small river Cher, down the field path to Châteauroux. Farther on, near the city of Nontron, weapons were being surrendered. It was the beginning of peace, which is the extension of war.

General Dunoyer wrote a thank-you letter to Olin. It was the 23rd of May.

In Chlumec, I let go Alice's hand and enticed by Edvin who was holding a bag of candy, (already of the "confiscated" kind), I made my first independent invasion of a region, in the vicinity of the rabbit hutch. More precisely: I started to fall into space but I managed to counteract the fall by quickly extending one leg and then the other, so that I was actually walking. It was only when I reached the rabbit hutch, after seven complete steps, that I flopped to the ground, clutching a handful of lilac blossoms torn off the bush during my struggles for step No. 8.

"In spite of present misfortunes," General Dunoyer wrote my Uncle Olin, "in spite of these bitter days which unite our two unhappy peoples in a bond of pain, let us keep faith in the future. Our hopes will be realized!"

I, however, shook the lilac blossoms off my hands in order to make room for the hard candy (brand name Largior), and I called Uncle Olin "cousin" (*mon cousin*, in French) in order to distinguish him from my other uncle, namely Uncle Bonek, who had dripped wax from his candle during my baptism.

4. LARGIOR

That maneuver of stretching forth a leg when about to
fall—that was one of my best ideas, Comr. Pavlenda.
The leg is simply extended right in the middle of a fall
and this maneuver produces walking, independent motion through space. This discovery probably fits best under question . . . Question 11? Yes, perhaps it should
be considered part of my *Educational Background*. But
I am not sure. I merely suggest that a special category be
set aside for discoveries of this kind. I believe it would
be just as important a category as Question 6, *Origin*.
You'll find no better way of analyzing people, Comr.
Pavlenda, than by their manner of making discoveries of
this kind.

However, as far as number 6 is concerned, the first
thing they looked into was whether or not I was of Aryan
descent. This was started in Chlumec by the candy manu-
facturer, Mr. Hatus. He wanted to be sure that his
Largior chocolate (as well as the drops by the same
name) was truly Aryan. Not that Jews took any part in
their manufacture—there was just a handful of them
in Chlumec, and their names were Czech: Chadima,
Kopecky, Vohryzek. No, Mr. Hatus was completely befuddled by the army which had occupied the town and
taken up quarters in the pavilion behind the Pleasure
Park. Pipers and drummers bedecked with horsehair
exercised in the big yard right in front of his eyes, because the Hatus villa looked out on this very yard. And
no doubt it was because he had to watch them all day
that Mr. Hatus gave orders—even before he had received any communication to that effect from the so-

called Landrat—that all persons who wished to hold positions of any consequence in his plant had to submit birth certificates, baptismal certificates, and a number of other documents.

Bonek, my godfather and uncle, came to see his brother Edvin and led him out to the soccer field in front of our house (see Question 5) and said: "What are we going to do about her?"

"About whom?"

Thereupon my godfather motioned with his shoulder toward the kitchen window, behind which Alice and I were just practicing the Ride of the Lords and Clowns (perhaps you know this game, Comr. Pavlenda: the child bounces happily on the adult's knee, to the recitation of a nursery rhyme about the different way Lords and Clowns ride a horse). At the same moment, the soccer match between Chlumec and Hradek was tied at 0:0.

"You mean Alice?"

Bonek nodded his typical Bonekian nod. He conducts all conversations in such a way that others are led to express his thought and he only approves it, as it were. Bonek was really a Socrates. And above all he was just, at least in comparison with Edvin, who was merely handsome. This was how they were always regarded. It was always assumed that when it came to basic matters, my uncle was the one to make the decisions.

This assumption was even shared by Edvin Sr., grandpa and bookbinder, who was to die in fourteen days (this having been Sunday, October 8; the Chlumec vs. Hradek score remained unchanged), without my ever having seen him. Already on the day of my birth he had been so bound by cirrhosis that he could not be moved from Prague to Chlumec, and now he was working—no, driving—himself to death.

His story: he had that bookbindery in Prague, and of course he also had a daughter, Alzbeta + Bonek + Edvin

Jr., my father. But he bound books with such a generous spirit, with so little thought of profit (the house in a suburban section of Prague in which they lived bore the inscription: NEITHER GAIN NOR GLORY), that if it hadn't been for Bonek I doubt I would ever have ended up with such an educated father.

The grandpa who was dying (and whose face I would never see) bound not only books but hundred-crown notes. Whenever the growing stack of brochures, diplomas, ledgers, and other bound items was matched by a pile of hundred-crown bills bearing the noble head of our President Liberator, he reached for this latter pile and fixed a golden clip around the stack in such a way that the clip clutched the President by the neck. And while Grandpa's eyes glowed red from the velvet reflected from plush couches on which reclined the Misses Melanka and Tylka (common whores, according to Bonek; angels, according to Edvin Sr.), the President kept losing his head again and again as one bill after another slid past the golden guillotine of the clip. After the last President had been dispatched, the clip that had been choking him began to choke remorseful Grandpa, who felt as if he had a weight on his chest and a dumpling in his soul.

Thus dampened, he would return home to his wife.

She was an angel, too; her name was Angelina and her voice had something angelic about it. She never said: "Edvin, you're soused again!" but always: "Edvin dear, you've been drinking," so that it was up to Grandpa himself to say: "Angelina my pet, I was guzzling like a fish. You know my benders: three days at a stretch."

Bonek, on the other hand, never used the word "drinking" in connection with his father. During the intervals when Grandpa disappeared—and they could not be determined in advance, though the silent, morose way he sat at his press was a clue—at such times Bonek would sit in the small cubicle behind the office, pet the dog

Astor, and remark about his father: "He's pissed everything away again. With those bitches, the son of a bitch!"

Then he would go out in the yard behind the cubicle, toss a stick in the air for Astor to retrieve, and when that German shepherd fetched the saliva-slick stick, even he, the dog, would be treated to a few remarks about getting soused. Then Bonek would ask: "Astor, who is your master?"

He loved to see the dog jump up, place his front paws on his chest, and lick the master's, i.e., Bonek's, face.

Bonek was eager to attain the status of lord and master; he trained Astor to this end, and to some extent even Edvin Jr. Whereupon: when he had succeeded in producing the best trained and best astorized of all Astors, he went to see Angelina. He walked into the living room, the windows of which had a commanding view of town, and said: "Mother, I've had enough!"

Mother asked enough of what, and he repeated to her what he had been saying to the dog.

"You mustn't talk that way," she whispered, and perhaps she meant it as a reprimand. But as she looked at her firstborn son and on his left saw the dog Astor with uplifted ears and on the right Edvin Jr., the future Mr. Handsome, it seemed to her that she ought to cross over to the other side of the room, to the couch, join the three of them—and she decided that she must not cry, for Bonek would be sure to reprimand her for it. She started in that direction, but to save face she continued right on into the kitchen and filled the big kettle with water. Only then did she join her sons and, as if apropos nothing in particular, she mentioned a new catalogue for which the company Melango had given them an order. Bonek knew perfectly well, however, that on his side of the room was arrayed a group whose spokesman he had become, and he was determined to wait at their head until—far away, in the kitchen door on the other side of the room (in Bonek's eyes the distance had grown until the room became transformed into a momentous battlefield)—until the crestfallen figure of Edvin Sr. appeared in the door.

Grandpa quietly closed the door behind him, he was being very careful, but then he stumbled and realized that he had not fooled anyone, for all those who were to have been spared the sight of his return were standing right in front of him, watching him intently: the dog was there, and his son, and the other son, and Angelina on the verge of saying: "Edvin dear, you've been drinking." This confused him so much that he attempted a smile. An apologetic smile, which made it all the more provocative. At least, that's how it affected Bonek. When Angelina started to say "You've been drinking," Bonek raised his arm as if silencing applause, and proceeded to bawl out his piss-away father.

Angelina gasped. Astor snarled, bared his teeth, stepped in front of Bonek, and acted the meanest Astor he could, even though by nature he had nothing of the wolf in him. The hand that was preparing to strike Bonek froze in midair.

"Sit down," Bonek commanded his father, "sit down, damn it!"

Grandpa was still befuddled, the barking, commanding, sobbing, and staring (of little Edvin) still had to penetrate the fog of his hangover, it needed time, forbearance, perhaps even mercy. This would have been rewarded by grandpa with tears of guilt, he would have collapsed in a chair with boozy trickles running down his cheeks. He loved self-recrimination; he would have gladly given himself a talking-to, but when that squirt (as he called Bonek) shoved him rudely in a chair, he was not at all sure he could learn to tolerate such behavior.

"I have given birth to a snake in the grass. I have

nurtured a serpent on my breast," he said, not too concerned with the lack of originality of his metaphors. "A serpent! You hear me, Angelina?"

But as it was impossible to tell whether Angelina's sobbing signified approval or rebellion, Grandpa began to stomp his feet in rhythm to the word *ser-pent*, until he had worked himself up into a state close to delirium.

Whereupon: Bonek walked over to the stove, on which stood the big kettle of hot water for dishes and other household needs. Bonek picked up the kettle, approached his father in a manner almost ceremonial, and emptied it to the last drop over his head.

Grandfather gasped, then stiffened, stopped stomping his feet or shouting about serpents. His eyes filled with tears, sorrow, plaint, confession. He said (as soon as he fully revived): "Nothing is more awful, my dearest ones, than a father who guzzles away his children's happiness and doesn't give a hoot for anything."

And later, in the company of the whores, he would add: "No, I do not deserve your caresses, sweethearts, or your kisses. You should hit me over the head or kick me in the balls, because I am an unworthy and sinful person."

All the same, there was no doubt that hereafter the office-desk drawer would contain brochures and delivery orders rather than bound banknotes. Not that Grandpa was never again to visit his favorite establishment, but he never again succeeded in spending every last hundred-crown bill. The golden clip would choke only the few Presidents he was able to set aside in secret.

Furthermore, he no longer talked of Bonek as a serpent but as someone destined to go far in this world (eyes full of tears), not a man meant to sweat and slave all his life but a gentleman. So you see, Comr. Pavlenda, this class business is rather complicated; I, for instance, never had to struggle to become a gentleman. My very first

ride on Alice's knees introduced me to the ride of the
Lords (high-stepping gait of nimble Lipizzaner horses),
whereas Bonek had to do it the hard way, by training
old Astor.

He shouted at the dog: "Stay!" i.e., he ordered him to
sit in the yard adjoining the house of NEITHER GAIN NOR
GLORY. This maneuver is called "down stay" and Astor
stayed there for two hours and thirty-six minutes before
Bonek returned and showed him his certificate. This
stated that Astor's master was duly enrolled as a first-
year student of the trade school for bakers and confectioners and that after the requisite number of years he
would even be qualified to make caramel-topped Dobosh
cakes . . . delicate seven-layer cakes on lace-paper doilies
which the Misses Melanka and Tylka would daintily cut
into small morsels, lift to their mouths on silver spoons,
and drop into the dark warmth of . . . no, Banek's fancy
did not dare go any further, but he felt a hard-palate
kind of faith that once he was master of the Dobosh-cake
secret, justice was sure to follow.

And so he said to Astor: "Up!"

And after two hours and thirty-six minutes the dog
got up and was rewarded with a piece of that same cake
favored by the two ladies. Uncle had bought it in their
establishment for this very purpose.

His revenge was thus sweet in the truest sense of the
word.

And just, too, because it was implemented by Bonek,
who was already a just man and becoming still more just
with each passing year. True, with the passage of time
he tended to forget about his pledge of revenge, and his
original intention would have faded entirely were it not
for that sweetness which he felt after each act of justice.

Then Bonek began to study how to ride like a Lord,
then Astor died, and shortly after his death Angelina and
the two Edvins received a letter from Bonek telling

them *there was hope* he might become an agent for the chocolate-manufacturing establishment Largior in Chlumec. In a P.S., Bonek did not fail to mention that the word *largior* was Latin and meant *to bestow liberally, to spread largesse*, which seemed to bode well for the future. But the P.S. also contained a message for Edvin Jr., my father. Bonek informed my father that he had enrolled him in the same school for bakers and confectioners where he himself was just finishing, and exhorted Edvin to exert "great diligence and tenacity" (the very terms Bonek used).

Edvin Jr., Edvin the Handsome, felt his throat tighten at this bit of news which indicated all too clearly that he would never be a sailor or an aviator like the famous F. Novak—"admired by all Europe and across the seas" —but only Edvin, brother of Bonek, head of the shipping department of the firm Largior in Chlumec.

But Angelina read farther, to the part where Bonek held out the promise of financial support to help Edvin achieve this goal (i.e., of ending up in the shipping department of Largior), provided:

(a) that Mr. Hatus, the owner, keep his promise of giving Bonek a bonus on all orders he negotiated;

(b) that Edvin maintain a solid scholastic level of achievement.

Hell, thought Edvin, if I've got to study I will, but only hard enough to get by. And later, too, after he had succeeded in landing a job in the shipping department, he continued to work there more for Bonek's sake than his own. My father was not interested in chocolate, he wrapped it and shipped it and that was all, it never occurred to him to figure out what its brand name meant and he did not even realize that the diadem-adorned lady underneath the gold lettering represented Fortuna, the goddess of fortune, or that the carnations pouring from

the horn of plenty were the owner's favorite flower—
Dianthus superbus. Dad left such concerns to Bonek,
because Bonek knew more and had need for such knowledge. In less than a year Bonek became the second-best
salesman, right after the Jew Herman Vohryzek, and
Bonek even gave up smoking when he learned that Mr.
Hatus did not like it and that Vohryzek did not indulge
either. He wanted to become just as indispensable a nonsmoker and sales executive as "that Jew," but that Jew
continued to surpass him by a whisker and even addressed Uncle as "my dear colleague," in a jovial but
slightly condescending tone.

For example, when Vohryzek was leaving for Holland
to negotiate an order for chocolate beans, a matter which
Uncle was convinced he could have handled equally well
himself, Vohryzek said to him: "My dear colleague,
Largior not only means to bestow liberally but to bribe
liberally! Look it up in the dictionary, you'll see it in
black and white. We bribe so we can bestow, and the
more liberally we bestow, the more liberal the commission bestowed upon us, and the more liberal the commission, the more we love Largior."

And Jew Vohryzek boarded the Chlumec–Hradek–
Amsterdam express, off to visit Van Houten, while Bonek
was trying to think up a good reason for holding
Vohryzek in contempt. Then he realized what it was he
disliked about that Largior tirade and about Vohryzek
in general: ambiguity! A man who mixed everything up,
turned everything topsy-turvy, such a man could have no
respect for anything great or super-personal! Such a man
was without greatness or nobility of heart. And so Bonek
launched one of his scorns, as a man might launch a
hunger strike. He thought about Mr. Hatus, too, trying
to decide whether the owner should not also be held in
contempt, for his blindness toward Vohryzek and his

lack of taste. After all, the face on Mr. Hatus's chocolate
wrappers doubtless belonged to one of his little whores,
some Melanie or Otilie; Bonek guessed that at once. It
was a tart, not a goddess, and she was not scattering any
superb *Dianthus* blossoms but plain ordinary carnations.
Anyway, Fortuna certainly was not Mrs. Hatus; Bonek
had an eye for such things. He squinted at the wrapper
until the world diminished to a slit around a tiny, ridiculous Hatus.

But the punier and more ridiculous Hatus seemed to
Bonek, the better a salesman Bonek was becoming. The
time had not yet come to dispatch his boss, to pronounce
a malediction with the impact of "pissing away"—it was
still the time to act the indispensable salesman and to
train a new, more trainable dog to stand guard, alongside and inside Bonek, over everything great and just.

"Yes, it is in poor taste," he said, unwrapping one of
the Fortunas which had found its way into his pocket,
"and it hurts sales. Do you know what our volume could
be if that woman weren't so disgustingly plump?"

"Or if she had on the kind of bonnet worn by the
peasant girl on Droste's cocoa!" replied Edvin. "And if
she were holding in her hand a bar of chocolate, with the
same peasant girl wearing the same cap on the wrapper,
and that girl holding a chocolate bar . . . to infinity, to
the vanishing point. That's what I would like to see,
Bonek, because that would truly be a work of art."

"Good God," said Uncle to Dad. "Are you pulling my
leg, or are you really so dumb?"

"I mean it quite seriously," said Edvin, smiling that
hint of a smile which appears on his face very rarely; i.e.,
when he means something quite seriously. It is an infuri-
ating sneery smile, at least Bonek gets pissed off every
time Edvin pulls it on him. It lengthens Edvin's face,
makes his cheekbones stand out, the cheeks collapse and

the lips grimace as if they were about to spread wide and reveal a dazzling, jazzy set of teeth. At such times the face of Edvin the Handsome radiates a magic triangle, for in accordance with the law of Pythagoras (transmuted into the law of Edvin the Handsome), two beams of light emanating from the eye sockets engender a third bolt emanating from dental ivory, disarming and conquering all.

Even Bonek is conquered by this lightning bolt of Edvin's. Bonek is helpless. He has nothing of Edvin's beauty, even though their features are quite similar.

Edvin, on the other hand, attracts smiles, and electricity crackles around him wherever he goes. For example, the conveyor belt in the plant conveys to him not only cooling, stiffening chocolate bars but also greetings from all the eight women working at the wrapping machines. And even the two old ladies in the corner, who knock the bars out of the forms and send them, tinfoiled, to Lady Fortuna, are aflutter and full of regret that their operational age has passed.

But Edvin is more keenly aware of the effects of his smile on men, especially its effect on that sour, contemptuous mug of his brother's. Men resent him, and if they had their way, Father would have worn dentures years ago. Only with women can he be his own self; they truly grasp him (with their minds and their tentacles).

Quite pedantically, he keeps a credit-debit ledger in these matters. *Shall I pay?* he asks himself when he feels that they are opening up to him, and if he answers himself in the positive, the corresponding number appears on the credit side of the ledger marked *paid*. Literally, a *number*. Only then comes the event: love, etc. And so, at the core of his being, Edvin remains absolutely calm. In the midst of the factory women (or any other women) he thinks of just one, who wears a Dutch bonnet on her head, holds a tray with a tin of Droste's cocoa, the tin contains Chlumec and Edvin (still without Alice), on the tin there is an illustration of another woman wearing a bonnet, a smaller bonnet, with a smaller tray, with a smaller Chlumec inside, and so on and on, to the vanishing point in infinity.

But since my father is no one-sided, narrow-minded person, he knows of course that even the tray with Edvin and Chlumec, i.e., this tray of his, does not really extend into infinity along a single straight line but that over and behind it there is another woman, a bigger and more capable woman, who grasps him while being herself grasped and held aloft and borne toward a still greater unfolding, toward still more extensive, more comprehensive wholes.

It would suffice, thought Edvin, if I took my stand between the over-women and the under-women, at the point of the hold, the shifting center of action: to become the eyes of the world.

That's how my father imagined it, gripped by the picture of Droste's farm girl, and a halo began to glow over his head—no, a *love light*, the light which brought him so much love, and of course protection, too, in moments of temptation. The love halo shone over his head, the score on the Chlumec soccer field was 0:0, and Bonek wanted to seize his brother's halo and gnaw it like a wafer with his canine tooth.

If I have not mentioned that special canine until now, Comr. Pavlenda, it is because I am the only male descendant on Father's side who is lacking it. My canine does not stick out, my third tooth on the left is in no way remarkable. When I bare my teeth, I do not look at all threatening, whereas when Bonek or Edvin do so, it looks as if they could readily bite someone if they wished. Right now, for example: Edvin was very angry, he realized what the conversation had been about, answered

Bonek with a cutting remark, finally told his brother to kiss his ass, and bared his pointed tusk as a warning: not another word about Alice!

Of course, Bonek's maxilla (jawbone, Comr. Pavlenda) is also equipped with just such a *dens caninus* (the Latin name expresses its purpose very well). But Bonek generally does not flash it right away, he does not believe in unnecessary warnings, and when he feels like biting and there is nothing to bite or the time is *not yet ripe*, he covers his already exposed canine with his lip, so that his face shows . . . a smile, actually, but that special Bonekian smile.

And so the two of them stood there facing one another, on the playing field of the Chlumec Athletic Club, smiling at each other and showing their canines.

It was the first time each of them noticed how sharp the other's *dens* was.

Edvin's canine actually seemed longer, it had a more massive cutting edge. Looking at that edge, Bonek told himself that in the future he would not acquaint his brother with his decisions beforehand but would tell him only whatever was necessary in a given situation.

At the same time, it occurred to Bonek that perhaps he should start treating his brother with a bit of scorn.

"Well, whatever you think, Edvy. After all, you're doing it for a *woman's* sake."

He did not like Alice, and besides, in his vocabulary, doing something for a woman's sake was equivalent to demeaning oneself.

"You won't believe me," said Edvin, "but I am doing it for my own sake."

. . .

A word of explanation, Comr. Pavlenda. At that time Hatus employees were supposed to fill out Questionnaire No. 184/L, which is relevant to Question 6 of *Our Questionnaire* (hereafter O.Q.) No. 012400. We were supposed to make a declaration about our origin: *Erklärung über die Abstammung.* And Bonek mistrusted Alice's eyes, he suspected them of being Jewish, and that's why he questioned Father so urgently, that's why he had asked, "What are we going to do about her?," i.e., *we,* in order to put us on the spot while at the same time giving the matter a more majestic ring.

5. THE PORTAL

Largior, Comr. Pavlenda, also means to forgive, that's another meaning of the expression, but H. Vohryzek failed to mention this one and Bonek did not have time to look it up in the dictionary because he was very busy. First of all, he had to fill in for Vohryzek, and secondly, he had to deal with people who lacked a responsible nature (e.g., Edvin), had no sense of values, and forced others to take care of their affairs. These cares drove Bonek all the way to the chancery to talk to Msgr. Rosin, and in effect were responsible for his encounter with Marta Vohryzek. Bonek knew that the Vohryzeks no longer lived in the Cepin villa, but somehow he had forgotten that they had been forced to move out here, to Franciscan Street, No. 12, into the loft of a run-down building that had once housed a wax factory.

Bonek would not have chosen this route if there had been some other way to get to the chancery, and Marta would have been at home if the shopping hours for Jews had not coincided with Msgr. Rosin's office hours. Bonek needed seven documents attesting to our origin, those seven documents regarding Alice's side of the family which Edvin had refused to concern himself about; Marta Vohryzek needed bones. They had been promised to her, she was happy that for once she would not have to cook soup from scraps of skin and dried blood but from the proper ingredients: pieces of meat still left on bones, and of course the bones themselves, big bones, so big they would stick out of the pot and Herman (formerly the best agent in the employ of Mr. Hatus) would snap out of his torpor, then pick up a cleaver and start chop-

ping at them with such gusto that the blows could be
heard far and wide and the neighbors would say to themselves: "Well now, listen to that, old Vohryzek is still
alive and kicking."

Whereupon: Marta picked up her shopping bag and
walked out of No. 12, Bonek picked up his briefcase
containing form Lg. No. 184/L, and they both set out in
the same direction, until they were so close they could
not ignore each other.

Marta lifted her Jewish, almond eyes (Alice's eyes)
toward Bonek, Bonek shuddered at the likeness (to
Alice), bowed his head, and said softly: "Good day."
It was out before he realized it, but he kept on walking
without stopping, he hurried on, frightened, he saw how
white Marta was, as if in that house of wax she herself
had turned into a wax figure.

Marta was hurrying too, she answered the greeting
with a whisper, not wishing to stop in the street either,
for she had come to learn that this was generally dangerous, and she was glad that Bonek had greeted her. She
thought she would tell Herman, perhaps that would cheer
him up, revive him a bit (he, too, had turned to wax),
perhaps he would stop squatting over the little iron
stove, burning up old furniture, and instead start hammering away at the bones . . . or even start a conversation.

The intersection of their paths, Bonek's and Marta's,
was marked by an autumnal sun chiseled in stone, as part
of the old Franciscan emblem on the wall of the house.
The sun was rising over an upright cross, but it was the
Sun of Death, and the real number of the house was not
12 but 8, like the DOMUS MORTIS of my horoscope.

I was born with the Sun in that house, and it shines
there for me still. I am greatly aware of its glow; on that
Wednesday in October (10/11) when Bonek encountered
Marta, I had felt it for the first time. For the first time,
I had smelled the death of those "diers." Some of those

around me who were still alive were already passing into another state, to their dying; they didn't realize it, but I did. Later this knowledge caused me pain and I felt guilty, though, to tell the truth, there is nothing very remarkable about my nose, I am just an ordinary sniffer of mortality.

So then: Bonek absorbed some of those deadly rays and carried them to Msgr. Rosin (I felt that, too) and the Dean caught their glow and from that day he began to resemble more and more the figures of angels in stained-glass windows of the presbytery, and from that day he also began to include exhortations in his services in which he alluded to the Sermon on the Mount in a voice that seemed to belong to some other, recessive ancestor. I should have become a priest like Msgr. Rosin, but I was not born similarly endowed. He spoke of the Light of the World (himself already illuminated) and warned his congregation that a city built atop a mountain cannot hide.

He was partly thinking of Chlumec, city of the crown royal, for Chlumec stood on a high plateau rising from the White River, visible and unconcealable.

The monsignor knew the city extremely well. He had been writing about it for some fourteen years, on and off, he had published blue-covered pamphlets on the *History of Chlumec*, "beloved seat of my labors," and there were altogether nineteen such booklets, making up three volumes of a projected four-volume set that covered the story of Chlumec from its earliest beginning to the year 1914. The last, fourth volume, consisting of six pamphlets, and entitled *Religious Life*, was still to be issued. The dedication on the title page had already been composed: "To Dean Stach, my predecessor, and faithful servant of the Lord." However, aside from this dedication and a pen drawing of St. Barbora's Church in winter, the pages were as blank and white as St. Barbora's snow-covered roof. The personages which were to fill the blue pamphlets—clergymen, monks, Utraquists, Jews—were still on file cards in old dusty drawers, waiting to make the move into Monsignor's history but hesitating because the time was unfavorable. The shelves were lined with parish registers, too. A green one, *Liber baptisatorum decanalis Chlumecensis*, contained an entry about the birth of a certain Jan known as Trubac, and the leather-covered register from the sister church at Zehun knew of Jakub Strela, who died all the way in the Balkans. These books knew a great deal, and knowingly they waited for Bonek in order to tell him who had begotten whom and in what generation. Yet Bonek was uneasy. In the hall downstairs he had met Christ in a terribly lifelike, life-size picture, and on the stairs he saw St. Jan Nepomuk. Henchmen of the Sluggard King were throwing the saint into the Moldau. He was in midair, falling and rising at the same time, and any one passing the canvas gasped at this uncanny blast of eternity. It affected Bonek, too. He felt ill at ease, trapped, the way he used to feel as a boy when visiting the fair and taking a ride through the castle of horrors.

And he fared no better upstairs. He saw two priests. One was thin and tall, looming up life-size over the desk. The other, very fat, was standing on a ladder alongside the topmost shelf.

"Your Reverence," he said to the fat one, casting an uneasy glance at the painted, thin one. "Your Reverence, I have a favor to ask of you."

"I know, you're from the Hatus plant," said Rosin, hitching up his cassock and wheezing down at Bonek. "Show me that certificate. Yes. Seven copies should be sufficient for you." He reached for the documents relating to my mother and the other Vachals all the way to Jan the Baptist, who had engendered them in Chlumec.

"Please understand," said Bonek, to whom the whole

affair with Lg. No. 184/L suddenly seemed embarrassing, "I'm only doing it for the sake of my brother's position."

Rosin said: "I understand, you're doing it for his sake, *date que sunt Caesaris Caesari* . . ." (this is Latin, Comr. Pavlenda, it's about giving unto Caesar what is Caesar's, etc., I'm sure you know the quotation). But when he saw Bonek glancing out of the corner of his eye at the picture hanging over the writing desk, he added: "That's my distant predecessor, Dean Stach, with those uncanny eyes of his. They're painted in such a way that he stares at you no matter where you stand."

"He looks alive," said Uncle.

"He is," replied Rosin.

Item: Bonek shot out of there as quickly as he could, while Pater Stach climbed out of the frame, walked down to the garden and right on through the gate toward the embankment.

It was the 2nd of June 1866. The sound of canon fire was muffled by heavy rain. Guns had been booming since early morning, from the Cepin side. Water streamed down Franciscan Street all the way to the chancery as eleven soldiers of the Nobili regiment slogged toward the gate.

Mud splashed under their boots, the troops looked so bedraggled that a pall spread over the town even before the decisive defeat on the following day. Now and again they turned and on the run fired salvos from their muskets (front-loading, Lorenz system) in order to slow down the invaders, but those Prussians were already pouring into Chlumec from all sides and through all the portals except the small chancery gate, to which only Pater Stach had the key. He shouted to the soldiers of the Nobili regiment, opened the gate for them so that they could live another night and die—all but one man— the next day. *Item*: They slipped and slid on the muddy bank, throwing away their white-strapped packs, soiling

their blue trousers, pulling off their boots, they jumped
into the water, that dirty stinking canal pelted by rain,
they held their muskets high over their heads as all
around them cocked hats were floating like ships, the rain
soaked the hats but they would only sink by evening,
when Chlumec had already been conquered and occupied
and at peace, and they would all set out for Sendruzice—
all but one, the eleventh, who slid all the way to the edge
of the stream but no farther. Pater Stach saw him, called
out: "*Hörst du mich?*" He hitched up his cassock and
came skidding down the embankment. "*Verwundet?*"
The soldier's white coat was soaked with blood at the
ribs, (matching the color of the epaulettes). "*Was ist
mit dir?*" "I don't know how to swim, your Reverence,"
said the soldier in Czech.

Pater Stach helped him up the slope, still marked by
the tracks dug in the mud by the rears of sliding comrades, helped him to reach Chlumec &—years later—the
heavenly kingdom as well.

.   .   .

At the same time the Prussian crown prince entered
Chlumec and was about to converse with a certain
K. Trubac, without an interpreter.

The conversation was about to take place, and it was
an important one from the viewpoint of Lg. No. 184/L.
A short distance from the spot where Pater Stach had
rescued Jan Baptist Vachal—that nonswimmer—sat
Alzbeta Trubac. She was locked up in a basement room
by her father to keep her safe from the Prussians, and
even though it was summer she had taken along a knitted
blanket and a warm pair of stockings. Alzbeta pushed a
wooden box of shoe polish next to the window (the cover
of the box showed a monkey polishing his shoes), she
stepped on that monkey and peered through the small
window at Jost Square, at the legs of the town councillors

who were lining up at St. Mary's Column to greet the Prussian prince.

But the simple act of sliding the shoe-polish box to the window provided a definite basis for calculating the degree of Aryanism, according to Section A, para. 1, of government directive 156/40 (*Regierungsverordnung*). The situation at the time was thus as follows:

a) Pater Stach was changing his cassock.

b) Jan Baptist Vachal, lodged in a small room in the chancery, was feeling much better in spite of having been told that he had lost a great deal of blood.

c) Prince Friedrich had passed the Anchor Inn on Jost Square, and was approaching St. Mary's statue.

d) Kaspar Trubac was standing in front of his boarded-up store, trying to look as if the store was someone else's property.

e) Alzbeta was peering through many human, and soon also equine, legs.

Gunfire still resounded but interludes of a peculiar silence could now be discerned amid the tumult.

Thereupon the prince told the town councillors that his war was with the emperor's army, not the people, and he requested the mayor to supply 3,370 loaves of bread, 5,000 measures of grain, 20 hundredweights of rice, 200 pounds of meat. He dismounted, sat down on the stone bench circling the column and fountain, stretched his legs, and began chatting with his officers and the Duke of Coburg. They were all dead-tired but nobody dared to dip his face in the fountain unless the prince did so first. But the prince wanted to show them that he was suffering the same tribulations as they (if not worse), and in order to make his point he made them suffer a bit longer. He was therefore in no hurry, the fountain was flowing, the storm was over, birds sat once again on the heads of the statues and on the starry diadem of the Virgin Mary. It was a moment of reconciliation of something or other with something else, though it would have been difficult to say just who was being reconciled with what. Kaspar Trubac therefore concluded that everything that was destined to happen that day (6/2/1866) had already happened. He turned toward his shop and saw a Prussian soldier lifting the butt of his musket to strike the padlock off the outer sheet-metal-covered door of *General Store—Merchandise of All Kinds—K. Trubac, Proprietor.* And so Kaspar made an about-face, turning once more toward the prince.

K. Trubac was eager to know whether the crown prince had seen the soldier, too, but the prince's view was partly blocked by the Duke of Coburg, and thus it was not clear whether the prince could see all the way *there.* Ah, what uncertainty! And Kaspar Trubac assumed the stance of a supplicant, that is to say, he was looking up at the statue of Mary but at the same time his head was bowed down toward the gray basalt under his feet. It was he who had provided Chlumec with this pavement, during his administration as mayor. Now it seemed, however, that not even the most obvious cough would arouse attention, especially since more and more rifle butts were banging on shop doors, Berta's store was being ransacked, and so was Just's. Trubac turned (it was his third about-face in the center of Chlumec, *versio in pedem*). The little shops gaped open, the sidewalk in front of Zuska's was piled with awls, whetstones, rolls of winding-sheet cloth, soap. From Trubac's shop they started carrying preserves, seeds, tins of yeast. Kaspar could no longer bear to watch, he turned away, i.e., he performed his fourth turn (*versio in capitem*) in the center of Chlumec, facing once again the crown prince, who was at last gulping water from the fountain, for the time of self-control had passed and the time of communal drinking had come. But how can one talk to anyone whose mouth is full of water? With due regard for the exceptional nature of the moment (and of course with due regard for his long-standing contributions in the office of mayor), Trubac made the following attempt: "Your Excellency," he said (*Sie Excelenz!*). But it came out sounding unseemly, unceremonious. "Ah, gentlemen," he continued, as if the others were in a position to help him, "perhaps . . ." And he reached out his arm to indicate his utter bewilderment.

Whereupon: The just Lord in heaven saw his gesture, saw all the previous turns of Kaspar Trubac, his attempts to change his unfavorable position in the center of town, and He clasped Kaspar by his outstretched arm and lifted him to Himself, for:

A soldier who did not like Kaspar's gesture stepped up (from behind), lifted his rifle (Dreys-type rifle), and fired a shot in the air, so close to Kaspar's head that K. Trubac leaped forward, took three steps in the direction of St. Mary's statue, and died of fright.

Crown Prince Friedrich spat water out of his mouth and asked: "*Was ist los?*"

And that is a precise record of their conversation.

.   .   .

Belehrung, or Instruction
Whereas,
according to para. 1 of the *Reg.Vdg.Slg.Br.* No. 136, a "Jew" is defined as "someone who is descended from at least three Jewish (*der Rasse nach volljüdischen*) forebears," it is clear from the aforementioned definition that neither I nor my mother's ancestors could be considered "volljüdisch." I was delivered into Chlumec in a racially impeccable manner.

• • •

The doors of the store were wide open and the few soldiers who were not busy carrying anything at the moment picked up Kaspar's body and laid it on the counter between two large glass jars containing hard candy, one at his head and one at his feet. And he lay there, Kaspar Trubac did, till seven o'clock that night, because only he knew where he had locked his daughter to keep her safe from the Prussians, and there was no longer any way he could tell it to the soldiers searching for her. Alzbeta heard the rifle shot, it terrified her, she slumped down on her wooden crate . . . and before she dared to stand up again, Kaspar was already lying upstairs in the looted store. She had simply missed the crucial moment. She was very scared, because the pounding and stamping above her head seemed to be coming closer, down the stairway and—God forbid—right to her bolted door. She recited her Hail Marys until evening, when Pater Stach found her and took her to his house, i.e., to Jan Baptist Vachal, so they could beget a son, Nepomuk, who begot Jan Evangelist, who in turn begot my mother, Alice with the black-olive eyes.

And believe me, Comr. Pavlenda, whenever she looked at anyone with those eyes (and I should add that those eyes were with her constantly, in other words I am not talking of occasional bolts of lightning), they turned an even darker, blacker olive.

The more intensely they gazed, the more their iris darkened and her pupils took on a pearly sheen. That is why in my childhood days I used to believe that Mother was able to turn her eyes on and off like lamps, and I was not afraid to go with her to the Pleasure Park after nightfall. I was also convinced that her pearly beam consisted of four smaller lights. Once I watched Alice, counted them, and then asked why she needed four lights in her eyes. "Lights? What lights?" She ran to look in the mirror. "But those are our windows!" (Facing the play-ground, Comr. Pavlenda.) "That's just a reflection, silly."

But she patted me even more tenderly than usual. Of course, I did not believe her, I was convinced that her eyes held a dark secret which she did not want me to know. And I was probably right. Even though it may have looked like a reflection of the windows, she answered me in such a peculiar manner that I was sure there was more to it. After all, my suspicion was further confirmed by Olin after he returned to Chlumec. He had not seen Alice for more than six years, but he immediately mentioned her eyes. He said that they had become even more equatorial, that they had begun to resemble a precious chrysoberyl-colored stone known as alex-andrite, and that they contained mirrors like the eyes of the cat Fatima.

Of course, Olin was not referring to the equator only in the geographic sense (or in the sense of women from tropical regions), but he was thinking of the *equator oculi*, which was especially prominent in Mother's case.

Olin also declared that Mother was "a Jewess of the Jewish breed, Jewish to the bone," which was a kind of saying.

Whereupon Edvin brought out document Lg. No. 184/L, *Uber die Abstammung*, and showed Olin Mother's certification, in black and white, but Olin was unconvinced, because paper is only paper, but eyes are eyes.

I thus began to realize, Comr. Pavlenda, that those eyes knew something special, otherwise they would not have acted that way. And I realized, too, that by its very thoroughness form Lg. No. 184/L was actually quite misleading. It was strict in demanding information of a specific kind, but it left no room for the respondent's self-analysis. The questions should not have been aimed at unambiguous declarations of the declarer (*der*

Erklärende), but the declarer after detailed analysis of all his or her basic attitudes should finally pose the question: Am I not really a Jew? It is not enough to trace the roots, it is the seed which counts. Form Lg. No. 184/L could be outwitted. Someone like myself, whose descent had been thoroughly investigated, could be harboring Jewishness (*das Volljüdische*) better than a Jew. It was therefore most important to examine the source, to study the origin of those eyes, to bring their submersiveness to light, to study how they were able to appear in one generation and disappear in another, and also to investigate who was responsible for smuggling those eyes into Chlumec—myself excepted.

. . .

Re: submersiveness. (For Comr. Pavlenda.)

Msgr. Rosin's *Liber baptisatorum*, in blue marbled covers, had an entry for the date II/29/1776 (leap year), recording the birth of a child, that made it possible for the eyes either to submerse or come to light, as they pleased. But the *dies natalis* of this boy was immediately changed to February 28, 1776; somebody had either made a mistake or had good-naturedly decided to make Ignac Trubac a day younger. In any case, it is clear that this uncertainty (quite fundamental astrologically, i.e., from the viewpoint of a chronoscope) expressed that general eccentricity and vagueness which I. Trubac was to inject into our stock (*mütterlicherseits im Sinne der Verordnung Lg. Nr. 184/L*).

Ignac was subject to rash decisions, and he would launch long arguments extolling the advantages of opposite alternatives; he rowed, as it were, with oars perpetually at cross-purposes. He would soon be twenty-seven, he was supposed to get married but did not yet know to whom. He was guided by the good rule that beyond a certain point all women are the same, and he was therefore waiting for Mother to pick an especially same one for him. *Item*: On that day, too, the 28th of February, 1803, he was rushing to see Mother. The metal of the harness rang merrily, the sleigh flew along, snow crunched under the runners. If his birth certificate had not shifted his true birthday, he would surely have stopped in Odslava or Prosek, but now he had to urge the horses on and scramble up the Moran hills, toward the forest with the Swedish crosses sticking out of the snow in memory of General Tortensson. Those crosses were a traditional place for coachmen to ease the load by getting off and walking. Ignac stopped, hung a lantern on the side brace; it was dark and starting to snow. His eyes were narrowed by hoarfrost—and also by fear, for this place was notorious for robbery and murder. There was a ballad about it, "The Robbers of the Moran Woods," telling of the death of passengers and of highwaymen, too, "dragged by horses, bellies gaping wide." Brrr! The wind picked up and blew against the horses, whistled through the clearing in the woods where the road passed the lonely spot known as Svetlice (i.e., Light-Crest). There God himself had once stood looking down into the valley, when He ordered the people to build Chlumec and Cepin and those thirty-three settlements scattered around them. Ignac mumbled a prayer, the wind died down, and behind the crests of the hills reappeared the starry sky of a clear winter night.

Smoke from a chimney rose straight in the frosty air. The harness jingled once more, the lantern swung into a curve, and the moon emerged from the clouds. Ignac looked toward Chlumec and it seemed far away, far behind the lights of Svetlice. *Item*: He pounded on the door of the cabin, Katerina Strela's door, and Katerina went forth to meet Ignac. She was still bundled up in her shawl, she was still hidden from him. Ignac was wrapped up too, his kerchief was tied over his mouth, white with frost. He kicked his boots against the side of the cabin, a sparkling shower of ice and snow came flying to the ground. Katerina asked him to come in. Inside, they both took off their wraps and were beautiful in each other's eyes. Ignac saw Katerina's four-point, chrysoberyl eyes with the rainbow arcs.

Whereupon: Quoth Katerina, 1803 A.D., February 28; glancing up at Ignac: "Unharness the sleigh, I'll take care of the horses."

Ignac looked into Katerina's eyes, and beyond them he saw other eyes and beyond those still others, still more penetrating; he saw all the way to the leaves in Jiven, where Alice was to press close to Edvin and squeeze me into life. It was the same convergence of images as the series of pictures on Droste's cocoa, so intriguing to my father.

Katerina Strela, too, looked at Ignac, saw the hoarfrost on his eyebrows and lashes slowly melting; drops of water trickled down, revealing his eyes: blue, perfectly blue.

．　　．　　．

About that smuggling, Comr. Pavlenda! Here's where it all started: Katerina gave birth to Kaspar (1804), the one lying on the counter, the corpse stretched out between jars of hard candy. He was the first smuggler, the first underground link. His own eyes had no pearls or inner glow. He did not use them to look back into time or forward into the gorge looming ahead, but looked from his small shop to the statue of Mary and further to Town Hall, and he kept looking at that Town Hall so intently that he became mayor. In fact, whatever he focused his eyes on submitted to him at once. And so he picked out Camila, daughter of Peregrin Holan, because she was beautiful and also because Peregrin owned the Anchor House and Tavern. Kaspar focused his eyes on her and she put aside her maiden wreath and then her pen, i.e., she never finished her poem "The Pilgrim," even though she was the only poetess in the entire history of Chlumec and had composed an "Ode to the Black Steed" on the occasion of the first train to arrive in Chlumec. But not even she, beautiful as she was (her portrait hung in the Mint House; Rosin's history contained a reproduction of it)—not even she had any trace of chrysoberyl in her eyes. Her eyes were veronica-blue, there was nothing *volljüdisch* about them, or about her hair, which was raven-black but without that suspicious coppery undertone.

I had come to love her very much, Comr. Pavlenda, not by her ordinary name but by her poetic pseudonym, Astrid Zorska, (and by that painting). She was, in the real sense of the term, a short-lived, shooting star.

She and Kaspar Trubac: there could have been no greater disharmony in a union, or a surer way to extinguish all chrysoberylness. Ignac had only introduced a bit of blue, he made the chrysoberyl submerge under a blue surface, but these two—Kaspar + Camila—had the power to drown it once and for all.

Camila (Oh, Astrid!) wrote:

> Trembling star in lonely flight,
> Tell, oh tell what fate is mine?

This is the question she posed in the First Song of her "Pilgrim," and Kaspar Trubac, i.e., his invisible penis, answered by impregnating her so thoroughly that it almost killed her progeny. Oh no, Camila had no appetite left for writing. She lay buried in her quilts, and even though it was the middle of July, her teeth were chattering. It seemed to her as if her offspring—that newborn part of her womb they were taking away—was being torn out of her body with a piece of her own flesh. Her gaping wound burned, fire spread through the ripped flesh without warming her, it burned with icy tongues.

Red-and-white flags flutter in the chilly wind as a train

arrives with the governor, the Archbishop of Prague, the Hungarian Prince Palatine, and of course the Archduke Franz Karl. Artillerymen fire cannon in Pleasure Park (Camila wrote a poem about that, too), the guests get off the train for a brief breakfast stop, the archduke emerges from the door of his parlor car, and behold: four hussars immediately spread out a carpet on which his Excellency walks to the canopy, draped red and white, where Astrid Zorska is standing with a bouquet in her hand, and under the flowers an ode "composed in celebration of the steam locomotive." No Kaspar Trubac is in sight, the air is full of "Hurrah!" and "Long Live" and garlands, tradesmen are holding up banners of their guilds, and sharpshooters provide an honor guard. And those pyramids of wreaths and foliage which the city fathers erected to stand on both sides of Astrid as if it were she who had so gloriously arrived in Chlumec . . . and not this pain, this pain which makes it hard for her to lift her arm and to present the bouquet and poem to his Excellency the archduke. Ah, sighs Astrid, I *must* give him the poem, she stretches out her arm with all her strength, the archduke smiles, peony petals rain down until they cover everything, and not even the most intense glare of Kaspar Trubac will ever manage to penetrate this glory and shrivel Astrid into mere Camila.

Item: Kaspar Trubac at last tossed a handful of soil on the coffin and when he saw Camila in her grave he began to love her. He had planted *her* in the ground, but sorrow was sprouting in *him*. And so Kaspar came to believe that his wife had been taken from him by God but that she had contributed to this end by being so fragile and by writing poems about Pleasure Park and the Black Steed and the Homeland. So Kaspar bought up all the copies of Camila's poems, locked them up in the upper drawer of his desk, which bore the mysterious inscription SUCCUS, so that nobody could ever again reach her, and especially not those Czech patriots (*diese Patrioten*) who dared to write to her even after her death.

A week after the funeral a letter came from them, addressing Camila as if she were still alive: Dear Lady, they asked, how are you progressing with your Pilgrim? Not at all, Kaspar answered on her behalf, for she hath died, her soul blasted by that poison of yours.

He resented these nationalists and performed his mayoral duties as if they didn't exist. And in March of the year '48, when they marched jubilantly through the streets, he strode toward them across Jost Square leading a little dog with a patriotic red-and-white banner tied to its tail. That's how he killed the dog, too. The animal disappeared and K. Trubac wrote to the District Superintendent: *Diese Patrioten haben auch meinen Hund gefressen!* They've eaten my dog! It was an insult which they never forgot. Even now, as he lay on the counter among candy jars, a corpse, they were saying it served him right that God had punished him.

.   .   .

Seminal Declaration

But to return to those eyes, Comr. Pavlenda! To those chrysoberyl eyes. Suddenly they reappeared. Torn out of Camila Holan's body with Alzbeta, bride of Jan Baptist, they survived. Perhaps it was this very graft that had killed Camila. What had Kaspar implanted in her, anyway? He himself did not know that he had it! But whatever it was, it had torn her in half.

Because I am aware, Comr. Pavlenda, that anyone deliberately providing false information (*wissentlich falsche Angaben*) will be prosecuted, I hereby declare that this "something" was first sired in Svetlice, 425 m. above sea level, on the Radec hill bordering the Moran woods, and that the first woman to transmit it (it can be assumed as proven that transmission takes place entirely on the distaff side) was Katerina Strela. She got it directly from the originator.

"You're the spitting image of him" (i.e., of the originator), her mother used to tell her. "I see him looking at me out of the pupils of your eyes, and I don't know if it's a sin or if this is the good Lord's way of letting me know that Jakub [the originator] is dead, buried in that Balkan earth under a Christian cross."

Whenever this conversation came up, both of these women

(a) Katerina Strela; and

(b) her progenitor Barbora

would step out into the garden. This garden was bordered by woods, sloping down the side of the Radec hill toward Chlumec. It had no fence but was marked off by a stream and some crab-apple trees in the midst of which stood a Christless iron cross, and Barbora used to hang wreaths of flowers on it depending on the season of the year and she taught Katerina to weave such wreaths and to hang them on the cross and to pray to the Holy Virgin because both women hoped to learn whether Jakub had found salvation in the Balkans or whether he was lying in some godforsaken Balkan wheat field, unburied, fertilizing what was supposedly the best soil in the whole empire. Then, too, Barbora the progenitor used to tell Katerina the transmitter that here in the garden lay their forefathers, buried at a time when the dead were not yet being interred in cemeteries but in their own soil, close to home. But Katerina found it hard to believe it was possible to put a human to rest in unhallowed ground.

And Barbora the progenitor also used to tell Katerina the transmitter that Jakub Strela had at first believed in Joseph II as a ruler sincerely desiring his people's good.

In this belief he had descended into the valley to see with his own eyes—in which chrysoberyl was already sprouting—the emperor's Patent of Tolerance. He duly perused the document, returned to Svetlice, looked up David's fortieth psalm in the Good Book, and said to his neighbors, that is, to his *lambs*: "I waited patiently for the Lord; and he inclined unto me, and heard my cry. He brought me up also out of a horrible pit, out of the miry clay, and set my feet upon a rock, and established my goings."

Thus spoke Jakub to the assembled multitude, heretic among heretics, among his Adamite lambs who had come from villages like Jiven (i.e., Willowgrove) and Odloucen (i.e., Wedgewood, the home of Barbora), from Jilem and Velc; he prayed with them and promised to attest to their faith, exhorted them to proclaim their faith openly, and having uttered this, he descended once more into the valley to see Bailiff Zellhofer.

"How many do you number?" asked the bailiff.

"We are fifty-three," replied Jakub, "and this is what we believe: not that the Lamb had become man, but that we are all lambs and sons of God. Whoever is just will most particularly partake of God's filiation."

Whereupon Bailiff Zellhofer said unto Jakub Strela, A.D. Martii 1782: "Mark me well. Your words deserve one hundred and twenty blows."

And Jakub replied: "Wherefore speak you this way?"

And the bailiff said: "By the emperor's command. This is how his Majesty wishes to treat with all deists."

. . .

The snow melted, even the Radec hills were bare except for two brownish-white patches still holding out in the garden; in the stream bordering Svetlice, water lapped against the boards of the bridge across which fellow lambs were bringing back their badly thrashed comrade.

When they deposited him in the house and straightened out the blankets on which he had been lying throughout the journey, he asked for the Holy Book and said to them: "The wicked have drawn out the sword, and have bent their bow to slay such as be of upright conversation."

He was pale, but a chrysoberyl flame flickered in his eyes, the first of four lights that were to resemble, now and again, a reflection of four windowpanes. His back was livid and swollen. Barbora lifted the folded sheet that served as a dressing and dipped it into a basin filled with icy water from the stream. The bloody smudges on the sheet were still fresh enough to soak off easily, staining the water red.

Item: Barbora kept changing the dressings all night and pulled out splinters stuck in the wound, but Jakub did not complain, only his face was drawn, his eyes lit up with beam No. 2, and his lips trembled. By morning he had recovered sufficiently to be able to walk to the window.

"If you like, I'll stay with you today, too," she said.

And he answered: "Stay."

But he had in mind a longer period of time than she had asked about. And so she rushed to Odloucena to fetch her things.

He was thirty-two and she was sixteen. Later, after he had completely recovered and had gazed for a long time into the valley, directed by the third chrysoberyl light, he asked Barbora to bring him his writing equipment. He wrote to Bailiff Zellhofer: "There was one additional thing I wished to impart to you, Honorable Sir, on the subject of the Third People, on the subject of us who are Vessels of the Lord and silenced lambs: there is a Soul in the human body which is immortal and which will recompense us for our suffering; we also believe in the Holy Ghost as our helper and supporter. We do not believe in punishment, particularly not the torments of hell, which are so contrary to the nature of our most merciful Father."

Then an extraordinary thing happened. A carriage containing his Excellency the bishop and a number of priests from various parishes drove out of town, climbed the Radec hill until the road became too narrow and H.E. the bishop had to proceed the rest of the way on foot, along with a cluster of clerics. Mowers dropped their scythes, knelt by the side of the road and humbly asked to be blessed, handed the bishop bouquets of wheat and cornflowers, while praying for Jakub Strela, praying that God in His mercy soften Jakub's stubborn heart.

But Jakub Strela prayed to the Lord: "Dear God, strengthen my spirit, fortify me and put me to the test."

Then his Excellency the bishop and Jakub Strela conversed for five hours alone in that big room, Jakub answering his Excellency with the greatest respect and in perfect gentleness; yet his mind could not encompass the mystery of the Christian faith.

A.D. Iulii 1782, five hours later, the bishop left the house, ignored the proffered bouquets, and in deep contemplation resembling sorrow walked back to the carriage.

Item: A court decree was duly issued and riders were dispatched to seize the deists. Six soldiers arrived at Svetlice, tied Jakub's hands with a rope, and attached the other end to their standard-bearer's saddle.

Barbora did not dare weep, she was even afraid to pray, for she saw that her mind was unwittingly turning for help to the Virgin Mary, the Heavenly Intercessor, and not to that severe Lord with whom communed Jakub Strela.

This frightened her very much, because of her love for Jakub, which included corporal love, for this too was one way of loving the lamb: having taken her, he entered her.

They encountered other soldiers who were leading

other lambs, until there was a whole procession and this finally reached the drill field of the Pleasure Park at the edge of Chlumec.

In the evening they were visited by Fra Mauritius-Marik, Superior of the Franciscan order in Chlumec, who implored them to abjure their obstinacy for the sake of their immortal souls. Nevertheless, by early morning the regimental drums began to beat, the governor nodded to the major and the major to the commandant. Their eyes met in silent agreement, they scanned their assembled troops, which formed a square wedged under the overhanging roofs of the barracks and stables. They also scanned all the lambs, the clerk read out their names, and each one answered that it was indeed he and that he was indeed present, even though no doubt could possibly have existed on that account.

Thereupon the commandant said: "Jakub Strela/and Metej Rubin and Josef Postrihac, etc., etc./are you aware of the frequent warnings and instructions (*Belehrung*) issued for your edification by offices of his Imperial Highness?"

Jakub assented.

"And do you even now hold fast to your fallacies?"

"I do," Jakub replied, and they immediately stripped him of his flannel jacket, leather trousers, white wool stockings, and sandals, and handed him a white coat of coarse worsted and long blue trousers.

And the other lambs, too, were put into uniform and were issued boots of the kind worn in Hungary. All were then enrolled in Croatian regiments of his Imperial Highness.

And so it came to pass that they fell into the hands of an unmerciful, yea vengeful foe.

.   .   .

They also led out the women of those lambs, admonished them and condemned them; those that were carrying children were deprived of them, for it is written: Rachel wept for her children, and would not be comforted, because they are not.

But they could not pull Katerina out of Barbora's body, for she was still so tiny and fresh that the midwife whom they had called could not swab or scrape her out.

It was only when they reached Temesvar, Comr. Pavlenda, at 22 degrees longitude and 40 degrees latitude, that they discovered this fetus. In other words, it was very far from our lands; it was in the Balkans, which those lambs had reached after two months of travel on foot and in silence, for they were forbidden to talk among themselves. That was why Barbora could not ask Jakub anything and why she felt ever more lonely and solitary, and when she happened to catch Jakub's eye she found no trace of response or encouragement, but on the contrary those eyes seemed to drain her of every remnant of courage. They reflected nothing. They looked right through Barbora's belly as if it were transparent, and they began to glow with a fourth light. And Barbora in fact began to feel transparent, vulnerable, and she therefore again turned to the Virgin Mary, but now without pangs of conscience—and with even greater fervor.

It was night when they entered Temesvar (they always entered towns at night), and her fervor turned to fever and delirium. Barbora called for help. A priest came, the district school inspector or superintendent, and gave orders for Barbora to get some chicken broth. Barbora told the priest about her transparency. He said that . . . that it was a vision sent by the Queen of Virgins, for the Virgin was the refuge of sinners and the purest of mothers.

.   .   .

And so they prayed to the Virgin, Barbora and the priest, but they did not utter one word about Jakub.

However, the story of the Spanish martyr which the priest recounted had a bearing on Jakub:

She—the celebrated Spanish beauty—had also been under the protection of the Virgin. When she fell into the hands of a nobleman who tried through violent means to deprive her of a maid's most precious possession, in despair she implored the villain to tell her which of her attributes he found the most beautiful. Your eyes, answered the nobleman. She grasped a knife, gouged out her eyeball, and threw it at the blackguard's feet.

Barbora burst into tears and pleaded for permission to talk to Jakub.

Permission was granted.

Jakub grasped Barbora by the hands, pulled her close, and said that she was free to follow her conscience. As proof that he bore no resentment, he gazed at her with untroubled eyes.

But they already contained all four lights.

On the 17th of June, in the local church, Barbora made a confession of faith.

On the 25th of November, in Svetlice, she bore a daughter, who was given the name corresponding to Tuesday of that date, i.e., Katerina. The infant had the eyes of silenced lamb Jakub Strela.

Barbora's dream that night: she called out to Jakub to turn around. He turned to her and asked: What attribute of mine pleases you the best, and when she answered that it was his eyes, he gouged out his eyeball and threw it at her feet. The color of the eye was chrysoberyl. Then, and ever more.

Item: I am enclosing a chart, Comr. Pavlenda, which delineates the propagation of those eyes. Please note that the transmitters are exclusively women and that the manifestation of the phenomenon always skips one generation.

The following sign denotes those eyes:

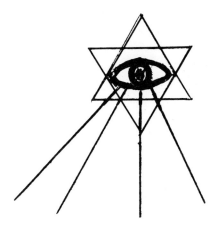

The chart is intended only as a basis for a pedigree which would trace not merely the stock but also the seed:

DECLARATION REGARDING SEMINAL ORIGIN

ERKLARUNG UBER DEN SAMEN

СЕМЕННОЕ ЗАЯВЛЕНИЕ

6. PLEASURE PARK 01

Fra Mauritius-Marik knelt in the Chapel of St. Damian (soon it would become a wax manufactory), but he was not praying for the lambs, he prayed for his own Franciscans. They, too, were about to depart from Chlumec. Emperor Joseph II was getting ready to write to them, too. He had already composed so many orders and patents (6,200 items), he was single-handedly reforming the realm and reprimanding the disobedient—like Jakub, and like Fra Marik . . . now kneeling in the chapel. He would have finished praying long ago (even in the time of Joseph II) if he did not have to wait for a cat to jump off his uplifted arms. That cat was SOROR FELIS, just as all creatures were *fratres* and *sorores*. And it would take her ages because she was quite content being where she was. Only after she had jumped off would Father Superior Marik accede to the wishes of H.I.H. Joseph and leave town with his priests, his alms collectors, sacristans, and Latin preceptors, leaving behind them Chlumec and Franciscan Street and the house marked by a stone emblem of a flaming sword growing out of a pair of outstretched arms. They would walk in silence, having lived here *anno currentis* some 550 years. Of course, they would not set out in the direction of Hradek (they had not been ordered to go all the way to the Balkans); they would leave by way of the Pleasure Park about which Astrid Zorska had written:

> *When trees are growing old*
> *And days are getting dark*
> *In this autumn's noble gold*
> *Find peace in Pleasure Park!*

Let its grace to grace incline
Use well this hour
While in thy power
For the next may not be thine!

Actually, the whole poem can be found in Msgr. Rosin's *History*, Vol. 8, i.e., Part I, p. 142, in the chapter entitled "Ferment in the Empire." I know that quite precisely, because we used to subscribe to Rosin's *History*, for the sake of Astrid, so that when the conversation came around to this subject, Aunt Ludmila could prove that our predecessor *really* had handed a poem to the Archduke. I had fantasies about this scene, imagining I was the Archduke Karl Franz, standing by the window and graciously acknowledging the Chlumec welcome, the festoons and carpets and of course also my beautiful great-aunt, to whom I showed the highest courtesy. Then the train jolted into motion and carried me to the next station, to Cepin and Aunt Vlaciha, who was always angry that I rode trains all by myself, without adult supervision; she would have preferred my coming on foot.

But I liked trains, even in the sense of Question 16 (*Secondary Occupations and Favorite Pastimes*). We had a bicycle, brand name Eska, and Dad would give me rides around the rail sidings and loading platforms behind the Hatus factory. I liked to watch the trains, especially the freight trains, and I classified them as *belchers*, *fumers*, and *nonsmokers*, depending on how much smoke they emitted and also how quickly they passed through Chlumec or how long they remained stuck here.

Edvin laughed at me and tried to find out whether I was careless with those names or whether I was really consistent in keeping to my system.

"There goes a belcher," he tried to trap me as a nonsmoker rolled by.

But I never made a mistake.

The seat of my Eska bike was equipped with a special pillow sewn by Alice. My feet on the pedals, I held the handlebar with one hand and with the other I rang the four-leaf-clover bell. (The clover design was stamped into the cover of the bell and was colored green.)

One morning we were coming down the hill and I was enjoying the speed and the wind against my face. For once we might be home in time for lunch. Lately we had been coming late, for Edvin had been taking me for over a week now to the municipal swimming pool under the Green Bridge. He was no longer working for Hatus; he told Bonek that he had found a job at the bakery but he was not supposed to start there until the following Monday. Today was Wednesday. We raced down the hill, the wind blew into my eyes from the north (the Pleasure Park). I looked down the hill and was sorry that the slope ended so soon, down at the post with the loudspeaker, next to Capousek's tavern. There I would have to stop ringing my bell and get ready for a dish of rabbit stew, but today Edvin wanted me to stop ringing when we were only halfway down, because some kind of message was coming out of the loudspeaker. I did not obey right away and so Dad covered the four-leaf clover with his palm to muffle the bell. Of course, I tried to ring all the harder, and the effort made me suddenly swerve; my right foot slid off the pedal and got caught in the spokes, so that both of us, Dad and I, went flying through the air, leaving the bicycle behind us, and before the bike had hit the ground we landed in a pile of roadside gravel. The dust slowly settled, I could hear the cover of the bell rolling toward the locust trees, I saw Edvin's pants torn and bloody at the knees. He bent over me and felt my leg. I began to cry.

An announcement was again coming over the loud-speaker. Two men came out of the tavern, but not in our direction, although at first that seemed to be their intention. Edvin picked me up and carried me toward them, and as we passed the locust tree he reached down for the clover bell cover and stuck it in the pocket of his bloodstained trousers. He did it for luck, because they had just announced a state of marshal law (*Ausnahmezustand*).

Thanks to this state of emergency, it can be ascertained that I had stuck my foot into the spokes precisely at 1232 hours on 5/27/1942. Thereafter, i.e., for the next five days, I lay in a small metal bed which had on its prow—for I pretended it was a ship—a picture of an angel, actually a cupid, sitting under a four-leaf clover as big as a tree, so big in fact that, in the grass beneath it, bells were springing up like mushrooms.

There was a belief about me that I had been born lucky, for I was continually surrounded by symbols of good fortune, and when I was asleep (or when they *thought* I was asleep), Edvin & Alice would touch me for good luck as people would touch a chimney sweep.

Oh, this touching was most valuable, for it transmitted Alice's and Edvin's vibrations to my body and I floated upward on this pulse, up toward sleep. In return, my own rhythm penetrated into them, into Alice & Edvin, as I absorbed their oscillation and transformed it into sound just before falling asleep, to make my music protect them from the Sun of my eighth house and bring them luck.

This was especially important when the deadly Sun rose over Chlumec and celebrated its high noon. Commissar Boldt was preparing the execution ground, in the drill field in back of the Pleasure Park, behind the sandlot, while Mother kept changing the vinegar dressing on my injured leg, worried about tetanus, for there was plenty of horse manure in front of Capousek's place where we had fallen off the bike.

The face of Father Rosin had already been irradiated

by that deadly sun, X-rayed, so that it was no more than a skull. On Friday he preached in the Church of St. Barbora, taking as his theme the city atop a hill, the city which cannot hide, and he deliberately pointed north in the direction of the drill field. He already knew about the commissar's execution ground, and was appalled by this irregularity: in Chlumec, nobody had *ever* been executed behind the Pleasure Park! As a historian, Rosin was highly mistrustful of such newfangled ideas. Everything arbitrary and disconnected from the past seemed evil and corrosive to him. When they decided to put a gendarmerie station on the site of the old gallows, he saw no reason to complain. After all, this had traditionally been a spot where life hung in the balance, so to speak, a clearly defined and fateful spot. But now Commissar Boldt, by means of a single arbitrary act, broke the old bounds. He barred mares from the grounds, expelled foals from their enclosure, and the riding school was turned into a makeshift prison for Chlumecians. From there the Chlumecians—not of the equine variety, the breeding of which had made the town famous, but of the human variety, listed in Rosin's archives—would be led to their fate. The pedigree records of Chlumec horses would soon be lost forever, just as nobody would ever be able to piece together an exact roster of executed hostages.

But from Commissar Boldt's viewpoint the location he had chosen was ideal. It was conveniently near the barracks of the special police squads (*Schupo*), and furthermore there was no need for building a protective wall as was usually the case in other towns, because here the bullets would stick in the sandbank and the same sand could be used at once to cover up the blood.

This was the place toward which the right hand of Father Rosin pointed like a magnetic needle that had shifted toward a new north, the north of the sixth part of the *History of Chlumec.*

And this was the place toward which a blue-green bus with whitewashed windows began to shuttle day after day, transporting people picked to die.

Its route went by our house. I could tell each time it passed, by watching Mother. I did not see it directly, I was not yet allowed to get up, and the headboard of my bed blocked my view of the window. But Mother betrayed each passage of the bus unmistakably. Every unusual street sound drew her toward the window, but when other vehicles passed by, she would step all the way to the head of my bed, whereas in the case of the bus she froze in her tracks, her lips moved, and for my sake she tried to suppress her sobs. Then, quite a while after the sound of the bus had died down, she would sit at the Petrof in the next room and play one of the three pieces she had learned during four years of piano lessons. Most often, it was my favorite minuet. She held back her tears until Edvin arrived, but then she cried tears of joy.

Edvin always kissed her and told her how happy he was, working in the bakery, yet he too avoided the window when the bus went by. Unlike Alice, he did not play the piano, but opened the door between kitchen and living room and walked up and down until his monotonous pacing put me to sleep. Actually, I was not uneasy, because I had faith in our four-leaf clover and I was confident that nothing bad could happen to us.

Around eight o'clock, when it began to get dark, the shooting would start. It woke me up and I listened. It did not sound like automatic weapons, more like individual rifle shots or salvos fired in quick succession. It generally lasted a little more than an hour. By then it would be nighttime and we kept vigil; i.e., Alice, Edvin, and I. And of course so did all of Chlumec, for the shooting could be heard everywhere, although it was especially loud in the areas adjoining Pleasure Park, such as ours. And the longer people listened, the more it resembled a malediction, a curse. At last Edvin said: Shit! And he repeated it several times. Then he rushed out into the yard, to the rabbit hutch, and gave our rabbit some lettuce even though she had already been fed. We got her because we wanted the meat of her young; she was expected to bear a big litter—and after my birthday she would do just that—but now she was up and calmly gazed through the wire mesh at Edvin, not the least bit surprised to see him bring another head of lettuce.

"Here, eat," he said.

And she replied: "You still haven't fixed that bicycle wheel!"

She nibbled the lettuce, crunching up the green leaf which was at the same time disappearing inside of her. It was comical.

Edvin heeded her admonishment. He placed the wheel in a clamp, turned it this way and that, straightened and tightened and balanced the spokes till they could be plucked like harp strings.

It was absolutely necessary, Comr. Pavlenda, to stroke an animal or to balance a wheel in order to keep that sound from unhinging a person, for those who merely kept on listening died many times over, whereas those in the sandlot died so quickly that it gave Boldt hardly any pleasure.

Msgr. Rosin, for example, kept leafing through the second part of the *History of Chlumec* all through the firing, and in the chapter entitled "The Hangman and His Work" (p. 162) he found the passage about Salomyna Trubac. In the year 1671, she established a special fund to provide in perpetuity all persons condemned to death with "a Dram of Wine to cheer the Heart and Two Masses to follow Execution." Monsignor

Rosin also searched his papers for a note about the metal ring on the wall of Town Hall to which the condemned were fastened. With the help of a stepladder he reached for one of those boxes where notes for the second part of the History were stored. He found the card and saw that he should actually rewrite the whole section in order to include the ring, and the linen shirt (paid for by the town) which the condemned person wore—not as a warning, but as a means of imploring alms and forgiveness. Thus tied and robed, he held out a plate to passersby, collecting contributions for a service to be conducted for the salvation of his soul in St. Barbora's Church the following day.

Rosin sat down on the top of the stepladder, placed the box on his knees, and using its cover as a support, he wrote the additional information on the card. He always carried a well-sharpened pencil with him for such purposes, so that he wouldn't have to keep climbing up and down—he was sixty-seven years old and that stepladder had seen some use! In a certain sense, the note he wrote on the card headed *Salomyna Trubac* really implied that

this circle represented *imago mentalis*, the spiritual picture, the symbol of the soul. Theirs, but also ours (?). That is why the condemned was fastened to a *ring* (how many other possibilities had been bypassed!), so that even face to face with death—a humiliating and extraordinary death—he still could delineate for himself a point in space which restored balance, for this point was first delimited, circumscribed, then grasped finally and transferred to the soul, so that the soul too could be *transferred* to the highest center of all activity. This circle is OUROBOROS ($ουροβόρος$), a serpent that has formed a circle by grasping its tail in its mouth and is thus consuming its own self. He too has closed himself, locked in space, drowned in space.

And finally our own eternal King, St. Wenceslas, *rex perpetuus*, the only true ruler of this realm, to the vain resentment of all merely temporal kings—St. Wenceslas clings to the ring on the basilica door, for he has to find support for the kingdom his sagging body is about to leave, while *malefici occiderunt eum in ecclesia ianua*: malefactors surround him in the church door. And if we pray to him to preserve us and our realm, what are we doing but reminding ourselves of the destiny to which he has inspired us, so that together with him we shall see the heavenly Crown which is also symbolized by a circle and which . . .

But here Msgr. Rosin put aside the card and the box, for the malefactors of Commissar Boldt had just entered: Chief Criminal Assistant Groh, the interpreter Hlawatsch, and a squad of armed men. Two black Opels were generally used for these missions. They took Rosin away in his clerical garb, without eyeglasses or breviary; in spite of his request, they refused to let him take those things along.

The ride to the summer pavilion took eleven minutes.

More than thirty people were crowded in the small cellar. The room was so stifling that Judge Bily and Major Ocko took turns at the skylight, fanning a shirt back and forth, to give people a breath of air. Rosin knew both these men, but because the judge was chairman of a Protestant society, he first greeted the major. The major smiled and said: "It's stuffy in here." Somebody wanted to know when martial law would come to an end, and somebody —not Rosin—answered: in heaven.

Then they listened to the hammering as crosses were being prepared. This was the task of Rüthel, the commissar's driver, and it was his invention: two planks the length of a man, placed side by side, and crossed by two shorter pieces. A person was tied to this contraption before execution, and afterwards it was used like a stretcher to transport the body to the crematorium, where according to standing orders the ovens were always ready by 1900 hours.

"Does anybody know," Judge Bily said to Monsignor Rosin, "whether Cucelli beat Asboth?"

"I'm sorry," replied the cleric, "I don't know." It pained him that he was unable to be of even that much help, when no other solace was permitted or indeed possible, in that tiny overcrowded cellar in such a short interval between arrival and departure. After all, some people found solace in thinking about the Genoa 42 tournament, and Judge Bily was not only chairman of the Protestant Society but also of the Lawn Tennis Club. They had arrested him right on the courts of the L.T.C. and taken him along in white shorts and white sports shirt monogrammed by Vasata & Co. It was his thirty-fourth birthday, and now that he realized he would never reach his thirty-fifth, the judge at least wanted to maintain the ironic stance which he had been cultivating in the belief that it went well with his sporty figure.

Whereupon: they were summoned, i.e., Major Ocko,

Msgr. Rosin, Judge Bily, and the two Tomeks, father and son. Executions generally proceeded in groups of five.

The Tomeks kept blinking their eyes; among the bodies of the first group lay Mrs. Tomek, wife and mother.

The men of the Schupo squads $(1 + 24)$ were lined up in a rough semicircle about twenty paces from the crosses. They did not show any special discipline. Half of them were just resting. They stood in a cluster and chatted with members of the guard. The rest were beginning to fall in rank, and this formation, too, was from a military standpoint rather loose (thought Major Ocko). But the helmets were strapped tight under the chin.

This day it was the turn of Oberleutnant Kretzer and his squad. Hauptmann Sadeler's battalion had a day off.

On the benches in front of the cantine sat employees of the Oberlandrat with their children and families, according to Commissar Boldt's wishes. Little Amdas, that beautiful child, was among them. His daddy put a stone and a pistol on top of the lists lying on the table, so that the wind would not blow the papers away. There was a light breeze. The perspiration had dried on young Tomek's forehead. They blindfolded him and his eyes teared under the cloth.

Ocko shook his head: "*Nicht binden.*" And Commissar Boldt praised his behavior—as one soldier to another. Judge Bily welcomed the breeze, he was glad he no longer had to squeeze against other bodies; he was again the man in white. They approached him with the blindfold and he smiled at them and when they tied it he said: Thank you (*auf deutsch: Danke schön*, Comr. Pavlenda). But Rosin's blindfold covered up the birds which he had been watching as they began settling back in the trees surrounding the sandlot. He knew that they were about to be startled again. *Item*: He said in the direction of the birds: "Be praised, my Lord, for our sister, Death, which no living man can escape."

This was from the "Canticle of the Creatures," which the blessed St. Francis had composed to the praise and glory of God.

Then the shooting started again.

. . .

And then I left, after all. To Cepin, on the 14:32 train. But I was not standing near the window, nor was I dreaming about Astrid Zorska, for this was before anyone had told me about her.

In any case, I would have found it difficult to believe that a person could have so many names. At that time I was firmly convinced that there could be only one single name, just as a creature can only be its own single self. I was even convinced that the mere act of naming could give birth to a being. For example, I made a train by setting up a row of kitchen utensils, from the biggest pot to the smallest frying pan, and as I was about to seat myself in the locomotive I noticed a box of soap flakes (brand: Hellada) under the sofa. I turned the big pot representing the locomotive right-side up, filled it with water, poured in that extremely valuable (wartime!) hoard of soap, and stirred until it dissolved. I had a straw for blowing bubbles, I sucked in the soapy water and made colored spheres float to the ceiling, where they burst with an almost audible pop. Up until then, I had not yet been struck by any doubts regarding my identity; it had never occurred to me that I might be myself and at the same time somebody else. It was only when Edvin came in and shouted—no, raged—"Who did this??" that I realized it might have been somebody else, and so willy-nilly I selected as the perpetrator a boy named Mirek, i.e., I uttered this name in order to create a being who was not living permanently at our house but dropped in now and then to do naughty things. Edvin thought that I was lying. Alice, however, understood that someone other than I must have done it. When she heard Edvin yelling, she came running from her laundry, took Mirek by the hand, led him into the next room, and I could hear him get a good hiding. I stopped crying, for it was now quite clear that I was not Mirek but Jan Chrysostom and a good boy. From that time, Comr. Pavlenda, I have always tried to name all things with which I came in contact as quickly as possible. This was so that they could not surprise me or, as it were, elude my grasp. And to this day I believe that any name, uttered into the blue, rises like a bubble and gives birth to something or other. Do you believe that I could have known what Rosin was praying for, had I not been his namesake? I am now almost a third of the way through my questionnaire and I am just learning what Father Rosin saw *under* his blindfold: the stigmata on the hands of St. Francis, burning with light. Thus, he was not any less resolute than Major Ocko; he had simply chosen a different way. The major wanted to *see* death, not merely to die. By seeing it, and by being seen seeing it, he was returning it to those who had sent it. Whereas Rosin absorbed it into himself, and had no wish to send it back to anyone, not even to those soldiers. Strangely enough, the marksmen were impressed by the major rather than by the priest. After work they stopped by at the Capousek tavern and continued to praise Ocko's behavior. But at that time I was already on my way to Cepin on the aforementioned train, at 14:32 on the 16th day of June.

Cucelli beat Asboth, 6:3, 6:3.

7. VAZOOM

Everyone asked me about the Vazoom. But I did not see him. I had arrived by carriage because I was expected by Aunt Vlaciha and by Mr. Vostarek, who had come to pick us up. My aunt held a basket of cherries in her lap, I was busily gobbling them up, and nobody noticed how many I was taking because they were busy talking in a hushed voice so that I would not hear. Mother was talking about Chlumec, my aunt about Amdas. The carriage climbed up the hill, we saw the Amdas villa, where Herman Vohryzek used to live before he was forbidden to buy raisins, travel by boat, etc. (in landlocked Chlumec —where the only body of water was the White River), and before they chased him into the former wax factory, where he mutely pounded beef bones. From the carriage I saw the villa and in the garden a gazebo and in the gazebo young Amdas, that beautiful child, who was grazing peacocks. He was strolling in front of the gazebo holding a long willow branch and with its leafy end he gently prodded those birds to make them spread their tails into wheels full of eyes that glittered with metallic colors. Little Amdas seemed like a magician to me: he waved his magic rod and giant flowers sprang up, burst into a spectrum of greens and blues, wavy contours undulated and merged with the fin-de-siècle outlines of the iron fence and the fin-de-siècle villa on the slope of the Cepin hill.

"Mom, isn't that beautiful!" I said.

"That bird comes from Java. From the East," said my aunt.

"A beast from the East," I said, and they smiled.

But Mr. Vostarek added that too much fuss was made over those birds, that they were just another breed of pheasant, and then we entered the brewery yard and Mr. Tapster Klahn shook my hand, but as he squeezed it I felt a pang of heartburn, the cherries in my stomach splashed up my gullet, I tried to quench the burning feeling by gulping down several glasses of water, and for the second time that month I got sick. I kept vomiting, I felt worse and worse, as if my insides were all gone and I was turning lighter and lighter. And again I had a fever, though this time it was more colorful, full of green and blue flowers, and I felt blue in their midst, like the feather of a Javanese peacock.

"Auntie," I said, "I was riding in a carriage, but over water, and Mr. Vostarek was following me, carrying a suitcase on his shoulder, he was walking on the waves and he did not sink." And Aunt said: "That's a lovely dream. But promise me you'll never again drink water after gorging on cherries!" I promised (and I kept my word, Comr. Pavlenda; viz., Question 29). In return, my aunt promised to take me to the Cepin castle to show me where the rock opened before Mr. Tapster Klahn. I never knew exactly what a Tapster was; it sounded like someone who drank a lot of beer, but I was told that Mr. Tapster Klahn drank no beer at all, because he had all sorts of stomach ailments, for which he took herb teas.

"But when did the rock open?" I asked.

"When he was on the hill early in the morning, gathering herbs."

"This smells good, but it tastes awful. Must I drink it?"

"You must, to keep the cup happy."

My cup had eyes and a mouth and laughed, it was made that way.

"What if Mr. Tapster went back to the rock and complained about you," said Aunt.

"He can do that?"

"You bet. People who know about herbs can do many things."

"You mean like . . . like he might just twirl a dandelion and the rock would split open?"

"Maybe," said my aunt, and watched me gulp down a whole cupful.

"And whose voice was it?"

"What voice?"

"The voice that came from the rock."

"What makes you think there was a voice?"

"Somebody had to say something. Otherwise, why would the rock open?"

"That's true," admitted my aunt. She thought a while and then said: "When that rock opened up in front of Mr. Tapster Klahn, after he had twirled a dandelion in his fingers—though I think it was more likely sesame, because there is a saying 'Open sesame'—anyway, when the rock opened up, there was a girl standing there all dressed in white like a bridesmaid and she told Mr. Klahn that she had been waiting a long time. Then she led him to an opening in the rock through which one could look right into the inside of the mountain, and at the far end Mr. Tapster Klahn saw a burning light and he could clearly see a treasure trove and money and precious stones and jewels, and on top of it sat a white snake which shone with a strange light."

"How?" I asked. Aunt Ludmila thought some more, and then she said: "Just like that. The light came right out of its skin."

"Mr. Klahn should have stroked it," I said.

"He was afraid. Besides, he forgot to cut himself a witch-hazel branch, which protects a person from evil powers. He stood at the edge of the opening and didn't dare go a step farther. And so the girl brought him whatever she was able to gather up in her skirt."

"Gold coins?"

"Maybe silver too, I'm not sure. But if he had gone inside, all of us would now be set for life."

"Too bad," I said.

"Too bad," said my aunt.

She got up and brought me a coin which had a cross inside a circle and some lettering. "This is one of those coins," she said.

I took it, held it in my palm, and said I would like to take it to bed with me. Aunt permitted me to do so and stroked my hair, and I said *this* was the way Mr. Tapster should have stroked the snake.

"Certainly," she agreed.

"I feel much better," I said.

"You'll soon be all right."

"Auntie, could he go back there again?" I asked.

She shook her head.

"Why not?"

"Because we might all be gone by the time he got back. He was only standing at the edge, he spoke only a few words, he swore it lasted only a second or two, and so when people told him he'd been gone more than a year he couldn't believe it. He still doesn't believe it to this day."

I believed it, though. I held the coin in my hand and I was about to fall asleep. "Do you think his name might have been Vazoom?" I asked.

"Whose?"

"The snake's."

"Did you say Vazoon?"

"I said Vazoom, Auntie, z-o-o-m." (That year I had become very good at spelling, and I was proud of that ability.)

"Yes, that could be his name," said my aunt, "but now go to sleep."

And once again she caressed me precisely the way Mr. Tapster Klahn should have caressed the Vazoom.

. . .

The caress made me fall asleep at once and I slept until the second harvest, September 23, 1943. I woke up and found myself sitting on the box of a wagon loaded with hay. The wagon was standing on a hill, its wheels secured by oak wedges.

In other words: I lost more than a year, an interval about which I can say nothing—because of the Vazoom. I suppose I could have asked Ludmila Vlaciha, but at the moment I am writing this she is blind, her eyes are covered by a gray membrane, she stumbles against drainpipes, skins her arms and legs, and does not even see she has been hurt. Poor old lady! She is eighty-six, but in her mind time has shrunk so that she is chatting with me now as if I were one of her dead. May the earth lie easy on her grave! She will soon die and push me a step nearer to my own death. One cannot rely on her memory! You therefore have to take my word for it: a snake is coiled under Cepin hill. He is self-consuming, he keeps eating himself without diminishing. He is resting on a hoard of gold, but is not afraid of robbers. He is forcing all those caraway plants to shoot out buds until the whole mountain is full of reddish blossoms, which Mr. Tapster early each morning cuts with a scythe, threshes, and then screens for seedlings to make his caraway tea. I drank some of it and fell asleep, waking up on the day of the second harvest, 455 days later. Caraway tea, *carum carvi*, not the kind of seed people use in sauces or sprinkle on meat, but a real elixir. Don't piss me off, Comr. Pavlenda, or I'll drink some and jump 252 years ahead of you. Or I will pet the Vazoom and beat you by a whole light-year!

About that big sleep: I slept until Friday, September 23, but I too could swear that it did not take longer than an hour (two at the most). I sat on the wagon, in Cepin. Mr. Vostarek was driving up and down the Amdas meadow with a mower, all of us had to go to the Amdas fields to help out, women from the brewery raked the grass and pitched it, the grass was drying and they were singing songs to it which made it even more fragrant, on the dray the hay was stacked high, it intoxicated me until I saw everything below me sparkle and glitter. My mother was there, too, she was carrying a basket with loaves of bread and she kept passing Amdas, who strolled about in a black uniform and boots, hands crossed on his ass, squinting up at the sky like a farmer worried about an impending storm. But there was no hint of rain in the air, so most probably he simply wanted to savor the pose. The poplars rustled, a gentle wind blew, a breeze wafted the scent of fresh-mown hay past the brewery, past the peacock villa. Alice passed Amdas, from an as-yet un-mowed section of the field came the cry of a quail. There was the flutter of beating wings and the quail rose toward the woods. People lifted their heads, smiled, Amdas too was smiling, again in a farmerly way. He reached into his basket for a slice of bread, broke off a mouthful and munched on it, munched on the smile at the same time and nodded his head, indicating that everything was *sehr gut* (the bread, the weather, the world), *gut, gut,* and after he swallowed a morsel of bread he called after the bird *pück der Wück, a bück der Rück,* bye-bye birdie!

I turned to my right and whom do I see sitting next to me but Mirek—the fellow who had pulled that dirty trick on me with the Hellada soap flakes.

"Mirek," I said to him, "leave me alone!"

But he paid no attention, as if I didn't exist. And on top of that he was dressed exactly the same way as I. He, too, was wearing an apron decorated with two animals, an embroidered dog and an embroidered cat that resembled Fatima . . . at least the colors were similar, but I doubt Fatima ever carried a parasol. "Mirek, behave yourself!" I shouted. But he said: "Let's knock

Amdas down to teach him a lesson and make him keep his paws off Alice." "I watched him carefully, and he was only reaching for a slice of bread." "He almost touched Alice," replied Mirek, and reached for the brake, turned the handle, the shaft of the wagon started to oscillate back and forth like the barrel of a gun, i.e., it zeroed in on Amdas, who was standing with his back to the tank. He did not see me, he did not see me start up, gain speed . . . and Mirek—he always does this to me—jumped off and ran, whereas I kept going . . . and began to get scared. Fortunately, Alice heard the smack of bare feet hitting asphalt (she had a good ear for Mirek), and she spun around and screamed. The women in the fields dropped their rakes, Mr. Vostarek stopped the mower & Amdas jumped aside (out of the way of this highly improbable encounter). He got away, this time. But I landed in a pile of hay, I was buried, lost . . . they began looking for me, weeping as if I was dead, while I was actually trying to bury myself still deeper to escape a thrashing. But they dug away furiously, until they came upon my shoes, then the dog on my apron, then the cat with the parasol, and at last my face, with eyes closed . . .

Mr. Vostarek put his ear to my chest to find out if my heart was still beating. But because I had been holding my breath for a long time I was finally forced to gasp for air, my chest suddenly expanded with a jerk, startling Mr. Vostarek. I jumped up and ran as fast as I could after the quail, across the field and up the slope and up a crab-apple tree. Ah, now I was even higher than the box of the wagon before, now I could see the whole panorama—the overturned dray, Amdas in his high boots, Mother still shaken but all the same the first to arrive, and now the others were beginning to cluster around my tree.

"Come on down," said Vostarek, holding a whip in

his hand (he was very knowledgeable when it came to brakes; he never thought for a moment that the wagon might have started rolling all on its own).

"Get down," said Mother, and because she had been given such a terrible scare she was holding a rod.

Only Amdas was without an instrument of punishment, he was holding an apple from his orchard in his palm, pared it with his penknife, and said to them to leave me alone. He was not angry at me. I climbed down and killed him belatedly: I accepted half of his apple, held it in my hand, irradiated it with the rays of my eighth-house Sun, the lethal beams bounced off the skin of the apple and penetrated Amdas, and even though the apple was red and deliciously juicy its rays were deadly. Served you right, Amdas!

Mother was also watching that apple, the half that Amdas cut for me. She was convinced that by partaking of it I might become cursed. As soon as Amdas turned around, she grabbed it out of my hand and squashed it underfoot.

Mr. Vostarek took this opportunity to whack me with his whip.

That evening, because we were in Cepin and because I was feeling sad after the day's happening, I asked Aunt Ludmila to tell me more about the Vazoom. But she couldn't seem to remember anything about a snake by that name that guarded the Cepin rock. So I went to see Mr. Tapster Klahn at the Silver Poplar, and asked him to tell me about the time he had stood on the very edge of the treasure cave, afraid to go any farther.

"And who told you that story?" he asked, and laughed like mad.

"Ludmila, my aunt."

"You hear that, Mirena?" shouted Mr. Klahn in the direction of a little room behind the bar. Mirena, his beautiful wife, came out, and she, too, laughed so hard she had to hold her belly. But inside that belly was Erna, my bride, and because of all that laughing Erna was shaken loose and was about to be born a bit sooner than expected, i.e., this very same day.

8. TAKE IT EASY 01

Not even a cat can see in pitch darkness, the bandleader said to Olin in Southend during a period that I cannot reliably pin down (*viz.*, Vazoom). But it must have been around February 1944, or at the latest in April of that year. That bandleader came from Zdar. In Southend, of course, he was neither a bandleader nor a legionnaire but a fighter pilot. He wore the top button of his uniform open, in fighter-pilot fashion. Both of them had a Walt Disney cat painted on the nose of their Spitfires. For protection. They often chatted about Fatima from El Arish. Olin had told the bandleader about her and the bandleader then reminisced about the cats of Zdar, especially the yellowish ones with hazel eyes that thrived around the mill (he was a miller's son). Actually, if someone had taken the trouble, those cats could have been registered as a new breed, and given a special number in the Fédération Internationale Féline d'Europe. But the people of Zdar tended to think that the odd color was the result of disease or whatnot, and they looked on the animals with distaste. "Let's face it, I was stupid," said the bandleader. "I could have been a pioneer breeder and now I'm nothing."

"You're a P.O.," answered Olin (that's pronounced Pee Oh, Comrade Pavlenda, and it means Pilot Officer, which was the bandleader's rank, whereas Olin was F.O.; in other words, he was also an Officer, but Flying).

The bandleader then added (he had been thinking about the cat): ". . . She has whiskers on her lip and on her face and also above the eyes, and even if it was dark as hell she could get around because she sees with her whiskers."

"I know," said Olin. "She sees with her whole body." And he told the bandleader about Regent Street and about the girl he had met there.

But as far as you are concerned, Comr. Pavlenda, the important thing was the so-called *day off*. It must have been pouring, the weather must have been ghastly if they stopped fighting. Sunshine, on the other hand, is good for war.

. . .

Item: Said Olin to the bandleader:
the town was full of mud, I drank that foamless beer of theirs and then I strolled down the street (with a greater probability of surviving one more day, thanks to the day off—note by J.Ch.K.) and ahead of me walked a girl in uniform who kept hitching up her trousers every time she stepped over a puddle, as if she were wearing an enormously long skirt. On Brewer Street she paused in front of the antique shop and looked into the boarded-up window. I looked, too, the window was empty, there was nothing to see except wallpaper with monkeys swinging on garlands of flowers, and there also was a ceramic plate, the only item left in the window, decorated with a floral motif in the middle of which was lettered LET HIM DO WHAT HE CAN. The girl was standing with her back to me, but reflected in the window I saw her eyes looking at me. To these eyes, and to the back the head, I said: "Will you come with me?" The motto from the plate now seemed inscribed across her forehead, first as a question and then as a command. Let him do what he can! She smiled, and turning her smiling face toward me, she said: "Where to?"

"Wherever you like," I answered, and smiled too. Then we walked in silence until we reached a house

which had no number because it had been torn off by a
blast, along with a piece of the façade. I knew all the
same that it was the right house, or rather the wrong
house, i.e., bawdy. She knew it, too, because as soon as
we reached the stairway—blacked out, and of course all
the darker—she said: "What will you give me?" She did
not say it like a whore, but on the contrary as if to make
me dismiss any idea she was a professional. It was like
a correction, a small "X" next to an erroneously calculated
figure. I took her by the shoulder, kissed her somewhere
near the root of her nose, clumsily in other words, and
told her that I would give her whatever she gave me.
I ran down to pay for the room, and when I returned,
she was facing the fireplace and behind her back there
was a big bed with a somewhat worn red damask headboard. I locked the door, and the sound seemed to startle
the girl back into awareness of my presence. She lifted
her eyes toward me and her face was drawn and nervous,
her features guarded but still expressing consent. Her
mouth was half open and in the light of the two candles
standing on the mantel, glass candles set in hammered
bronze animal paws, her teeth glistened like a coin which
she was about to swallow. I liked her looks immensely.
I stretched out my arms to embrace her but she slipped
out of my grasp, abruptly and quite unexpectedly. She
took a deep breath as if about to say something, and a
moment later I felt her embracing and kissing me with
trembling lips as if she were weeping—a tearless, noiseless weeping. And then she started unbuttoning my shirt
and I felt her stripping me completely, she herself was
down to her black silk slip. She pressed the black silk
against my body; it felt cool even though the skin underneath was getting warmer and warmer. I did not understand, tried to take off her slip. "No, none of that," she
said, and held it tight at her hips, and in her refusal I
recognized fear. Then she pressed her leg against mine,

I felt her juice trickling toward my knee; that moisture set off a wave in me which I could not stop and I spurted it out. But the girl, who a while earlier had been so vigilant about her slip, now lifted it high over her breasts and stuck out her belly against my squirting to collect long, thick lines of splatter. Then she lay down on her back, rested her head against the shabby damask, her face smooth and long, crumpled black silk over her breasts; she rested as if she wanted to suck everything into herself, to drink it all up like a flower drinks the rain. I lay down next to her and saw that this was just what she wanted. I nestled my head on her bosom and it seemed to me that I too was disappearing, soaking into her. I had just lived through weeks of alerts, hours of briefings and operations, my body had learned to jump to the sound of a bell like a machine. Now, by the side of this girl, I could at last shut off my nerves and senses.

I tasted my fatigue, savored it. When I finally opened my eyes, it was still night. She was standing before the fireplace. While I slept, she made a fire, put out the light, and watched the flames licking the handful of logs, which, for all I knew, were in the room merely for decoration. She noticed that I was awake and turned to me. "You have beautiful legs," she said. This embarrassed me, for it seemed the kind of remark I should have been making to her.

She sat down in a low, comfortable armchair at the foot of the bed. She was still wearing that black slip, and I gazed at her like someone who had possessed her (after all, squirts count, too), and not merely like a hungry man. The fire suddenly died down, but only for a moment, as it licked at the knot in the last big piece of wood the girl had put in the fireplace while I was waking up. Then the log crackled, flames shot up and lit the whole room, a shadow broke in the angle of the ceiling behind the bed and then fell on me. And the shadow trembled, it was her shadow, the girl's. I saw her face where the light also flickered and shook because the spot where she sat was in the crossbeam of two mirrors, one over the fireplace and the other a big folding mirror next to the bed which was placed there for titillation but its big glass eye now reflected the girl, multiplied her, repeated the way she covered me with her shadow and the way firelight danced on her face until she got up and pulled the black silk over her head; for an instant it stuck there like a flag, but I was now seeing her in all her nakedness, she guided me to come inside her and I can honestly say that I've never enjoyed a girl so much in my whole life.

Toward morning I asked her whether I could see her again, because now I had to go back to Southend, but I was hoping to get another pass soon. She said she would certainly like that. Not here, of course. It would make her feel like a tramp. Understand? I understood. And she described a house which was called The Fires. I asked her to let me come in once more, but trucks could already be heard rumbling in the street, it was getting light and traffic was beginning to move past the boarded-up shops, through the gray confused dawn. An ambulance with a red cross on the rear door emerged and then disappeared. She kissed me. My cock, my heavy tail, stiffened. She was again covered by black silk, damp in the back along the curve of her bum, her pear, and I licked my lips so that something on my own skin could be drying, too. I saw that lick in the mirror which was there for those coming after us, those ordinary fuckers.

"You love me, don't you?" I said.

She got up. "Aye, you've got beautiful legs!"

The same words as earlier, but now I thought I knew what she meant. While she was putting on her uniform she kept testing me to see whether I remembered about The Fires: "I'll be there on Thursday, from one until morning; go right in, along the path, and if you can't make it, then you can come the following Thursday, again from one to midnight." By now she was dressed, completely impersonal. It was broad daylight.

.   .   .

"You jerk," the bandleader said to my cousin. "A cat figures her chances, she jumps only once, but it's for keeps. What kind of woman was she, anyway?"

"I don't know," said Olin. "At that shop with the plate, on Brewer Street, she crossed over to the other side. I remember the spot, there is a photograph of it in my soul—how she stepped over the puddle, lifting her trousers like a skirt, and I also kept seeing before me those white trickles on her belly. I saw it before my eyes. I was sitting in the plane praying for rain with all the religious fervor of my student days, I tried to recall the right words because I was convinced that this was the only way our alert would be called off, and I whispered: Almighty Father, who watered the Mount of Olives with your holy perspiration, hear me in your agony and forgive me if I blaspheme: drown this runway with a deluge of rain, oh Father!

And it was Thursday, my day off, and I was able to go to that house, I found everything as she had described it, even though most of the two-family houses on the street had been demolished by a bomb. The Fires was left standing, looking as sunny and cozy as a picture on a brochure: big garden, perfect rosebushes dotting the lawns. A curtain fluttered in an open ground-floor window. A hum was coming from the house as if a crowd of people were inside. Perplexed, I paced up and down the street a few times before I gathered enough courage to walk through the garden gate. I opened the house door—it was not locked—and entered the hall. Nobody came to meet me, nobody greeted me. I stood there, a stairway on my left and in front of me glass doors through which I saw the dining room and beyond that the terrace and back garden. The radio was on. Actually, it had been on all the time, but it was only now that I realized what it was playing: some old Scottish song, the words of which I could not make out. The sound of voices mingled with the song.

I knocked on the door, thinking that perhaps someone was expecting me after all. There were three men in the room, rolling up a thick carpet toward the piano, which was the sole piece of furniture except for some watercolors on the wall and a radio standing on the only chair. A fire burned in the fireplace, and the room stank of disinfectant. The three people set to work straightening up bodies on the floor. I could not make out how many bodies there were, because they were already covered, except for two almost nude corpses which did not fit into the corner. One body, a woman's, stuck out of the pile; her shoulder was propped up against the piano leg, and her head was covered by a sheet. The other body was barefoot, and blood was oozing through the white coat that covered it. I slammed the door behind me and ran, and as I pushed my way past a group of medics who asked me what I was doing there, I shouted never mind, just a mistake. But it was no mistake, not as far as the address was concerned. I seemed to have been the only one there who knew the girl.

Olin's arms sagged, and his companion (the bandleader, Comr. Pavlenda) began shuffling the deck. They were sitting in the barracks, waiting to be called for flight duty.

"Cut," said the bandleader.

Olin turned over a trump. The bandleader said: "I forgot to tell you. If a hole is big enough for a cat to stick its head through, it will manage to push its whole body through, too. That's a fact."

"Of course," said Olin, "it's quite possible that it wasn't her at all."

"Take it easy," replied the bandleader, and because this was the motto of their squadron, Olin stopped talking about the incident.

The card that came up was the king of clubs.

9. TREE OF THE REPUBLIC

It is of course questionable, Comr. Pavlenda, whether those cats of Zdar would ever produce a new breed deserving of a special number in the Fédération Internationale without the loving attention of the bandleader, the miller's son. But they had to erase his name from the blackboard after he drowned his Disney cat, his Spitfire, and himself in the English Channel—an event which also happened in the time of the Vazoom, and so I am unable to fix a precise date for it.

Among the bandleader's belongings which Olin inherited was a postcard. It showed a mummified cat from the British Museum, standing up in her lacquered bandages as straight as a human being. I saw the card after Olin's return. I could not believe it was a cat; it looked more like a chocolate Easter bunny. As an addendum to Question 27 I am enclosing a picture of this animal (*felis silvestris*, domestic cat) in order to document its rather rigid posture and to draw a connection with some of my own equally rigid stances.

According to Olin, I lack the suppleness of people born at night. Please understand me, Comr. Pavlenda, I am not slow or clumsy, but at those moments when I hear a smell (ah, how I wish I could express it more precisely—but it really is the aroma of hearing), at such moments I don't fly like those egger moths streaming to the pine where Mr. Vostarek attached his trap, but I freeze.

Mr. Vostarek was very fond of me (we were fellow hunters of these eggers and monarchs and swallowtails).

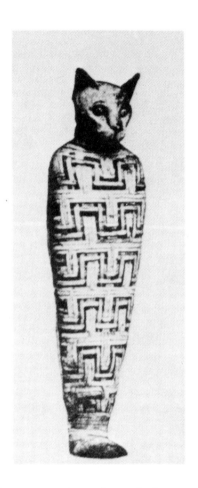

To the bark of a pine he had attached a cage, inside of which was the moth queen; around it he fastened a bull's-eye of sticky flypaper—and then we waited, Mr. Vostarek and I and little Erna Klahn (fancy that, she popped out of her mother's belly only the other day, and now she's already up and walking!), and we counted all the moths that came flying to the tree and stuck to the paper and died because their queen smelled so strong that they could scent her from several kilometers away. And I was praised for being able to count all the way to 262, the number of the dead moths.

Note regarding that rigidity: I *hear* smells too, but instead of flying I cover myself with pitch like that feline mummy; my senses simply stiffen. I become as stiff as a board and even if the ceiling was about to come down and crush me to bits, I would stay rooted to the spot; if anything, I might try to prop up the ceiling. But people born at night (the majority of people) are luckier, for they would simply fly away. Or else they would accept death without resisting. The odor of death is as inviting to them as their queen's scent was to the moths, or the aroma of *Dianthus superbus* was to Herr Hatus.

The Hatus villa was surrounded by beds of that noble breed of carnation, wafting their fragrance to the study and bedroom. From the bedroom the barracks yard was still visible (very discreetly, though, without in any way disturbing the sense of green privacy surrounding the villa), but there were no longer any soldiers lining up behind shrill pipers, only bandaged convalescents sitting at open windows, playing sad tunes on their harmonicas. Or else they were corpses en route to the Hradek crematorium to join Rosin and Ocko in that series of cremations begun by Herman Vohryzek, once the best salesman in the Hatus organization. Nowadays, the best salesman in the firm was Bonek. He did not know as many meanings of the word Largior as his predecessor, he did not know that Largior *inter alia* also meant to bestow, favor, and forgive, but he was indispensable. He looked upon Mr. Hatus with the calm, concentrated gaze of a man who had given up smoking for the sake of carnations and who was resolutely waiting for the moment when he would be able to demolish Mr. Hatus with the same few well-chosen words he had once used on Edvin Sr.

"Tell me," asked Mr. Hatus, "have you ever eaten a frog?" He showed Bonek a document entitled *Richtungen für das Leben unter einfachsten Verhältnissen*—guidelines for life under basic conditions. It was a confidential memorandum for people in the food industry, and therefore also for the F. Hatusch Kakaofabrik.

"You see," he again addressed Bonek (without transition, as if to sound him out), "first they create the most complicated situation possible and then they prepare you for the simplest, *einfachsten Verhältnissen.*" To tell the truth, Mr. Hatus (Hatusch) was not equipped to live under simple conditions. He wanted to continue with those beautiful Largior wrappers, but the demand for them kept shrinking. One day the demand reached zero, and since then he had been talking to himself, answering himself, and responding to his own answers as if they were just another kind of question.

"Hmmm, so you've never eaten a frog," he said to Bonek, the Indispensable One.

"Never, sir."

"And caterpillars?"

"Never."

"I ate a caterpillar once, as a boy," Mr. Hatus reminisced. "It was a bet, you understand?"

"Yes, sir."

"Not by itself. With a piece of bread. But on account of the bread they didn't give me credit."

In spite of his habit of divining everything in advance, Bonek asked: "Who?"

"The other boys," Mr. Hatus replied, with a vacant smile. "But haven't you read this?" (He was again referring to the guidelines.)

"I haven't yet had an opportunity," said Bonek.

"*Neuartige Nahrungsmittel*, that's what it literally says. Beets, roots . . ."

"But we're already producing those," said the Indispensable One.

"Yes, but now they're also talking about clover, alfalfa . . . mowed when the shoots are still very new. And then those frogs. Do you understand it?"

"It's a source of protein," said the All-Comprehending One.

"But there is the problem of catching them. Maybe I don't understand it right. It says here: *Fang mit bunten Lappen, die im Wasser am Ufer antlanggezogen werden.* You find that clear?"

"No."

"Multicolored strips are soaked in water on the shore and placed alongside . . . No, that can't be right! We need better instructions. How are we to catch those frogs? Will they cling to the rags? Or is the idea that the rags are slippery and the frogs won't be able to brace themselves to jump off?"

"I think they will slip," said Bonek.

"I guess they will skid and won't be able to brace themselves."

"Whatever you think, sir."

Hatus: "No, I want to know what *you* think. I'm interested in *your* opinion."

Bonek glanced at the five-page guidelines in the hand of Mr. Hatus, and focused on item No. 8, partly covered by the thick thumb of Mr. Hatus: "Perhaps they mean, sir, that the rags will simply be spread on the bank to lure the animals, and the capture will be conducted manually."

"All right," said Hatus. "And what then?"

"There is no *then*, sir," said Bonek severely. Hatus would have liked to hear more. (How he resembled me,

Jan Chrysostom! When Alice stopped in the middle of
The Sleeping Prince and he, Jan Chrysostom, kept begging for more, more!)

It was not lost on my uncle (Jan Chrysostom's uncle)
that item No. 8 dealt with the future: *Verbesserung der
Eiweissgrundlage durch Schlachtung aller greifbaren
Tiere.* Everything would soon get much better—especially
the *Protein Supply, through the Slaughter of all available
warm-blooded Animals.*

And then Bonek smiled at Mr. Hatus, bared his *dens
caninus*, that canine dog-tooth fang, that sticker and
killer, flashing at Mr. Hatus the message that the future
had arrived, the so-called right moment, i.e., the moment
of the decisive word—whereupon the warm-blooded Mr.
Hatus, fragile to the point of transparency, slumped in his
chair, stuck out his drooling lower lip, and breathed
heavily, a comical and slightly repulsive frog-bubble
pulsating on his jugular vein.

If I were to puncture it, thought Bonek, he would
deflate like an old tire . . . "Anyway, it's time," Bonek
heard himself say, "it is time, sir, for serious decisions."

"Yes," agreed Hatus.

"The time is ripe."

"Yes."

"Don't come to the plant any more," said my uncle,
and Mr. Hatus nodded again.

From then on, Mr. Hatus sat at home, smoking
Egyptian cigarettes (stashed away and turned into a
treasure by the war), but as he was a nonsmoker, his
head would spin. And those carnations smelled too strong.
He must have planted them when there was a rainbow
or on Good Friday . . . or when the moon was full, they
were so red. They were even bloodier than the ones on
the Largior wrappers; the carnations of Chlumec had
grown as lusty and red as if that plump lady with the

horn of plenty had scattered them all over town and filled the baskets of bridesmaids in celebration of imminent peace.

. . .

My mother could already sense that peace was coming. She got some lemon peel and butter from Aunt Vlaciha and I was put to pounding sugar with a bronze pestle in a mortar because we still only had sugar in lumps, from before the war, and then I stirred the dough until my arm hurt, but when Mother saw me licking the wooden spatula, she took the bowl away from me, added egg yolks and lemon peel and flour, plus egg white beautifully beaten into white snow by Edvin, my father, also happy that peace was coming; he kept testing the egg white until it was thick enough to stick to the beater, and after we had done all this, we poured the dough into the pan (about a finger's-breadth thick) and covered it with cherries—also from Aunt Vlaciha, who had put them up the day I met the Vazoom, the day I got so sick. But *these* cherries were different—we would eat *these* cherries in peacetime, and we would be happy; Uncle Bonek came over and agreed that it would be so. I recognized Uncle by his voice, not by his clothes, because he was dressed in a strange way. On his head he had a helmet with a strap going under his chin, which lengthened his face and gave him a look of great energy. Uncle was not wearing his usual striped suit and tie, but knickers and a sweater and a military-type belt, and in the flank of the deer (the sweater was decorated with a deer) was stuck a small Czech flag.

When he got a whiff of the sweet smell from the oven, he said: "Edvin, our liberated nation is about to settle the score with traitors and collaborators."

Dad said: "Where?"

"On the hill," said Uncle.

And so Edvin, too, stuck a small flag in his lapel, put

on a pair of knickers, and set out with Uncle toward the Pleasure Park to reconquer Chlumec.

Mother pulled the cherry cake out of the oven, set the pan on the windowsill to cool, and gazed after Edvin. He was climbing the hill. Mother's cheeks were flushed. I watched her, and it seemed to me her face was red not because of Edvin's dangerous expedition but because of the way the aroma of the cake wafted upward toward her face; that aroma was warmer than a day in May, i.e., it seemed to me that the hot fragrance shimmered around Mother's eyes. But before I was able to study this more thoroughly, Alice covered the cake with a napkin and said: "We have to sew a flag."

Little Erna Klahn was with us, already able to talk.

And there I was, holding a piece of blue cloth for Mother to cut the triangular wedge of our flag, and there was a wasp. It came flying in, circled the cooling pan, craving the sweet.

"Chase it away," Mother said, because she knew that the wasp was likely to sting me.

Item: I waved the blue triangle of the Czech flag-to-be and the wasp flew off. At least for the moment. It was not to harm me until Tuesday, May 8, and I was glad that I didn't have to ponder the question of what it would be doing in the meantime. That might have given me a headache. Whereas, by just shooing it off—shoo!—it was gone.

Erna helped me by applauding and also by reciting *Frankfurt is a city where* . . . and I chimed in with the second line (by now the wasp had disappeared): *Frankfurters fly through the air*.

The sky was clear. No frankfurters were flying. It would have been a sight to see, franks streaking through the air over Chlumec like pursuit planes, firing at the enemy. And then I really did hear a roar in the sky and the shadow of a Storch skimmed our yard. He was toward the Pleasure Park, probably reconnoitering, and Dad was probably shooting at him. I was proud of Dad. I imagined him firing his machine gun (actually, I used to call it an *automatic*, Comr. Pavlenda), with little flames shooting out of the barrel, the way I saw it in a magazine, and then I imagined the Storch listing to one side, wing aflame, making a rainbow of fire and smoke over Chlumec.

My father, alas, had no automatic, only a small pistol, and that's why he was lying in a ditch and the Storch was being fired at by Lubos Carek, Sr., Doctor of Jurisprudence, and Joseph Bezpalec, Graduate Engineer. But these gentlemen of course won no military glory; either they missed the plane, or else their bullets failed to reach it. Ratatata! "Target: low-flying aircraft! Fire!" shouted Eng. Bezpalec, and immediately obeyed his own order, until Bonek had to reprimand him because Bonek was Patrol Commander and he was the one empowered to issue orders. For the sake of discipline, he called out: "Brother Jerabek!" (*not* Brother Bezpalec!) And when Brother Jerabek answered "Here," Uncle commanded: "Take two men, direction tall tree, and set up an observation post!" "Yes, sir," said Brother Jerabek. He was very happy to be entrusted with setting up an observation post under the tall tree and acting brave. He had feathered his nest quite nicely during the war and yesterday at the station, when rifles were being handed out, he just barely managed to get one. The locomotive of a hospital train had been blown up by dive bombers. Everybody in Chlumec ran to capture his German. Brother Jerabek grabbed a sick soldier, took his rifle away, and the comically rubber-kneed German waddled off as fast as he could, as if he were skating.

Item: Brother Jerabek commanded "Fall in!" and two men, i.e., Brother Hajek and Comrade Aulik (I am providing their class background, Comr. Pavlenda), ambled in a most unmilitary way toward Brother Jerabek, who stuck out his chest, turned in the direction of the afore-mentioned tree, put on his beret, received two old egg-shaped grenades from Bonek, stuck them in his pockets, and after giving himself the order "Forward march!" obeyed at once and marched on Amdas, who was coming into sight on the right of the tall tree, driving down the Cepin slope in a one-ton brewery truck.

"Hey, something is coming down the road," said one of the Brothers (or rather, one of the Comrades).

"Brother," said Mr. Jerabek, "run over and report it."

"You mean to Bonek?"

"No, I mean to Brother Commander," Mr. Jerabek reprimanded the unmilitary bit of familiarity.

Bonek asked for the folding binoculars, and though it was getting dark he said: "I know that vehicle!"

Eng. Bezpalec said: "It's running on ersatz gas."

Amdas stepped on the accelerator and started to climb the hill toward Mr. Jerabek. All he wanted was to pass him. He was fleeing, the peacocks were running all over his garden making ugly noises as if the flowers on their tails had become carnivorous. Amdas was no longer wearing his German uniform or his boots and Tyrolean hat but a raincoat with a revolver in the pocket. At his feet crouched young Amdas, that beautiful child.

"*Halt!*" shouted Mr. Jerabek. And Amdas stopped.

"*Aussteigen!*"

Amdas did not get out. He was afraid to open the door and let them see his son. Instead, he shot Jerabek and was off. Soot came flying out of the tail pipe and this sudden backfire felled Bonek + his patrol + my father Edvin, all of whom thought the attack of General Schörner's army was about to begin.

Soot-covered Edvin was first to get up, and said: "Did we fuck that up!"

Bonek said: "Let us pay tribute to our dead!"

He took off his helmet and stood silently over Mr. Jerabek. The egg-shaped grenades had rolled out of his pockets, whereas the beret on his head had not moved an inch.

Bonek examined the body, the ceremonial moment was over, and Mr. Hajek said: "Sir, I wrote down the number."

Bonek looked at him, puzzled.

"I mean the number of that truck. You understand? It's a habit of mine, I like to make notes of everything. And now it will come in handy."

But Bonek couldn't imagine what for. He was quite familiar with the one-ton truck from the Vlaciha brewery, license number CH 434; he knew Amdas, too. There was no need for detective work. And so Mr. Hajek got praise only from Dad.

"You're a regular Sherlock Holmes," he said. But in reality Mr. Hajek was a clerk at the Chlumec undertakers. *Item*: He offered to place the firm's refrigeration room at the patrol's disposal. The men returned to town, passed our house, and when Bonek saw that Mother had finished the flag he asked whether she would lend it to him to give Mr. Jerabek a dignified funeral. But Mother said no, she would not do it, for *our* flag was not intended for such purposes. And she lifted it off the ironing board, called me, handed it to me, and asked me to take it into the bedroom to cool off. Thus, in Question 22, section marked MOTHER, I can put in evidence—aside from the apple which she pulled out of my hand (*viz.*, Chap. 7)— this flag, which instead she pressed *into* my hand. I could also state under this Question (or does it belong under Question 28, *Domestic Resistance?*) that I took that flag, still hot, into the bedroom and spread it over Edvin & Alice's double bed in such a way that the blue wedge lay at the head, the white stripe covered Mother's side, and the red, Father's side. As the flag cooled, they took Mr.

Jerabek to the refrigeration room, too, but they cooled him just long enough to find a coffin for a Class I funeral, then they put him in the hearse with the glass sides and silver angels in the corners and took him to the family crypt in the Chlumec cemetery. He's in a better world, they said along the way, or else: He's beyond pain now; and just as they began to climb the tree-lined road to the cemetery and neared the top of the hill which Mr. Jerabek had so recently been defending, German tanks came rumbling down, with soldiers sitting on them as thick as bees. They were retreating through Chlumec, but so heavily armed that they struck terror in everyone. They spotted the hearse standing in the middle of the hill, looking suspiciously deserted. Whereupon: they fired a cannon shot at it. The shell flew through the glass walls and dug into the dirt on the other side. Mr. Jerabek stayed put. He calmly remained in his coffin; the angels with bowed heads did not drop the torches from their hands, even though they were shaken quite a bit. But then, Comr. Pavlenda, a strange thing happened! The hearse, which had survived the cannon shot, suddenly up and exploded all on its own. Something twitched inside, the coffin flew apart, angels came tumbling down, and splinters flew all over. The big, imposing rear wheel came rolling toward Mr. Hajek (and toward the other members of the cortège, who had taken cover in nearby bushes).

"It's unbelievable! It's a miracle!" said Brother Hajek.

Bonek said: "It's quite simple. We forgot to take the grenades out of his pockets."

And another Brother said: "But even so, I'm not sure whether it's technically possible for grenades to go off like that."

The tanks disappeared.

"Brothers," said Eng. Hajek, "the murderer of Brother Jerabek must be punished!"

And the others said: "He will be!"

And they went off to catch him, while all around
Chlumec there was a mounting din of traffic, carts came
rattling down the hills with Russians sitting on the boxes,
whips snapped through the air, and grinning soldiers
waved.

.   .   .

I was still squatting on the windowsill, resting my
chin on my knees while my flag fluttered overhead. I
watched the soldiers in the carts, who were tossing
gingerbread cookies at me. I jumped in the flower bed
beneath the window and vaulted over the picket fence for
the cookies.

They were dusty from the road, but they made me
hungry for sweets, and I remembered that there was a
fresh cherry cake on the sideboard, which everybody had
forgotten about on account of the revolution.

I lifted the napkin and admired the fabulous cake,
and then I broke off a piece near the edge, which is the
part I like best. I munched on it and went back to my
perch on the windowsill. The Russkies were gone, but
I saw Brother Hajek with a gun, leading an Amdas.

Twelve other Brothers came marching along, with
twelve Amdases in tow.

"Twelve lovely maidens, each one fairer than the next"
flashed through my head, and I thought of the King's
words in the fairy tale in which a bee helps the hero
identify his true bride standing among eleven others, all
identically veiled: "If you guess your true love, she will
be yours."

I was puzzled how in this profusion of Amdases they
were going to find the right one when I heard a wasp,
the one I had chased away from the cake on Friday.
Now it was returning, first circling the piece of cake I
was holding in my hand and then flying straight to those
Amdases, flying from one to the other and buzzing "It
can't be this maiden, or this one, or this one," until at

last it landed on the right hand of a walking body and said: "Give me this maiden, oh King, this is the one I have earned through faithful service."

The right hand of that body was motionless, tied with wire, and stuck to the other hand, which smelled of blood because the wire cut into the flesh and blood trickled down the fingers; at the edge of the trickle it had dried almost black. The wasp, even though already gorged on our cherry cake, clamped her fuzzy mandibles (as well as that part under the root of the antennae) into the wound, right up to the opening of its mouth, and all its hairs and feelers were helping to work the proboscis deeper and deeper. Its hairy legs, too, were braced in flesh. The tiny veins on the folded wings pulsed and throbbed, joyously rather than watchfully. The ease with which the juices flowed promised that the hands would continue to be quiet and harmless and that the wasp could safely dig into the freshest part of the flesh, the lymph. Human lymph mixed with the saliva of the yellow-black insect which was clasped to this outlying part of the walking body. The walking did not produce any motion to startle the wasp, it was hardly perceptible to the insect except for the slight rhythmic lapping of the juices which filled the wasp's hairs with aroma. Only once was there any need for flight—when an indistinct shadow flitted over the wound and struck the walking body. This was accompanied by a flash of light, because the butt of the rifle which had so rudely prodded the body was covered with a metal plate and caught the rays of the sun. The body sprang forward, groaned, and began to jog, hands behind its back, and the wasp poised over them, hanging in the air, buzzing in a tiny shimmering circle. Trained to fly over meadows, earth, and stones, it knew how to swerve at the slightest movement, to hang suspended over its prey and to pursue it for miles. For example, it traveled from our house all the way to Happy

Living (an inexpensive but clean rooming house), and there it again alighted on its old spot. After the rifle-butt blow, none of the motions was sudden or violent. The body was twisting and struggling, but this only made the juices flow all the more easily.

It was the gasoline that finally chased· the wasp away, the gasoline stench as they doused the bodies and set them on fire. The wasp climbed to the top of the tree, high over the branch with the burning body. But it was chased out by the smoke even there.

"Mr. Hajek," said one of the Brothers, his eyes averted from the screaming, upside-down Amdas, "you have hung him on the Tree of the Republic!"

"So much the better," said the clerk, and started looking for another Amdas.

I was still sitting on the sill, but I was no longer eating the same piece of cake, I was polishing off the last piece. I saw Dad running home, his face ashen. Alice made him sniff ammonia, and he just kept repeating: "My God, Alice! If you had only seen it! If you had only seen it!"

I wanted to ask what it was Dad had seen, I opened my mouth to swallow the last morsel of the last piece of cake, and that same wasp was perched on it again. I bit into it and my palate blew up so fast I couldn't get out a single word.

10. THE BRIDE

I started to cry and Alice now had to shuttle between me
and Edvin, but she was more worried about me because
she thought I might choke to death. She forced me to
open my mouth, intending to fish out the stinger with a
pair of pincers. I kept yelling that there couldn't be any
stinger there, because I had been stung by a wasp and
not by a bee. They didn't understand me because my
speech was already too thick. Edvin forgot all about his
own suffering (my plight aroused him, or else the
ammonia had done its work), he held me by the shoulders,
clamped my legs between his knees and held me tight
while Alice searched for the stinger. But I was right, they
didn't find anything, so they merely put a slice of onion
on the bite.

When the smell of the onion died down, I fell asleep.
Even in my sleep, I heard Edvin railing at Dr. Hajek's
behavior at the Tree of the Republic. He kept insisting
that he could never again pass the center of Chlumec
and look at that tree—personally planted by our
President-Liberator—without recalling those gasoline-
soaked Amdases. Mother told Dad to stop thinking about
it, for heaven's sake, and then she said something to him
that I couldn't make out, and then in a louder voice she
said they should go out dancing. Edvin liked that idea.
"But what can I wear?" asked Mother. She said she had
no shoes or "anything decent to put on." And then: Who
would look after the boy (me)? I got up and said to her:
"Don't be sad!"

But my speech was still thick, they couldn't understand
me, so I repeated the words more slowly and told both

of them that they could go to the dance because I didn't mind being home alone and I would not parachute off the dresser onto my bed and the bottles of dandelion wine would be safe. (This promise about not jumping, however, was made with crossed fingers.)

Alice gave me a kiss and Edvin said we could put an ad in the paper

> exchnge vvt.jkt./hd.
> for eve. pmps. med. sze.

I asked Edvin what language he was speaking and he said it was our own, and meant that we would exchange a velvet jacket with hood for a pair of evening pumps, so that Mother could go dancing at the City Center.

I looked out the window at the playground to see who was camping there, I mumbled "Whooozoutthere," and Mother explained that those were Russkies baking bread in the penalty-kick area. Then I saw Uncle Bonek strolling among them in his deer sweater, but without the little flag. Instead, he was wearing a red armband. I asked Mom what Uncle was doing there and she said that he was earning his future bread.

I said: "They are pouring the dough into little forms, they are sure to ruin it!"

Dad remarked: "Bonek will straighten them out, Bonek is an old fox."

All of a sudden Bonek started walking toward our house. Three soldiers were with him. They walked past the cabins and the post office, along our garden fence, gesticulating with their hands and laughing. One was carrying a chicken, another a salami, and the third a bunch of onions.

They were bringing all this to Mother to cook up in a pot. Bonek had put them up to it!

"The Comrades want something to drink," said Uncle.

Alice retorted: "The *who* want something to drink?"

"The Comrades," Edvin quickly interjected because he saw how steamed up she was. "That's what they call each other."

"What's so strange about that?" said Bonek.

"Nothing," Alice answered, flashing her four-beam eyes at Uncle. He pretended not to notice, and asked in a loud voice: "What can we offer them?"

"Dandelion wine," said Edvin. He was proud of that wine. He went to the bedroom, took the big bottle off my parachute-jump dresser, and showed it to the Russkies. They shook their heads, took the stopper out of the bottle, examined the glass fermentation tube, which seemed to interest them more than Edvin's concoction, then they gulped the wine down but made faces to indicate that it wasn't the kind of drink they had in mind. Edvin was hurt, they hadn't even bothered to strain out the stalks, everything was gone and they had maligned his prize product in the bargain.

Bonek said: "What else can we offer them?"

"I also have some apple cider" (from those Cepin apples, Comr. Pavlenda!).

But the Russians were again making faces, and they gulped down the cider without pleasure. Then came the soup, Alice's, and this they praised. They waxed enthusiastic about the soup. And about Mother. "A beauty! *Krasavitsa*," they said, and Edvin was getting nervous.

"What are we going to drink?" they asked.

Mother threw up her hands. "This is all I've got left," she said. She showed them the bottle of ammonia that she had used for reviving Dad. And the Russian who had called her "*krasavitsa*" pulled out the stopper, sniffed the alcoholic tincture, and let his comrades smell it, too. They all rolled their eyes with approval, took a swig apiece, and the little bottle was empty.

"*Yishtcho*, more! *Krasavitsa*!" they shouted. They slapped their thighs to show that this was finally the right kind of stuff, while Bonek and Edvin were pale with fear, visualizing all those Russkies dead on the floor. Bonek said that the responsibility pointed at our mom, and he warned her: "You'll see, this will get *you* in a lot of trouble!"

(Actually, Comr. Pavlenda, there was some ammonia in that tincture, but mainly it was made from lime, which was put into a strong jar and slaked with brandy until it stopped bubbling, and then we decanted it into bottles to use like smelling salts when somebody felt faint.)

Bonek's dire prediction seemed to have been justified, for the Russkies were beginning to drop to the floor after polishing off that tincture. And Bonek warned us that if the Comrades died by morning he would have to make a report. All night long we kept peeking into the kitchen to see if the Russians were dying, but in the morning they got up and asked in their language what happened to the soup from their chicken; i.e., they were alive and we were safe, as even Bonek had to admit.

The one who had kept calling mother "*krasavitsa*" put his fingers in his mouth and whistled out the window toward the playground; somebody promptly brought him a horse, he climbed into the saddle, he was a captain, he reached for me, picked me up, and we were off galloping up the hill, direction tall tree; it was May 11, Friday, and we passed Erna Klahn near the tavern where I had lost that four-leaf-clover bell cover, I thought of that event and told myself—This is my lucky day and this is a lucky spot, I'll marry her, this lass, she is fair and comely; I fell in love with her the moment I saw her, just like Prince Oldrich atop his gallant steed.

To Erna, quoth I: "Erna, be true to me!"

To Mother (dismounting from my charger): "Bake another cake, Mother, for my wedding is near."

"And whom will you marry?"

"The Klahn girl, of course."

And Mom said: "Maybe she doesn't care for you."

"I'm sure she does, Mom. But . . . I could ask her."

"You'd better do that," said Mom, "before I grease the pan."

.   .   .

Item: I harnessed Astor to the cart (re Question 10, Comr. Pavlenda, *Property—Fixed & Movable*: we always had some kind of dog, and he'd always been called Astor) and I drove to Cepin to see Erna. No, I no longer went by train. I was grown up now, I had Astor & cart. Astor was almost a St. Bernard (i.e., mostly St. Bernard, the rest pure Chlumec dog [*Canis chlumecensis*]), born and bred in the Cepin brewery. And so, when I told him we were going to pass his birthplace, he smiled at me. He did this by opening his mouth and looking up from below, as it were. I harnessed him, stroked his head, and I was off in the cart, which Edvin had made for me out of my old baby carriage. I passed some Russkies, they laughed and saluted, and I drove direction tall tree, clucking at Astor, and he pounded along, traces shaking at his sides, and I imagined that I was not Jan Chrysostom but a water sprite pulled by four cats whose eyes cut through the night like the headlights of a car. Below me was Cepin and to the right belched a belcher, the local train that used to transport me at 14:31 hours before I had become independent thanks to my dogcart.

I traveled almost as fast as the train, since I didn't have to zigzag or make a detour to the station, which was almost as far from Cepin as it was from Chlumec.

Erna Klahn was beautiful, I could see that from my cart even better than from horseback. She was not wearing that white dress or the hat with the silk ribbon which she had on when I fell in love with her, but she was sitting on a swing, in the garden behind the inhabited wing of the brewery, wagging her legs and blowing soap bubbles into the sky. They were even more shiny and glittery than the glass balls that stuck out of the flower beds among the roses, ivy, and hyacinth bells. And when I looked on Erna's ponytail, tied with a kerchief as yellow as saffron (to make her hair even sunnier), I thought to myself: You have done well, J.Ch., to fall in love with the Klahn girl, because even though she is the daughter of a mere human she could easily be a nymph.

"Don't unleash your dog, you know I'm scared of him," she said.

"He isn't mean."

"But he's big."

"You want to see him smile? Astor, smile!"

Astor performed, and Erna said: "How do you make him do it?"

I lifted my index finger and shouted "Bark," and for each movement of the finger the dog let out one "arf."

"For that performance you ought to lend me your bubble water," I said.

"Here."

I blew a pearl toward the sky. "Let me give you a ride, Erna."

"Why?"

"Just for fun."

"I'm scared of Astor."

"And me?" I blew a few sparkling bubbles.

"I like you."

I was happy, I smiled, and when Astor saw that, he started smiling too and Erna the same, she saw Astor and broke up, so that all three of us were laughing. Because we liked each other. Her skin was like flower petals, soft, clean, her eyes like sulphur flames.

Suddenly Mrs. Klahn, music teacher, stepped into the garden and said: "Jan"—that's how she addressed me, in the manner of Aunt Vlaciha, i.e., in the Cepin manner —"what brings you here?"

Mrs. Klahn was almost as beautiful as my mom, she

had long arms and even at home wore long skirts (down to her ankles), and she did not play the piano but the clavier, which was black and stood in the room with the Venetian mirror. Mrs. Klahn knew many more compositions than my mom; e.g., she knew songs about the Trout or Death and the Maiden or the Beautiful Miller's Wife. She sang in an alto voice, and I watched her hands, which were like a kite in the sky, they trembled and plunged yet stayed in one place.

"I've come for Erna," I said. "We're going to get married."

"Really?" said Mrs. Klahn. "You should have told me sooner!"

All the same, she went out to pick some rosemary for us. It grew in a pot on the veranda, the pale blue flowers climbing to the ceiling.

I pointed at the prettiest sprig and Mrs. Klahn promised to keep it for me.

"We'll get you a streamer for it," she said, and because Erna wanted Astor to be included in the festivity, too, we stuck a spray of rosemary behind his trace.

I drove my cart back home to Alice, to see whether she had finished baking. I filled the cart with pastry and put some fruit and gingerbread under the seat and also a daisy wreath, another gift from Mom, and new shoes with snap-on buckles. I clicked my tongue at Astor, waved my rosemary sprig, and I was off to see my bride. Her hair was loose and the saffron kerchief which yesterday had held her ponytail was now tied around her neck to make the white dress underneath even whiter.

Near the swing had been placed an ash-wood bench covered with a napkin and sprinkled with rosemary flowers. I unloaded everything I had brought and set it all on the bench, while Mrs. Klahn brought raspberry juice (made from berries that grew at the foot of the Cepin castle) and poured each of us a glassful.

That was our wedding.

Then we went to the room with the clavier and Venetian mirror and Mrs. Klahn played for us, a two-handed rendition of *Vierhändige Klavierstücke*. Erna the dancer danced, standing now on one foot, now on the other, now on both, kicking up her heels at the whole wide world. I danced, too, but not nearly as gracefully as my bride. My brand-new shoes creaked, the tight buckle cut into my flesh, but I didn't care. "Oh, what a lovely wedding," said Erna. She was all out of breath from the dancing, her cheeks were flushed. "Tomorrow we'll have another one, all right? Tomorrow *I* will marry *you*!"

I was immensely happy that she liked me. I attached another streamer to my rosemary branch, which Alice had made by cutting a strip from a roll of crepe paper with scissors. The scissors were decorated with portraits of the Austrian emperor and empress, in such a way that each time the scissors closed, the imperial couple kissed. I was determined to kiss Erna, too.

I fixed the buckle on my shoes by putting some surgical cotton under it so that I wouldn't have to wear ordinary sneakers when I went to see my bride again.

A breeze was blowing; my red-and-white ribbons streamed from the rosemary rod as I stepped into the garden and said: "How can we tell that today *you* are marrying *me*?"

She thought it over. "Because we are eating pastry made by *my* mother."

"Spread with rhubarb jam."

"No, rhubarbara. We call it rhubarbara."

I agreed. Anyway, it was her pastry and her marriage. She asked me to chase off a gosling which had stuck its head through the fence into the gazebo. The gosling was watched over by an old goose that Erna was afraid of.

Shoooo, I waved at the yellow waddlers about to follow the first one through the fence. I picked it up. The old goose stuck out her neck at me and hissed, but the gosling felt so fuzzy and soft I didn't give it back to its mother but carried it to Erna.

"Feel how its heart is pounding," I said. "Here, stroke it, but gently."

Erna was sitting on the swing, trying to keep the gosling from slipping out of her grasp. She propped her legs against the bench, and as she placed the tiny bird on her lap, her skirt slid up from her knees—and look: the flower *Masdevallia ignea* appeared before my eyes. I did not know then what it was called but I sensed what it was. (As far as the actual flower goes, Comr. Pavlenda, I really saw it quite a bit later, on a school outing to the Botanical Garden. It was damp and stuffy in the greenhouse, big elongated leaves loomed overhead, and among their stalks I saw the same thing that I had seen under Erna's skirt. In the greenhouse I was reminded of Erna and I felt so giddy that I had to sit down.) But that day of my first vision, that day on the swing, I managed to hide my agitation. I stepped back just in time and picked up a burdock leaf. I handed it to Erna: "Here is a parasol for you."

She reached out her left hand to take the leaf, but as I was handing it to her I had to bend down and this motion made me lose my balance; I tumbled head over heels toward her girlplace and I kissed it with eyes open, while Erna kept petting the gosling with one hand and holding the parasol in the other. As she moved, the place I kissed kept moving, too; I observed everything very closely.

After a long while, at least it seemed long to me, she said: "Here!" and returned the yellow bird to me without mentioning the thing that had happened down below.

She straightened her legs, the flame of the *ignea* went out, to disappear on me for eight whole years until I saw it once again in the Botanical Garden.

On that occasion they told me, Comr. Pavlenda, that *ignea* meant *fiery*, but by then I was already well aware of that myself.

I didn't want us to break the mood of silence, and so I took Erna by the hand and we ran to the Cepin castle. Right behind the garden was the Silver Poplar, the tavern owned by the Klahns, then the brewery smokestack, and beyond that only a meadow rising to the old walls with gaping windows.

We skipped hand in hand through the greenery and I promised Erna that I would get a job as a waiter in her father's tavern, even though originally it had been agreed I would become President, like Dr. Beneš. I had read a story about him in the newspaper, how he returned to the castle from exile "with simple dignity." I was very moved by that, I imagined myself holding a pair of suede gloves in one hand while waving to the crowds with the other, my Erna—like the President's wife Hana—by my side; it was a beautiful scene, but now I would have to give all that up because my bride wished otherwise.

We kept on climbing, the wind died down, the liverworts were opening up. The higher we climbed, the better we could make out the outline of Chlumec and the spire of St. Barbora's, and then we stopped because we thought we heard the bells of the church. We must surely have been mistaken.

Then I said: "Show me where your dad saw the Vazoom."

Erna pointed to the spot. Then we both hopped around on one leg and shouted: "Vazoom, come forth!"

No luck.

"Maybe that's not his right name," objected Erna.

"Sure it is," I said. "There can be no mistake about

that." And so we resumed our stomping and hopping and I jumped so hard that the cotton inset fell out of my shoe and blood began to trickle beneath the buckle.

We tried to summon the Vazoom a few more times. Suddenly a man stepped out from behind the wall facing us.

"Who are you?" I asked him.

"Who are you?" he said.

"I am Jan Chrysostom."

"I see," he said, coming closer. He was wearing a military cap and a jacket with winged-crown insignia. "Then I am your uncle."

"No, you can't be!"

"Why not?"

"Because we already have an uncle. Bonek."

He guffawed, and said: "Now you have another one. Olin. And introduce me to the lady."

11. ORTHOPTERA

"On the Sabbath at Noone the Towne is to be shut," was the order issued by Sir Jost of Chlumec, as quoted in Chap. 3, p. 182 of Monsignor Rosin's *History* ("The Golden Era").

Item: I now give the same order, Comr. Pavlenda. All the people you are interested in are now present and accounted for, as per Question 21 through Question 26, inclusive: From Erna, my bride, to Olin (*Country, Purpose of Trip, Length of Stay*).

Even Cepin is here. I now close everything shut. Including the Vazoom. Let nothing stir or change places, except through its own natural inertia.

They were going to brew beer. Peace had come at last.

Klahn and Vostarek were planning to brew the same glorious beer that Olin's father, the one who died before the war, had brewed. They would spread out the grain on the threshing floor until it germinated to malt; Mr. Vostarek was not going to let it steep too long but whisk it just at the proper moment to the malt kiln and the drying mats. He was a master brewer; once he had even been offered a job in Pilsen (and if he hadn't met old Vlaciha in the Grodek trenches in 1915, who knows if he wouldn't have ended up in Pilsen), but instead he gained his eternity in Cepin. He realized it and was content to be where he was. Whereas Mr. Klahn felt that his eternalization was still ahead of him. During the war that had just ended he helped out Aunt Vlaciha, who was all alone, and now Olin was trying to lure him into a partnership.

VLACIHA & KLAHN: CEPIN BEER
*famous light lager beer
available only in the finest establishments*

In brown bottles with raised lettering; sold at the Silver Poplar and select restaurants. Modest scale, but sound. Sixty bushels per run, no more than sixteen barrels per fermentation vat.

That's how Mr. Klahn talked business with Olin, sounding like a businessman and not a mere tapster. Mrs. Klahn, in the meantime, was playing the piano at the Silver Poplar (at her house there was no instrument as shrill and twangy as this one, with *Mexico City* in gold lettering over the keyboard), and she relished her new role as Mrs. Klahn, the Partner's Wife.

Aunt Ludmila sat at the head of a long oak table, the vaulted ceiling behind her converged on a stone flower and it seemed as if the flower were there just to wreathe her head in a festive garland, i.e., to enable her to gaze more grandly into the bright future represented by her beloved Olin at the other end of the table.

He said: "They used to brew one hell of a strong beer in these parts." And Mr. Klahn retorted that it used to be called Spring Bock, whereas Mr. Vostarek claimed that it was called Martius Beer from way back, after the Latin name for the month of March.

"We'll hire a driver and make our deliveries," said Mr. Klahn. He thought of everything.

CH 434 turned up in the Odloucen woods. It had run out of fuel and couldn't go any further, the Amdases got out and died (if those dead bodies nearby were really theirs). Now this Praga truck was standing in the yard behind the vats, and Edvin, who was also present and also gazing at Olin as if the Future dawned on that side of the table, said: "They can shove the bakery job up their ass. I'll join up with you. Tomorrow I'll quit."

At the word "ass" Mirena Klahn pounded the piano keys to drown out Father. She didn't like such talk and she was getting uneasy; instead of *Vierhändige Klavierstücke*, she played the popular hit "Seven Canaries."

Olin got up, having finished his mug (here they served beer in mugs with hinged lids), and walked the length of the table to Aunt Ludmila to ask her for a dance. Aunt was not shy, she was in high spirits. With one hand she smoothed her hair, with the other she lifted the corner of her skirt so that the hem rose in an attractive arc, and then she danced with Olin around the stone pillar in the middle of the hall, and it was this pillar on which all the stone flowers converged.

Erna and I also danced to the tune of "Nine Canaries" (Eight are Even and One is Odd) during the festivities at the Silver Poplar, the day that was to inaugurate the rebirth of Cepin beer, but we two did not soar like Aunt Ludmila and Olin, we hopped around until our cheeks were red and blood pounded in our veins.

Item: As soon as Bonek found out that my father wanted to go into the brewing business, he called him over and said: "You know, that poor fellow Hatus is in deep trouble, he's going to get at least ten years."

Edvin asked what for, and Bonek said it was for owning the Hatusch Kakaofabrik.

"But that was hardly a crime," said Father.

And Bonek answered that perhaps it was not a crime from a personal point of view but it was from a class point of view.

Up until then, the only class Dad was familiar with had to do with school, and so he shrugged and asked: "And what will happen to *his* factory?"

Bonek replied that this was precisely what he wanted to discuss with Edvin. "The factory must go on operating," he said, and pointed his finger at an item in the newspaper *Labor* (formerly *Political Life*) which read: "*Trivia and personal matters must be swept aside! The following is a list of directives for organizing factory councils . . .*"

"We have already formed such a council, Edvin!"

"And what are you going to council about?"

Bonek looked severely at Dad and said: "One of these days you'll pay dearly for that big trap of yours!"

Dad, too, looked at Bonek, but there was no threat in his eyes; on the contrary, his manner was conciliatory as he too pointed his finger at the newspaper story. The finger pointed at the word *trivia*.

Uncle was nonplussed. But then he assumed Dad was being apologetic, and said: "Well then, Edvin, shall we buckle down to work?" And with these words he flung out his arm like a statue in the direction of the railroad station, i.e., toward the southeast, toward Prague, and added that our chief task was to accept historical responsibility and stand in the ranks of the struggle for the birth of a new life.

"You understand?"

Dad nodded, even though he could not imagine a struggle that had ranks.

"We are going to produce *Dianthus*, you understand?"

Dad shook his head to indicate he didn't.

"I'm talking about *chocolate. Dianthus* is going to be the new brand name. The woman will be taken off the wrapper, but the flowers will stay. Red flowers. One of them, the biggest, will kind of stick out over the others . . . and will be surrounded by lettering."

"Gold?"

"Gold on red."

"Then you'd better count me out, Bonek." Dad smiled at Uncle. "Factory council, that's fine. But now you want to get rid of the woman, and you're suggesting gold on red—no, I'm afraid I couldn't go along with that."

And he flashed his canine tooth in Uncle's face.

Bonek clenched his lips to the point of blanching, then said: "Just as you wish, Edvin. You could have been chairman."

"Or fireman," said Dad.

"You're a pest. I'll tell Mother on you."

But Edvin was already on his way out of the room.

. . .

A short time later Hatus died in prison, awaiting trial by a Special Court of the People. He was sensible. And the new vocabulary scared him. It seemed to him that in the old days "people" was always spelled with a small *p*, and "Special" was used in connection with trains added to the schedule at Christmastime. But then everything was getting mixed up and he only seemed to be in the way. Whereas our Bonek! He became national director of United Chocolate Works, Chlumec, and Fortuna duly disappeared from the wrappers. On the same day, I dismissed Astor from my employ, not of course because of dissatisfaction with his performance, but because Edvin had succeeded in reconverting Praga CH 434 to ordinary gasoline and I could hitch rides to Cepin. Besides, I was growing a bit too heavy for the dog. I was also growing too old for wedding games, and told Erna that I would no longer bring her wreaths or drink raspberry lemonade.

"Then what are we going to do?" she asked.

"We're going to watch Mr. Vostarek fly," I told her.

Next to Olin, my favorite adult was Mr. Vostarek. He was the only one who shared my belief in the Vazoom and he had succeeded in luring 262 moths to their death.

"How are we going to watch him if he hasn't flown yet?"

"We'll wait."

"You'll be waiting a long time." She frowned. "I'll have to find me another boy."

I felt a pang of sadness, I had an inkling, Comr.

Pavlenda, that this prediction would someday come true, and my foot smarted where the buckle had cut it during our wedding dance.

Item: I ran down the slope to the malt house, where Mr. Vostarek had a wooden shed with a workbench, and tools on the walls, arranged according to size. He even had a grinding wheel, he turned the whetstone with a handle, and underneath there was a tub filled with water to keep the round stone moist. When Erna and I had still been man and wife, she used to turn the handle while I held an old chisel to the dry stone, which threw off a shower of sparks, and this is how we created our make-believe fireworks display.

During the day, Mr. Vostarek used the place for building his *orthopter*, or flying machine. He referred to it both ways, depending on whether he was talking with an expert or a layman. Since Olin's return, Mr. Vostarek recognized no other expert but this Royal Flying Officer, although even Olin the F.O. had never flown in the literal sense of the word but had only ridden through the air with the help of various engines.

"I am going to build a vertical-flap device for true human flight."

"But it will never take off from the ground," said the F.O., who picked up a pencil and showed the brewmaster why not.

The brewmaster studied the calculations and said: "Of course, it's true that arms alone can never generate enough power. Fools always try to build wings for the arms alone. People will not fly like birds, horizontally, but standing up. And the flap axis will be horizontal."

"That won't produce enough lift, either," said Olin.

"They'll have to practice. From childhood, from babyhood." And Mr. Vostarek pointed at me, but the idea of being connected with childhood or babyhood didn't please me.

"I have thought up a good training device. An *auxiliary balloon*. It would make a person practically weightless. With such a device, one could easily leap to great heights and leap over obstacles like a grasshopper."

Mr. Vostarek opened his sketchbook to a sheet showing a man flying through the air attached to an auxiliary balloon. The sparse ruler-and-compass rendering of the balloon and its equipment contrasted with the lovingly drawn, detailed picture of Chlumec and Cepin. The flying figure clearly represented Mr. Vostarek himself, dressed in his Sunday best. A summary of the flight data was attached, including a description of the terrain traversed; i.e., Cepin and the brewery, and in the yard the onlookers, namely us, looking up at the sky and waving.

All traces of irony disappeared from Olin's eyes. He leafed through a sheaf of notebooks filled with paintings of moths with outstretched wings and analyses of their applicability to human-type flight. The egger moths were there, too, the ones we used to trap on sticky paper, with the remark that they were *unsuitable for flight and harmful to the forest.*

A similar remark was made about practically all of the insects. One of the exceptions was the Goliath butterfly (*Ornithoptera Goliath*). This entry did not even show the usual curve illustrating wing movement. The habitat of the Goliath is South America, so that Mr. Vostarek could not study its flight as he did in the case of the ordinary Cepin varieties, yet the skeleton of the wings he was constructing in the shed behind the brewery strikingly resembled the shape of this particular swallow-tail butterfly.

"Well then," Mr. Vostarek said, "once a person got used to the idea of flying, some kind of wings could be added, and the balloon would get smaller and smaller until a few hardy, well-trained individuals could do without the balloon altogether and fly using only my flying machine."

Olin said: "I'd love to have one of those painted butterflies." He smiled, and the affectionate glint was reflected in Mr. Vostarek's eyes, too; he promised to give Olin the picture of Goliath.

To me he promised a highwayman, because he knew that I didn't understand much about flying and that I had inherited Edvin's puppet theater with a set of battered puppets. They were made of plaster and now most of the noses were missing and some of them had only half a head. I would sit in front of the curtain, shift the scenery around to construct landscapes, castles, and forests and also a witches' den, but I kept postponing the actual performance. I had already printed tickets and invited Alice, my aunt, Olin, and even Erna, my former bride. But I was waiting to get the highwayman, so that I could present a piece about "The Highwaymen of Moran Forest" and the treasure which this band had hidden in an old oak tree. Mr. Vostarek made an oak for me, then he made the robber chief Bellengardo, and one by one he constructed the whole gang, including Bonecrusher and Cutthroat, and when I said to him that the devil was sure to get them he produced a devil, too. I liked him best of all, because he was covered with black rabbit skin and a long red tongue hung out of his mouth. It was only after all these figures had been assembled that I rang the bell three times (not the four-leaf-clover bell, but a Christmas bell), and hoisted the curtain by pulling a string over miniature pulleys. Bellengardo the Magician sat under the oak and I said in a raspy, rascally voice: "Zounds, didn't we have the devil of a warm night! And there was toil and trouble aplenty to finish by the rise of the moon!" And in a different voice (but from the same text) I spoke for Cutthroat: "Yet methinks this will prove a profitable piece of work, for those merchants are worth five hundred guilders if they're worth a farthing. Not counting spices and brocade!"

Alice managed to watch the performance and at the same time sew a skirt for a peasant woman and a gown for a princess (to be ready when their turn came). She even sprinkled the gown with gold dust from the mask she had worn at the Lent masquerade dance.

"Mom," I asked, "do you think devils can fly?" The spangles on the veil of the princess sparkled.

"They should," she said. "After all, they were angels originally."

"And did you ever see an angel fly?"

"Almost."

"When?"

"One night when you were asleep. But that was quite some time ago."

"Hmmm," I said, disappointed. "That was only my guardian angel."

"And isn't that good enough for you?"

"He wouldn't be able to fly me as far as I want to go."

"And where is that?"

"Further than Mr. Vostarek."

"Whoever heard of such a thing, putting angels in harness," Alice said in mock annoyance, smiling.

"Suppose instead of Astor I hitched up some birds to my cart, like wild geese?"

"They'd have to be specially trained and then they wouldn't be wild any longer. And you'd need an awful lot of them . . ."

But I didn't hear the rest of what she said because she dropped the veil over the face of the princess, the spangles glittered, and this was not just a flash which disappeared in a moment but light that remained before my eyes, a dazzling platform onto which I stepped and which grew bigger and bigger until there was room for my whole cart, birds alighted on it, birds whose names I did not know, and then a flight of wild geese appeared in two long slanting lines and they called on me to hitch them up. I would have much preferred to harness the multicolored birds, but as I didn't know how to address them, I was afraid lest they answer me derisively. And so I hitched up the geese, my hands were full of reins, there were so many they scared me, especially as they were made of the same red leather as the tongue of my devil (isn't it a sin, to want to fly this way?), but I snapped the reins, sending a wave along the leather strips toward the necks of the geese, the cart took off, rose over the Pleasure Park and flew toward the South, toward the steeple of St. Barbora, which reassured me that I was not sinning but sailing, I clenched the knot of reins in my fist and drew it to my chest to make the cart hover motionless in the air while my avian steeds fluttered their wings . . . I hovered over the acacias and locust trees, over the gates in walls which from this height looked like dimples in the dough of a Christmas cake. I hovered in one spot and St. Barbora, whose head was bowed down under the sword of Father Dioscuros, lifted her face toward me and asked whether I, too, was ready to suffer for my faith. "Yes," I replied, "I am taking Holy Communion tomorrow, they are preparing a candle with a ribbon for me, you will see it burn with a clear flame!" "I will watch," she said. "And if you are speaking the truth, I will show you how to rise from Chlumec into heaven!" "I thank you kindly," I replied, but she had to stick her head back under the sword, her father having been holding her all the time by her flowing tresses. Tears came to my eyes. "Someday I will seize one of those Dioscuri. I will split him down the middle and Barbora's hair will slip out of his grasp and flow over Chlumec like jasmin."

Having made this promise, I loosened the reins, sailed twice around the church, and flew toward Cepin, in the direction the tip of the sword pointed. And lo: everyone was standing in the yard, they were shielding their eyes with their hands so as to watch my silhouette against the sun, Edvin and Olin were there, and the beautiful Mrs. Klahn and Aunt Ludmila, and—most remarkable of all— I was there, too, looking up, shielding my eyes with one hand and waving with the other.

.   .   .

"When I look at something, right away I start thinking how to improve it," Mr. Vostarek was saying to Mirena Klahn. "For instance, I am looking at that clavier of yours and right away I think: colors! An instrument like this could easily be converted into a device for playing colors. Every tone would correspond to one pastel hue, projected on the wall behind you, Mrs. Klahn!"

Mr. Klahn glanced nervously at his Bösendorfer. It was a rare instrument, Viennese workmanship.

"That sounds like a fine idea," said Mirena. "But if anything went wrong I'd hate to lose our fine piece."

"Your fine piece would be in fine pieces," I said, and they laughed. They ate their cake and sipped malt coffee.

Soon they had another celebration, this time in honor of the First Brewing.

I sat near the window on a stool upholstered in red velvet (I liked it, those tassels at the corners turned it into a royal throne) and I watched them, I saw their reflections in the Venetian mirror. They held their Rosenthal saucers with great care. The cups had gold rims, steam rose from the swan-shaped teapot.

"Sometimes I think that being an inventor must be some sort of mental disease. I'll be darned if I know what comes over me! Like right now, for example, my head is spinning with all those colors that could be played on your keyboard."

Mr. Vostarek stepped toward the piano, saucer in hand.

Mr. Klahn, too, rose to his feet and stepped between the Bösendorfer and the brewmaster.

"You know, Mr. Vostarek, I once knew a certain inventor. He invented a machine in the meat-processing line. An extremely ingenious machine. In one end you shoved meat, bacon fat, bones—and out the other end came . . . guess what?"

"Sausages," said Mr. Vostarek.

"Frankfurters," I said.

"Headcheese," said Mr. Vostarek.

"Not at all, my dear sir, out the other end dropped a jackass just like you!"

Mr. Vostarek put his cup and saucer down so hard the porcelain rang against the table, and said (without looking at Mr. Klahn): "*My* principle is to rise from the ground vertically, against crosswind, and then shift from sailing-type flight to spiral flight."

We all remained silent.

"Both wings are basically ready. The completion of certain details and the fins will require an additional six months. Then we shall see."

And he looked at Mr. Klahn. Quite indulgently! All of us (including me, J.Ch.K.) felt that Mr. Klahn's words had been out of keeping with the celebration. But that was a bad habit of his, to come out with something tactless at the worst possible moment. He wasn't really a vulgar person, it was his bad digestion that drove him to do this. His seven plagues, as Aunt Ludmila would say. He brewed teas and infusions for his ailments. These ailments weren't killing him, they cohabited with him, drank tea with him, enjoyed his infusions, induced him to leave the house early each morning to gather herbs, they kept pestering him so much that he was too flustered to go inside the rock when it opened up to him. How rich all of us might have become!

I held that against him.

And also that he insulted the brewmaster, even though he was the only one who knew how to brew *real* Cepin beer. Edvin and I carried a sample of the First Brewing to Capousek's tavern. There they tasted and quaffed and sipped and smacked their lips, and said: Old Vlaciha must have visited heaven, because this was brewed from a heavenly recipe.

．　　　．　　　．

And now I declare as follows: On Saturday, September 13, on that sunny-windy day, I peeked into the brewing chamber, through the low window accessible from the road. I was coming down from the gate of the Cepin castle (in ruins), the twisting S-shaped road wound past the lager storage room, straight in front of me stood a linden (tree) and the Silver Poplar (tavern), the tree was already showing a bit of autumnal yellow, the wind was blowing at the leaves from below so that they glistened like the hues of the still-to-be-invented color piano, the paper tail of my kite streamed behind me, for I was gently holding the wood frame of the kite head, on which Edvin had painted a toothy, grinning dragon. Our heads side by side, the kite and I were looking for Erna so that she could hold the ball of string during takeoff. The smoke rising from the brewery smokestack paralleled the tail of my kite. Whereupon: I looked in through the low window, the women inside were mixing barley in a vat, they saw the teeth of my kite and waved, and as I was peering in, it was like lifting the curtain of my little theater on "the witches' den" because the boiler was similar to the globe which was painted on my scenery, except that instead of the circles on the globe this boiler was circled by a ramp that Mr. Vostarek was standing on.

He called to me: "Where is Olin?"

"In town, with Dad."

And the brewmaster stepped along the ramp until he

almost reached my window, and said: "Wait for me, we'll do some flying together!"

I was proud that I was going to fly a kite with Mr. Vostarek and not just with mere Erna; I forgot all about her. She stepped out of the icehouse door; i.e., she appeared just as I stopped looking for her—that's one of her habits. She shouted: "Come here, I want you to hear this!" And she sang:

> *Come good people,*
> *one and all,*
> *see Vostarek's rise and fall.*
>
> *When he goes up,*
> *we'll give a yell;*
> *when he drops, we'll run like hell.*

At that moment I think I really despised Erna. "You're stupid," I said. "I bet your father thought that up for you!" I picked up the kite, the red tail blazed up at Erna in farewell, and I climbed back up to the castle gate.

Mr. Vostarek showed up around two o'clock in the afternoon. He was carrying his wings and was accompanied by a whole crowd of Cepin people, especially the women who had been mixing the barley, and also Aunt Vlaciha, Mrs. Klahn + her daughter.

"Erna," I said, "you have some nerve!"

"I've changed my mind. He'll make it. He'll fly over Cepin and land in our garden."

We crossed the rubble-filled yard to the steep northern slope. Those who were eager for a closer look descended to the bottom and stood about three hundred yards below us. From their vantage point they saw us framed in the huge window of Jost's ancient hall, dilapidated and gaping, as if we were standing in a gate leading straight to heaven. And I saw that Mr. Vostarek was not assembling the butterfly Goliath but a flying machine, and

I was proud that we'd be able to surprise Olin with news of a successful flight.

Actually, Mr. Vostarek had brought along only one big wing, made of bamboo rods and white parachute cloth (left behind by the Germans in their Chlumec depot). The wing bellied out and fluttered in the wind, sounding like a snorting horse. Then I realized (once again) that this was not a wing for flapping but for soaring; i.e., that Mr. Vostarek was not going to move it up and down but to glide. Erna and I and the other children were here to dramatize that only minuscule power was needed to make the wing airborne. We took hold of the rope which Mr. Vostarek handed us and ran down the slope until the rope tightened and seemed to stick, but that was only to give the flyer greater traction for takeoff. He took three big strides into the crosswind and the people at the bottom buzzed with awe because he really rose in the air. He hung by the straps, turning slightly to the left, toward Chlumec. Erna and I ran underneath him. We waved our arms, crazy with joy. He unhooked the rope, lurched, the rope dropped to the ground like a dancing snake, the wing filled with air and lifted the flyer high over the countryside.

With his legs trailing behind him, he looked to me like a butterfly from one of his drawings. He must have been able to see beyond the pine grove where horses were plowing the manor fields and the plowman stopped in amazement, not believing his eyes. And Vostarek in the sky must have seen the brewery truck coming down the road from Chlumec, and it too stopped, Olin and Edvin jumped out, shielded their eyes with the palm of their hand like the plowman, but Olin also crossed himself and at this signal a gust of crosswind came out of the northwest, jerked the flying machine, tugged at the right half of the wing until the seams over the flyer's head creaked, the joints loosened, ends of ropes and leather thongs flapped freely, the wind leaned into the tilted part and drove the orthopter toward the rock, toward the never-conquered side of Cepin hill. Erna and I raced over there and stopped at the very edge of the cliff.

"My God!" I shouted. "He'll be killed!" and I clutched Erna by the hand as if she were still my bride.

I got a last glimpse of the flyer, pulling himself up by his arms, legs bent, chin over his left shoulder, as he looked down in the direction of his fall and disappeared among the pines.

All the onlookers converged, and soon the gully was surrounded by people. Edvin and Olin ran off the road and called out to Mr. Vostarek. "Where are you?" they shouted, but there was no response. Mr. Vostarek was stuck in the branches, jackknifed, snagged in a jumble of ropes and thongs. He was all tangled up but wheezing, i.e., still alive. And so they stretched him out on the remaining half of the wing, which had knifed into the ground but was undamaged, and they carried him off. Tiny pebbles kept trickling out of his shoes and left a trail along the route.

My father Edvin and my uncle Olin drove Mr. Vostarek to the Chlumec hospital in the old Praga truck. Olin ordered that Mr. Vostarek's body was to be kept as motionless as possible. They drove slowly and Aunt Ludmila sat in the back to make sure he wouldn't slide around in the curves, watching over him and comforting him. He was covered up to his chin, his eyes were closed. Then they returned to pick up the wing. The irregular circle of blood made it resemble the wing of a Red Admiral butterfly.

The only reason I didn't cry was that Alice told me about all kinds of people who got well even though they had been in worse shape than the brewmaster. In the evening, however, I avoided my favorite book about June Bug, because I remembered the sad picture that showed June Bug stuck on a rosebush thorn. And I prayed for Mr. Vostarek. St. Barbora had promised to show me the gate to heaven, but I prayed that the ancient gate on the Cepin slope would not turn out to be a heavenly portal for Mr. Vostarek.

I said to the devil with the red tongue: "Is your name Zorobelin, Kharar, or Romila?"

"My name is Schtricks," he answered.

"Well, then, Schtricks, tell me why Mr. Vostarek should die, when he was nice enough to create you."

"To keep me from having power over him."

"How can you be exorcised?"

"By means of the mighty and mysterious words BRABARACHAM and ARMABACHAR."

"I invoke the power of those mighty words! Begone!" I said, to get rid of him.

Then I set up scenery for the witches' den. I put the globe in the right rear corner, to stand for the brewery boiler, and I placed the pulpit with the magic book in the spot where Mr. Vostarek had his stand with the logbook in which he kept records of malt and barley. I did that to lure Mr. Vostarek back to the boiler ramp where I had last seen him before his ill-fated flight.

On Sunday, September 20, I went to make my First Communion, hoping to be heard in heaven and gain grace. (I know that date precisely, because I was given a souvenir picture, and I was the only one with a sprig of rosemary tied to the ribbon of my candle, whereas all the others photographed with me in the chancery garden had myrtle.)

In the afternoon I was permitted to visit Mr. Vostarek in the hospital. Mother led me to his bed, over which hung a small blackboard with VOSTAREK, VINC. printed in chalk.

At first we had trouble seeing each other, because he was encased in plaster and couldn't turn his head, and due to my small stature I was not able to see past the foot of his bed. So I climbed on a chair and saw him, his face pale and shrunk.

"I must be quite a sight, eh?" he said.

"Well," I answered, "it should not have been called orthopter but glider."

"Sinker, more likely," he said, and smiled at the ceiling. "At least this will serve one good purpose," he added, tapping his cast with his free right hand. "It will be a good model for a knight in armor when I make Sir Wolfram for you."

"Which knight was he?" I asked.

"The one who grazed lions."

"You mean lions can be grazed? I never heard of such a thing."

"It was a very tame lion."

"But I've never seen a *grazing* one."

"Then I'll make one for you. Out of painted cardboard. And I'll make grass for him to eat, too."

That's what he promised me. I was happy. I had a clear conscience and I looked forward to more puppets.

Erna and I definitely broke up, until Three Kings' Day. On that holiday I was in Cepin to earn a fiver from Aunt for my caroling and I met my Erna girl, who asked me whether I was going to the children's masked ball. And so when I got home I begged Alice to make a costume for me.

"What would you like to go as?"

I thought it over. "As a butterfly," I said.

So she sewed a butterfly costume for me.

It was made of blue-green cloth which shone and shimmered. I had a pair of wings which started on my back and were attached the whole length of my sleeves, so that when I spread my arms to fly, I flitted. She even sewed gold spangles on my sleeves. I got in and out of this butterfly costume through a zippered opening on the side, that was the only way to put it on, and then you stuck your head out through a slit where the collar would normally be. There was a headpiece with antennae, held in place with snap fasteners, which also served as a mask.

It was snowing as Edvin and I walked across the park to Town Hall. I could hardly see, my headpiece was covered with snow and the eye-slits were beginning to freeze up, but I wouldn't have put on my own face for anything, because I didn't want to be recognized. But then it dawned on me that a person could be recognized by the company he or she was with. So when I saw Mr. Klahn and Little Red Ridinghood on the stairway I tore myself away from my parents and stayed as far away from them as possible so as to guard my mysterious identity.

First I danced with a salamander and then with two robbers. We whirled near the stage, right underneath the band, held hands, and I yelled at the gang of robbers to go out and capture Little Red Ridinghood. We surrounded her and she was ours. I said to her: "Are you supposed to be Snow White?" I guessed wrong on purpose, to tease her, but she didn't seem to mind and said quite cheerfully: "Butterfly, look what I have!" She tossed a paper streamer which kept unwinding and unwinding, and at last got caught in my antennae.

"And I've got this!" I showed her a bag filled with colorful confetti.

"We'll sprinkle it down from the balcony," she decided.

I took her by the hand and we ran up the stairs and in the rush I skidded and fell, rolled down to the landing, my headpiece fell off and my antennae got bent out of shape.

"Jan!" She clapped her hands. "It's you!"

"Yeah, it's me," I said in disgust, rubbing my knee and trying to get up. She straightened out the wires in my antennae, but as she touched them I felt a quiver pass through my body, without quite knowing why.

"Did you come only with your dad?" I asked.

"Mom is with Vostarek."

"Why?"

"He's delirious."

I rose to my feet and the confetti which we were going to shower on the dancers spilled to the floor.

"Erna, I *must* go there."

She didn't understand.

"I mean, to see Vostarek."

"Now?"

I put my finger on her lips as a signal to keep quiet about it. She took off her lace mask and her wide-open eyes showed how startled she was.

"I have to," I said. "I keep seeing him before me."

"If you only saw yourself! But go, go!"

I rushed out. Light snow was falling into the darkness and I was catching it on my wings. I took a shortcut past the peacock villa, ran through Cepin, and as I approached the lager cellar I suddenly saw Mrs. Klahn burst out of Vostarek's door and run across the whitened outdoor veranda, leaving tracks in the snow. She rushed to the phone, not even bothering to slam the door behind her. I had hardly reached the linden tree and yet in the stillness I could hear the clock inside the house strike four-thirty. I ran through the door and came upon Mr. Vostarek, looking at me from beneath the grandfather clock. He was lying on a couch, his head propped up on pillows, and he was stretching his arm toward me.

"Here you are," he said. "Help me take off my shoe."

I shook the snow off my wings and tried to pull off the headpiece. I had trouble undoing the fasteners and I was in a hurry, so I simply pushed it back like a hood.

"Which shoe?"

"It's heavy," he said, and again strained forward, leaning on his elbows, which were chafed from all the straining and stretching. But I saw no shoe.

"There," he said, "down there!"

One foot was bare and the other was covered with a sock. I touched it. The wool sock was damp with perspiration.

"Untie it."

I hesitated, perplexed.

"Please!" he said.

I pulled off the sock and he heaved a sigh so deep that it rattled in his throat. Then he sank back in the pillows, collapsed into them. I didn't know what to do next.

There was something he was asking of me in that wheezy rattle.

"Mr. Vostarek, can you hear me?"

I meant to ask it in a loud voice, but it barely squeaked out.

He answered quite distinctly: "*Unhitch me*," and motioned with his head that he wanted me to help him up. He was heavy, my wings got in the way, and so I only managed to hold him in a clumsy hug. He gasped for air, lifting his shoulders so abruptly that he almost tumbled out of my grasp. His mouth was close to mine, his lips reached out for a wave of air which he wanted to inhale, his eyes widened in anticipation, grew transparent, then darkened.

He opened his mouth slightly, as if about to smile, but this expression froze on his face.

I let him go, no, he was falling on me, pushing me back into the pillows, the yellow spangles on my wings were rubbing off and sparkled on the bedcover.

Mirena Klahn rushed into the room. She took one look and told me he was dead. Oh God!

Item: We knelt on the floor, she and I, the lady and the butterfly, and we prayed.

12. CHOCHLAKOV

I, too, came down with pneumonia after running through the snow from the Town Hall to Cepin, but I did not die like Mr. Vostarek. I got well, and in the meantime truck CH 434 & the brewing business had both perished.

Three officials came to see Olin and requested the books of Vlaciha & Klahn, the company's production records and other property. One of them sat down on Olin's office desk and asked to see the safe containing family valuables. Olin crooked his little finger, stuck it in the left corner of his mouth, and pulled his lip out of the way to reveal tooth No. 7.

The gold crown—the only piece of gold in the whole mouth—glistened, and he said: "Here! Take it!"

And when he saw that the man continued to sit on his desk, he added: "If you don't mind, dear Comr." (Comr. = Comrade, as I already indicated, Comr. Pavlenda; i.e., mate, companion, associate; e.g., the mates that came to see Olin in order to ensure that the Cepin brewery belonged to our entire nation), "if you don't mind, you're breaking wind where I break bread. So please get your ass off my desk."

The Comrade complied, but on the still warm desktop he left an order which prohibited, as of immediately, any further brewing of Cepin beer, "on account of leakage from the cemetery into the brewery water supply." "Good Lord," gasped Erna's dad when Olin showed him the document. "That same well has been used for seventy-three years now, and the cemetery is all the way in Chlumec! They must be joking!"

But it was the end of Cepin beer.

I don't know exactly on what day they stopped brewing (because of my illness; *viz.*, Question 8), but it was certainly in the early part of that year.

And on Christmas morning a group of officials came for Olin Vlaciha. They took him to the district jail and there they immediately proceeded to knock out the golden crown which he had shown to their comrades.

It flew out of his mouth, but they were busy pummeling him and didn't even notice it.

Olin saw it, however, saw it roll under the washstand in the corner of the interrogation chamber, and he said to himself: "Next time they hit me with a right hook I'll throw myself over there and grab it. Everything depends on the right move."

The right fist of Comr. Investigator flew through the air, Olin caught it, the blow threw his head straight back. For an instant he remained motionless and then he fell . . . lifelessly and as believably as possible (i.e., he landed on his side with a heavy thud).

The crown was lying just a handbreadth away from his palm. And yet the distance was insurmountable. "That idiot," Olin said to himself. "He missed."

He realized that it was necessary to reach the gold by means of a single blow, he knew that one of those men (either Comr. Dlab or Comr. Fafka) was sure to score a hit sooner or later. But the right direction and the right force had to be suggested to those two through proper posing and through feigned resistance to precisely the most desirable blows.

Comr. Pavlenda: As Olin later explained to me (while taking care of a certain cat's shelter), this was one method (fainting aside) that enabled a person not to feel blows and to see oneself as a kind of third entity between *I* and *they*. Olin maintained that after a certain point he had even stopped being aware of the blows, and that he had smiled at this realization.

Neither Comr. Dlab nor Comr. Fafka was aware of this, for at the moment it happened Olin was already lying on top of the crown, he grabbed and covered it up, and his torn, tattered gums smiled with joy.

(I would categorize this smile as *inner/outer*, because in contrast to merely outer smiles, when a certain amount of energy is smiled away at other people, and in contrast to inner smiles, which involve nobody except the smiler— here was an instance when an outer manifestation co-existed with its total concealment.)

Olin kept his crown even in solitary. He kept thinking about it when it seemed to him he was going mad. He squeezed it and this helped; for example, it restored his sense of time. The muscles of sorrow relaxed (according to O. Vlaciha, sorrow has its own set of musculature), and even though he still had the feeling that he was gaping out of a coffin, so to speak, it was no longer a timeless void. He kept clutching the crown, and also began to construct a mathematical system (so as to ensure maintaining a sense of measure) in which the highest number was 6 (in the Questionnaire this number designates *Class and Social Origin*) and in which $5 \times 5 = 41$. After eight months Olin mastered this system to such an extent that he could have discussed it with highly educated persons.

But the only discussion to which he was invited took place in the courtroom, with the judges declaring that in *their* logarithm tables eight months equaled ten years, and Olin promptly disappeared underground, in the coal mine.

·   ·   ·

Many people lived in the mine, but only one horse. His name was Bighead. Olin's name was Croaker. He got

that name because of his skinniness. Of course, skinny
or not, he had to push carts full of coal. They rattled
along the rails, and at the bottom they were counted up.
5 times 5 once again equaled 25, and that was good.

Bighead's eyes were good, too, bulging like scarabs.

I recovered from pneumonia and saw the coronation
of Elizabeth II as Queen of England.

She rode in a carriage and I liked it very much. But
I didn't remember the second film, the main feature, because suddenly there was a blackout. Electricity had been
shut off in Chlumec, in Cepin, everywhere. Everything
turned completely dark.

I asked Alice: "If you were queen, what would be the
first thing you'd do?"

"Have the lights turned back on."

"Why are they out?"

"They don't have enough electricity."

"Who?"

"*They*," answered Alice; she found my hand and we
went out. And by the way she had answered me I understood in principle that "they" were the people controlling
light switches.

And that wasn't bad.

.　　.　　.

"Mom," I said to Alice as she placed an oil lamp on
the cupboard in front of a row of flannel-polished apples
(Edvin!), and another in front of the mirror to double
its glow, "what would you do *afterwards*?"

"After what?"

"Well, after the lights came back on. What would be
your next order?"

"If I were queen?"

"Yes."

She didn't have to think very hard. "I'd set Olin free!"

The oil lamps were burning; the apples lined up on the

cupboard with the usual precision reflected the glow, as did the mirror on the opposite wall, and the rose-hip wine in the big bottle shone like an eternal flame.

And that felt good.

.   .   .

The carts stopped. Within some fifteen feet of Olin, the first one had started to wobble, then derailed and smashed against the wall. The other two piled into it, filling the shaft with a mass of coal, iron, gravel, and wood.

Olin saw that he was going to live, and at the same time felt the warmth of the horse's body. The animal's heart was pounding.

That felt good, too.

The gold crown kept moving on. It was given to the Sudeten-German, Polifka, who had charge of the underground horse. But he didn't call him Bighead, he called him Rapp. He was so happy the horse had survived the accident that the next day he brought Olin some bread and bacon. Olin pulled out his gold to pay for these things. But the German said: "One time I also felt how is beating the heart of mine horse."

He didn't want anything. He told Olin about his former Rapp: one day he'd been riding his horse in a field where there were some mechanical reapers covered by canvas. Rapp was frightened by this apparition and his heart beat so hard the German felt the pulsation right through his legs. They also spoke of cavalrymen who had similar experiences before a charge. During this conversation Olin secretly put the gold crown into the German's breast pocket (i.e., he crowned his heart, which had such a strong affection for Rapp alias Bighead. Or am I talking nonsense?). The German came up from his shift (he was not a prisoner in the mines; his punishment consisted in exclusion from other forms of employment), and the next time he came he brought some pastry stuffed with cabbage . . . and inside the cabbage was the gold ringlet—hereafter destined to be a wayfaring crown.

. . .

I watched Edvin. He took the oil lamp out of the cupboard, and because it was Saturday he went out to kill the rabbit—a direct descendant of the female petted during the shooting—for our Saturday dinner. Rabbits are great: they eat grass and weeds and potato slops, the meat comes cheap, and then there are the skins into the bargain. A lanky boy would pass by on his bike, calling out: "Rabbit skins!" He rolled the first word in his mouth, the second came out fast, as if spat out. I would bring him a skin, it had to be in good shape and dry, and he would give me a crown—candy money. This rabbit business was a holdover from the war. Edvin promised we wouldn't get any more rabbits, but we kept on eating them all the same. Either as chopped meat or soup or in paprika sauce, or just plain roast rabbit. The roast I didn't like because that way they kept their shape as if they were still alive. I watched Edvin lighting his way to a rabbit's death. He set the lamp down on the roof of the hutch and hung a pair of hooks on a branch of the plum tree. As soon as he did that, the rabbit whose turn it was started to squeal. How did he know, Comr. Pavlenda? Explain that to me! I closed my eyes, Alice said: if it must die, let it die. I opened my eyes, the rabbit was already hanging by his rear legs, half skinned, as if Edvin had taken off his pants. The upper part glistened, the lamp shone its light on it. Dad had quick hands.

I whispered: "Mom, if you were queen, what would that make me?"

She smiled: "A prince."

"And I'd still have to eat rabbit?"

"No," she said. "As prince, you could pick anything you wanted."

Whereupon: Olin stepped into the stable and saw Bighead lying on the ground, all stretched out, his eyes meek and sad. Olin begged him to get up. The horse could barely lift himself to his knees. Polifka arrived, talked to the horse, rubbed his neck, the horse stretched his neck, smacked his lips as if cleaning another horse, as if those others were still there.

"I'll get the foreman," said the German. But this was just an excuse for leaving. The gold crown was in his pocket; he did not have time to return it.

On the ground in front of Olin stood a canteen containing tea with a bit of rum.

.   .   .

Note about Bighead:

They took him up top so he could remember what a gallop was like, and there was still some life left in him. He was so happy to see the light of day that he pawed the ground with his hoofs. He lifted his forehead, bruised by beams like Olin's, gazed toward the offices where a guard was seated on a bench sipping a bowl of soup, the sun shone in the blue June sky, against the distant mountains a column of smoke rose high and thick out of the machine-shop chimney. Bighead neighed, broke into a run, i.e., stumbled, but he was merry and coltish even in his stumbling, as if he were running in a mallow-strewn meadow, trying not to step on the darting farmer's boy or his dog, and as if the pain in his legs was only caused by thorns. He'd just show his hoof to the boy and everything would be all right.

The butcher arrived and asked them to put the horse in the waiting slaughterhouse truck.

.   .   .

Olin took a swig out of the canteen. And another, and another. And because his stomach was always empty he got drunk almost immediately. They took him away, too, a week after the horse. The camp was being disbanded. Buses with whitewashed windows arrived. Olin sat jammed against one of the windows; someone had scratched out a small rhombus symbolizing a cunt, and through it Olin peered out at the road. When the bus made its third turn to the west, it was clear that they were heading Toward the Krusne (i.e., Hard) Mountains. He told the others.

"In those hills you already feel the frost by August," somebody said. But the first thing they actually felt was gunfire. They were lined up in a row, and guards were standing on watchtowers known as Peace and Solidarity (that was their official designation), firing down. Just for the hell of it. Or, more precisely: to establish the right feeling, so that nobody would have any wrong ideas as to what lay ahead.

And perhaps it was also a salvo saluting that engineer of human souls, Trifon Fyodorovich Chochlakov, the fat giant with a voice that sometimes skipped on him and turned hoarse. "*Krugom!*" he wheezed to a guard standing alongside. He himself never gave orders to prisoners. And the guard yelled: "About-face!"

The prisoners turned.

Trifon Fyodorovich inspected them. Especially their backs, the curve of the back. He had a method of sorts but nobody could quite figure it out. If he liked the way someone's back looked, the man was marched off on the double to the soul-engineer's office. He examined everyone, felt their muscles, inspected their skin and the appearance of the eyes. And, of course, the teeth. All those who still had any gold in their mouths made a left turn.

Those who had already been defillinged turned to the right. They could go straight to work, without any delay.

Olin was among those, and he appealed to Chochlakov.

He was still skinny, but he had become more wiry, he was no longer a croaker. The engineer felt the hard muscles of his arms, smiled, and promised Uncle that he would send him out on especially interesting assignments. *Kurit budyes*, tobacco, he promised, and motioned to him to open his mouth. When he saw no metallic gleam, he added: *Kusat budyes*, you'll eat, and dispatched Olin to join his goldless colleagues. As a final gesture he shook his fat finger at him in a fatherly way and forbade fucking, i.e., he said: *"No nye yebat! Yebat vospreshchayetsa!"* He guffawed heartily, and the guards laughed, too, even though they had heard this joke many, many times.

Item: O. Vlaciha laughed, too.

In terms of category, his smile was again of the inner/outer kind.

of course, all those languages in which I am Chrysostom the golden-mouthed, for since they knocked out Olin's teeth the power of gold is now in my mouth. For example, I said: Open sesame, let Olin pass! And the rock opened and Olin walked out.

13. LANGUAGE SKILLS

To Bighead, c/o The Lord (above slaughterhouse)
Bighead, you who are now grazing in that big mallow-filled gazebo in the sky over the slaughterhouse where slaughtered animals go after death, behold my Uncle Olin: they are giving him a new pair of boots, but first they gouged holes in them so that his feet would always be wet; they are giving him a fisherman's hat, they are aiming harpoons at him, they want to shoot him full of lead, he is sloshing through wet ore, in the midst of beep-beep-beep—the beeping of detectors. Listen to their voices, beep-beep. May daisies bloom over his head, the daisies that would be growing on your grave if you had a grave. Birds are chirping overhead, beep-beep, squirrels and deer hear the beat of Olin's heart and bring me news that he is alive.

To Comr. Pavlenda, c/o Granit
It is true that Olin was a prisoner (*viz.*, Question 28) and it is true that I love him.

But in Question 13 you ask about my language skills. To be brief: even though the number of that question is 13, I don't consider that an unlucky sign. Even according to Olin, 13 is just an ordinary cardinal numeral, a prime number in just one of many possible number systems. At most, I would agree that this number can be at times somewhat troublesome. In its field of influence, things really do tend to become a bit more difficult, more energy is required. That's why I will not dwell too long on this subject. So then, to come to my language skills: I know how to speak Czech; i.e., my mother tongue. And also,

But before he got out, in fact while I was still bedridden with pneumonia, Alice went to plead for Olin. She went all the way to Bonek, for he was powerful.

For example, he would sit on a cloth-covered podium (red cloth) and I'd carry a Japanese lantern and wave it at Bonek, while he waved back or chatted with people seated around him, always leaning forward a bit from the waist, always smiling a little. Or I'd carry a pole with various slogans attached to it, waving it through the air and reciting lines written by Comr. Principal Kuruc— i.e., Shorty, whose pendant Alice had once emasculated, the French teacher, who now added Russian and prin- cipaling to his activities and composed slogans such as:

> *The working class is sure to smite*
> *Profiteer and parasite.*

Or:

> *The People's Army we can trust*
> *To make the rightists bite the dust.*

I wanted to recite those lines at the top of my voice, I always took a deep breath in order to start out as loud as possible, but then I just piped up and barely whispered the rest. I was ashamed, just as I was ashamed of peeing when Erna was around. When I was with her I preferred to suffer rather than run to the bushes and admit to her that I had an urge to urinate. No, Comr. Pavlenda, this bashfulness was not connected with the content of the slogans, I was too young to grasp what they meant, I simply felt uneasy shouting in unison with others, it didn't seem nearly as much fun as going home together across the park after the festivities. The girls always kept their Japanese lanterns lit, even in the park. They walked in groups of three or more and guarded their lights. But we waited in the shrubs, swooped down on the girls, and punched the lanterns from below, which made them go out or catch on fire.

On account of that, I was called up to the front of the class by Shorty. He thrashed me with a wooden pointer until I writhed on the floor like an overturned bug. He didn't really care much about the lanterns, he was still thinking of the time Alice had castrated him, he knew that I had been inside Alice at the time and that I somehow remembered the event, and that's why he was so furious.

But I'll get even with him, I'll give him a beating, no . . . I'll kill him, Comr. Pavlenda, as soon as my turn comes. You'll see, I'll knock him down with the palm of my hand like Edvin stunning a rabbit.

I was actually lucky that, because in Shorty's eyes Bonek was part of our family, he didn't dare go any further.

In my mother's eyes (those four-beam eyes) it was different: she didn't count Bonek as one of us.

She went to see him at the United Chocolate Works, Chlumec, where he sat in Hatus's old office, framed by flags on either side—one red and the other still redder, bordered all around by a golden yellow tassel like the curtain of my puppet theater. And Bonek's head kept bobbing out from behind the flags—now he was Bellengardo, the Illusionist, now Monsieur Franz, the Majordomo.

As Bellengardo, he said: "Behold this my castle, not thunder nor cannon can level these adamantine walls," while as Monsieur Franz quoth he: "If mine eyes do not deceive me, here is little Dorothy, the burgomaster's daughter, with a message for me. On what business dost come, dear child?"

Whereupon Mother replied that she wanted to see whether anything could be done for Olin. For Aunt's sake, if for no other reason, because she was alone and it would be the death of her if anything were to happen to Olin.

Bonek said: "This is a time for strict adherence to positive values."

Mother said: "Maybe we could at least send him a package."

Bonek said: "Nobody has a right to stand on the sidelines."

Alice said: "But he's not standing on the sidelines. He's a prisoner."

Bonek pursed his lips, nodded gravely, and to underscore his attitude of sympathy he added a bar of chocolate. He reached for it in the drawer of his enormous table, pulled out an enormous bar of Dianthus (Export, Superba) and asked Alice to give it to me.

It tasted so good that I didn't agree with Mother, who felt we should send it back.

"Once you accepted it, you had to keep it," Edvin came to my support.

"But I didn't remember it until we reached the bridge."

"Well, then you should have thrown it away."

"But that would have been a waste," I said, and while they were arguing, I polished off one square after another, all but the last two. After they had made peace I gave them those last two sections, they grabbed them and gulp!—*finis* Bonek.

. . .

So Edvin had to start from scratch, as if there had never been Astor No. 1, that Dobosh-cake eater. First he turned in the Praga truck, Plate No. CH 434, and then he went to the Moran hills to cut lumber. But he never returned the enamel sign from the side of that truck, Comr. Pavlenda. It had a bottle of old Cepin beer painted on it, in a realistic shade of brown, but against a dark blue background and light yellow lettering:

VLACIHA & KLAHN: CEPIN BEER
famous light lager beer
available only in the finest establishments

Then Dad went over to the bakery to find out whether they would take him back. They said they might, and gave him the same kind of questionnaire to fill out that you gave me, Comr. Pavlenda. The form was still quite new then, it had been in use only a few years. They asked us in the questionnaire whether we were workers. What they were really after were Alice's eyes: somehow they seemed to lack pure workerness (*das Vollarbeiterschaftliche*). Edvin couldn't make it out. One question called for *origin* (it was designated as Question 6, just as it is now, but in contrast to the current version of the form, which inquires in a round-about way about so-called *Original Occupation*, the question was put more directly). Edvin answered that he originated from the same printer, Edvin Sr., as his brother Bonek. However, they replied that he was not as "working-class" as Bonek.

Alice said: "They are giving you a hard time because of me. In our family we always voted for Drazan."

Edvin, a non-Chlumecian, said: "Who was he?"

"The man who died recently. The one who built the Red Army bridge."

After a pause, Dad said: "You know what? Make me some coffee."

He drank two cups and then went off to the Moran woods to cut pine, spruce, and hemlock; it was a mixed forest, a primeval forest. It gave Alice and me a chance to play "Guess the Smell."

After work Edvin would go to sleep with his clothes on. The only things he took off were his shoes, his stocking feet stuck out over the couch, his right hand kept slipping to the floor. Alice put her finger on her lips to shush me up, and then whispered: "Guess!"

I drew close to Edvin (quietly), sniffed his pitch- and resin-covered hands and said: "Pine?"

"Oh, no! Spruce!"

Sometimes I guessed right, sometimes she did.

Dad nailed the *Vlaciha & Klahn* sign to the side of the rabbit hutch. This gave a blue tinge to the hutch and when lilac was in bloom the whole southern part of the garden seemed to turn bluish. I liked that. I loved clear, bright colors. I had a sketch pad and water colors, and I used clear bright tones to paint Cepin and a walled city, all sorts of cities, but always old and ringed with fortifications. And I added some touches of my own: moats, steeples, towers of churches, and forts. Edvin had a helmet which they told him to wear while lumberjacking in the Moran woods, cutting down trees and stripping off the bark until his very skin breathed the smell of the forest. When Edvin brought this helmet home, I put it on and won victories in all the wars described in *Fields of Glory*. And because our house had the number 1278, the year of the decisive battle of Marchfeld, this was the battle I fought the hardest, and I crushed the traitors before they had a chance to betray me.

. . .

I also read the *History of Chlumec* by Msgr. Rosin. I found a picture of Mayor Drazan, who wore a medal on his chest and looked fat and grumpy. But Camila Holan was beautiful, with lovely hair tied into a bun, a long slender neck in a lace collar, her curved undulating lips complementing the curve of the lace, and those eyes—I imagined them alive, for I loved Camila, my heavenly Astrid. I felt it on the lawn of the Municipal Baths. I was lying just behind the bulrushes, the clock of St. Barbora's was striking 3:30; i.e., in eleven minutes I would be thirteen years old. I turned to face the sun, perspiration was trickling down my throat, I shielded my eyes with a burdock leaf so as to be able to watch a darning needle hover over the surface of the water, its straight glassy wings appearing motionless, I was fascinated by the arrested motion, the insect was about to do something that tensed me in anticipation, something my body sensed but couldn't understand, I stared from under the leaf at that hovering cigar until it suddenly shot out (so violently that blood splashed into my groin) and grasped its fellow needle. With legs and wings intertwined, they droned through the air; screwed into a murderous stranglehold, they skimmed the water, darted over the lawn, where I was lying on my back watching everything from under the leaf and then rolling over on my stomach (so that nobody could see what was happening under my swimsuit).

.   .   .

I don't mean to say, Comr. Pavlenda, that this had never happened before. The novelty consisted in my discovery of the usefulness of my so-called "member." He had become my rouser in the real sense of the word, for from now on I was to become a part of him, and not merely—as had been the case heretofore—was he a part of me. This is what I grasped during that single turning from my back to my stomach. From that moment I put an end to all other manipulations; i.e., I no longer let schoolmates handle my rouser or permitted myself to do anything with him in their company.

Lying on my stomach, I waited for the excitement to pass. But as it receded it traveled upward like a cool stream, contracted from within, and I felt after each shiver that the coolness was at the same time heat, a glow distinct from the sun scorching my back.

"Lord, she is beautiful!" I said to myself, because right after those darning needles I had a vision of the picture on page 164 of Monsignor Rosin's *History*, a vision of Camila—lovely Astrid—"hair raven-black, bewitching eye, smile somewhat haughty." Ah, why did Monsignor Rosin write about eye and hair? Surely to separate the eyes and hair of my feminine progenitor from commonplace hair and eyes, to make them unique. And so I approached Astrid, who handed me a memorial volume of her poems, not merely to thank her and nod as the archduke had done, but to grasp that outstretched hand and pull her close to me, to fold my arms around her, clutch her with my legs and fly with her through the air . . . Time to come to my senses.

Alice, my mother, was calling.

She was standing on an arch of the Green Bridge and was about to jump eight meters into the water. To match the bridge, she wore a green kerchief over her hair. She dove head-first into the water, a corner of the kerchief glistening green at the back of her head.

She wanted me to jump in after her. I scrunched low, and bent down, I ran into the water to quench the fire in my loins. Then I swam to the other shore, while Mom shouted at me to come join her on the bridge. The rivets hurt my feet, they were burning-hot. I looked down, the surface seemed farther than it really was, and the concrete at my back seemed very hard.

"Go ahead and jump," I said to Alice.

"No, you!"

"Feet first," I said. "I know how to do it that way."

"Head first."

People were watching from down below, hoping for something interesting to happen. Alice saw my bewilderment.

"You have to throw yourself into the water, not let yourself flop like a pancake. Look! Throw yourself at the water and knife through it." She jumped, showing me how to do it. She bobbed up to the surface and shouted: "How about it? What's stopping you?"

The rivets under my feet burned even hotter. I straightened up, stuck out my arms, and behold: once again I turned into a butterfly. Anyone who has ever tried to do what I did, Comr. Pavlenda, will never forget such a moment.

The closer I plunged to the bottom, the darker it got; I sank into mud up to my wrists, bubbles squeezed their way between my fingers. They looked white against the surrounding green. I followed the bubbles up to the surface, and came up alongside my mother.

"That was good," she praised me. "Next time, bring up your knees and it will be a real somersault."

Strange, as I was falling, i.e., as I was learning to fly on my own, I felt the same hot wave that had passed through my body a while earlier, while watching the darning needle.

And so I asked: "Mom, was Astrid Zorska really our *direct* ancestor?"

Alice, emerging from the water (Anadyomene), said: "She was your great-great-grandmother."

We went to eat birthday cake, and I pondered the word "great-great-grandmother." It did not appeal to me. In the photographs Camila was a young woman; no longer a girl, not quite a lady. Slender, metallic black hair (raven hair), high forehead with arched eyebrows, thick eyebrows to frame the eyes and bless me from the depths of her soul. I resented that fellow Kaspar Trubac. He *had* to have caused her death, his picture told the story quite clearly. I stripped his picture off page 96 ("Mayors of the Town of Chlumec") and threw it behind the bookcase. But I made it look like an accident, as if Trubac had landed there all on his own. In the etching he looked as if he'd been carved out of wood, his neck stuck stiffly out of his starched collar, his skin-tight coat buttoned high, eight buttons on each side from saber to chin. Jesus Christ, what a jackass he must have been! Served him right, to rot on the counter among the hard candies. But I pitied all those other Trubacs of Chlumec who were my ancestors on the male side, all those descendants of the sword which Kaspar clutched so fiercely. And then came the Vachals. The first one, Jan Baptist, slid into Chlumec on his ass, to stay. This is a pleasant place. I am part of the place, too, of course, sitting behind the stables, turning the pages of Rosin's *History*, until I come to a picture of a hanged man swinging from the beam of some sort of hut whose roof is missing. A crow sits next to the man's head, and the whole thing is entitled "Chlumec Justice and the Tombs of the Condemned." But the executed man was not one of our ancestors, at least there was no mention that he was from our family.

But then I read about Joachim the Trumpeter (Trubac = trumpeter or bugler), who might have been one of us. He was playing his horn from the ledge of St. Barbora's steeple when a storm broke out and hurled him to the ground, ledge and all. (That indicated that he and I might be of the same blood: I held on to a weather vane while my horn slid down the steep roof of the church, hit a drainpipe, and bounded into the sky, flying in a south-southwesterly direction.)

Somebody shouted: "Joachim, hold tight, unhand not the vane. After yon storm blows over, you will rule once more over your domain and you will be given fourscore doubloons and a cord of wood and you will be founder of the Trumpeter line."

.　　.　　.

A Word about Orchids (amendment to earlier testimony)

(To Comr. Pavlenda, c/o GRANIT)

I confessed about the flaming flower *Masdevallia*, but I have to amend my testimony somewhat.

We were on an outing with Shorty to the Botanical Garden. Shorty stood under a heavy, hanging flowerpot overflowing with leaves, and it seemed to me that if the cord attaching the pot to the glass ceiling were to snap, Shorty could get killed. I was beseeching the cord to break, I looked up to see whether it was complying with my wish and suddenly I saw the clear red of the open *Masdevallia* flower. My ears pounded, blood splashed through every sluice of my body, I grew weak, my legs buckled under me (or I under them?), my backside slid into the potted palm *Ptychosperma alexandrae*. I sat in the dirt of that plant while they loosened my shirt collar. I explained that I had felt faint from the heat, but actually I had a vision of Erna sitting on the swing, petting the gosling while I leaned forward and kissed her lap.

I stepped out of the greenhouse to stop the world from spinning, and out in the open I decided that I would like to see this flower once again, on a human body.

Because Astor II, my steed, was getting too old for such work, I jumped on my bike and rode off to see whether Erna still had it.

I coasted down the Cepin hill past the monument to the here-departed Brother Jerabek, who had died on that spot. I was hunched over the ram-horn bars, which I had obtained in exchange for Edvin's old, straight handlebars. A ribbon of front-tire rubber, blackened and shiny from the hot asphalt, flowed steadily under the mudguard. There was no shimmy or swerve, I had trued and balanced the wheels myself. I yearned for the day I'd own racing tires and overdrive and really burn up the road between Chlumec and Cepin.

Mrs. Klahn was still in mourning clothes. They were heavy, she must have felt hot. She was sitting on the ash-wood bench under the swing, reading a book.

She was a widow.

Mr. Klahn did not tell any commissars where to get off, they didn't take him to prison like Olin, but he was forced to leave for the steel mill, and there he bled to death. Out of the blue he felt a stabbing pain, it was Saturday night and he was lying in the barracks all alone, he clutched his stomach and began to moan, he was without his herb tea. He crawled to the washroom to get a drink of water but he vomited blood all over the tiles, and this was where they found him when it was too late.

Last year I went to his funeral. I saw Erna there, we dropped clods of earth on the coffin, but at that time the kind of thoughts I was to have were still far from my mind.

I rang the bell of my bike (still that four-leaf-clover bell), Mrs. Klahn lifted her head from the book and said happily: "It's about time you came to see us!" And I answered casually that I was visiting my aunt and . . . "What is Erna doing?"

"She is rinsing the wash."

I noticed Mirena Klahn's long neck and that widowish hairdo, which looked good on her and reminded me of Camila's hair.

"What are you reading?"

"Oh, it's called *The Well of Loneliness.*" She snapped the book shut.

"Strange title," I said. But I really thought it was a stupid title.

I went off to look for Erna. Near the malt house, between the apple trees, seven squares of linen were spread on the grass, sopping wet and slightly bulging from the pressure of the grass. A barefoot girl held the watering can, the stream of water made a rainbow against the sun, but only from the point where I was standing at the moment. As soon as I took a step, the rainbow disappeared, only Erna was left, she noticed me but

continued soaking the laundry. I observed that her neck
was not as slender as her mother's, but she had a sharper
chin and straight eyebrows. Her hair was tied in a
ponytail, with a rubber band twisted around its base. She
was barefoot, in shorts.

I said "Erna, I haven't seen you for a long time."

She called out: "Ahoy there!"

I answered her greeting the same way. And then we
just stood there, while she watered on and on.

"Listen," I said. "If you like, we can go for a swim."

She carried the empty can to the well. (A different well
—the *Well of Promise?*)

"Where would we go?"

"To the Municipal."

"I don't have the right bathing suit for that place."

"To the pond, then."

"That frog-hole?"

I was stuck. She could have watched me jump head-
first from the bridge, but now? Mrs. Klahn came over
and asked if I felt like having a bite to eat. In the room
with the clavier there was again some cake, a pile of
notes (including those pieces for four hands), and even
though the house was in mourning I was served on a
plate of Rosenthal china. I ate my slice of cake, and Mrs.
Klahn ran her hands across the keyboard as she walked
by the piano, just a shower of tones. She now taught at
the music school and took the 7:12 train to Chlumec
every morning. Except for the changed Erna, everything
was almost the same as it used to be. But she was no
longer the same. The time was gone when I could talk
to her as my one-and-only. Now I had to try to catch
her. And I couldn't go after her with a stick, though I
would have loved to let her have it! It made me mad, the
way she suddenly changed her tune and said she'd like
to go swimming after all, and asked her mother whether
it was all right for *us* to go. Was she making fun of me,

or was this how girls were supposed to act—first drawing near and then pulling away? When I closed my eyes, that's how things appeared.

They were talking about my pictures. Mirena Klahn had heard about them! Why don't you bring them over to show me! I promised to bring the one of Cepin; a reconstruction, the way it looked at the time of the battle of Marchfeld. It wasn't finished, but I was ready to promise anything just so there would be no more delay and I could put Erna on the bar of my bike and take her away.

But once she was seated on the bike her head was so close to mine that it got in my way. Her hair and ears smelled good. Again, that flower got to me. My head felt giddy and I forgot about the tricky hill where I had once taken that spill with Edvin. Erna and I took a spill, too. But with her it was a far easier fall. I lay on top of her for a few moments, then I helped her up. I held her left hand in my right, her palm was green from the grass.

"You didn't hurt yourself?" I asked. I examined her hand and didn't let go, I held it a long time, until it became evident it was extra-long, and both of us knew it.

But nothing happened of the kind I'd been reading about in books; i.e., she didn't break away and flee, "flustered and blushing." It was I who pulled back.

Item: Erna's right hand dropped and the air between us turned cold enough to turn rain to snow.

Oh, I had to call that hand back, I had to hold it once more! I decided that she would become my steady girl again. I leaned the bike against the wall of the Capousek tavern and asked my girl whether she'd like something to drink, a lemonade perhaps. She nodded. We sat down in the garden under the maples, a winged maple seed came spiraling down on our table. I pried open the sticky end and glued the green wing to Erna's nose. She crossed her eyes, trying to see the tip of her new appendage. I looked at her through my glass of lemonade. "Erna," I said, "you look sooty!" That remark didn't really make sense, but the way she looked reminded me of the way she did when I watched her through the yellow glass wall of their veranda, the time we smeared the glass with candle soot to observe the sun. Anyway, I had to say something, I had to use my voice on her, and it didn't much matter what the words meant. I tried to entice her into pecking at me with her gobbler nose.

Later I swam under her—with my eyes open, of course. Here the bottom was not as muddy as it was under the bridge, it was firm and strewn with clean pebbles, the water was full of sparks, I floated on my back and blinked at the flattened disk of the sun, I could almost touch its oozing rays, I let Erna pass overhead to scatter the sparks and slide over me with her shadow. I saw the *Masdevallia*. Here I could safely examine it.

On land I didn't have the strength to do it, I was always forced to look elsewhere. I didn't admit to myself that the flower was always with her. I forgot *it* (as I shall refer to it henceforth), but even forgotten, *it* still gave me pleasure similar to the joy I used to feel in church during early Mass when they started singing "Heavenly Dew." A similar wave of emotion passed through me, I was on the verge of tears, of which I had formerly been ashamed.

Forgive me, Lord!

I even promised my girl I'd do her portrait, even though I didn't paint people, only towns. I would paint her with long hair, a gosling in her hand. If only I could do it delicately enough!

I kept on chattering. On the way back, I walked the bike (I didn't dare have her sit so close to me again, with that aroma of hers), I kept prattling, but my mind was preoccupied with the thought of a kiss. When I finally shut my mouth, Erna too lapsed into silence, and we walked side by side like a pair of hunters in the woods.

Then I asked her: "Are you sad?"

"No ... Why?"

"Neither am I."

"That's good." She smiled.

I smiled too, and encouraged by our mutually smiling bodies, I swore to myself that I would kiss her as soon as we reached the railroad crossing, provided, of course, the barrier was closed.

Behind the chocolate factory, several belchers were waiting on the siding, snorting smoke, and because it was already dusky, red needles streamed out of their stacks. Those were the trains for which I used to wait with Edvin, sitting on the seat of this same Eska bike. The belchers were taking their sweet time. They moved along a bit until their snout almost reached the barrier, they managed to crawl as far as the signal tower, then suddenly there was a series of bumps and a freight train loaded with cocoa started rolling toward the insatiable maw of Uncle Bonek's enterprise.

"Stuff yourself, Uncle dear, at least you're good for something!"

But at last, from the direction of Cepin, came the whistle of the Prague express, it tooled right along without even stopping in Chlumec, the barrier came down, and I had to buss Erna as I swore to myself I would. I turned to her with my eyes closed, kissed her, i.e., plunged toward her as if leaping from the Green Bridge, the warning bell kept ringing bim-bam, bim-bam, I was sure the railroad bell must be decorated with a four-leaf clover because I was so happy, my lips ended up somewhere in the vicinity of Erna's clavicle, my bike lay on the ground where it fell when I tried to free my hands. The lanterns on the last car receded along the iron road

and I recalled Camila–Astrid's ode to the black steed
("Thou subdues the wind in speed . . .")

But Erna said: "Stop that! Promise you won't do that
again!" She smelled of smoke, she was inflammable and
kissable. I could tell.

I picked up the bike, the barrier slowly lifted.

I thought to myself: "Promise her anything . . ."

.   .   .

Another Note about Orchids (important testimony)

When you consider, Comr. Pavlenda, that the word
"orchid," which sounds so exotic, has come to mean to
me simply *testicle*, you'll understand the extent of my
unhappiness. You must admit the resonance and beauty
are gone! Perhaps it looks different from another viewpoint, through another pair of eyes, but that wasn't the
case when I looked at Erna. I wanted everything to be
exalted and yet to be able to touch it. But the more
orchidic I tried to act, the more testicular I became.
The first time I was aware of that transformation of
states was when I kissed her.

I went to see Erna, convinced that she was my girl
now, but she hardly spoke to me, and on the veranda she
shoved a piece of paper into my hand:

> *Dear Jan,*
> *what happened yesterday must never happen*
> *again. Only my husband will ever be allowed*
> *to kiss me. And not until I am eighteen, you*
> *understand? It was nice of you to ask me out,*
> *but I don't want to do anything I'd have to*
> *be ashamed of.*
>
> *E.*

So why did she entice me, I fumed. Was I supposed
to wait five years for the next kiss? And then she might
marry somebody else, anyway. I felt keenly that I was
being wronged. Once I got home, I thought of breaking

off with her. I went to look at Camila, hoping that her beauty would help me make a decision. I reached for the volume of Rosin's *History* which had her portrait, but instead my hand brushed against Dr. Simsa's *Household Medical Guide* on the next shelf, a tome containing five hundred illustrations, plus foldout inserts and forty supplements. I thumbed through it and stopped at "The Human Body," division *Woman*. There I found a lady with a door leading inside, each breast swung open like a folding altar, I opened a door and leafed through one organ after another, a lung, another lung, all the way to the kidney, also sectioned in half, until I thought I would pass out through the lady's back as if walking out the back door of a house. The unfolded lower section resembled the balloons which Mr. Vostarek used to draw over the heads of aviators. It didn't look very attractive, although the title appealed to me: *os sacrum*, with the number 110 printed underneath. Ah, Dr. Simsa, you did a much better job on betony and bugloss, those plant illustrations looked believable, I believed in their reality —but *external genitalia?* Vaginal orifice? Pudendal labia? Phoooey! Whoever dreamed up those names? Perhaps the perpetrator wanted to break off with some Erna of his. That would make sense, because once you thought of an Erna possessing labia and orifices, you already felt a lot calmer.

· · ·

Prayer for All Souls' Day (a confession)

During a long interval I had nobody to love except Astrid Zorska (I took up with one other girl, but she developed herpes and I lost interest in her). On All Souls' Day I met the two Klahn women at the cemetery. I was there to pray for Mr. Vostarek, and they for their daddy. It was already late afternoon and all the candles were burning, lighting up the approaching dusk. Erna placed a bouquet of cellophane-wrapped chrysanthemums on the grave. As she stood leaning over the tombstone, a white marble dove appeared over her shoulder. The bird's head hung mournfully over the side of the tomb, its little wings drooping; that dove was I, Comr. Pavlenda, mourning for my mate. When I looked at Erna, my eyes were full of sorrow.

"You promised me a picture of Cepin," said Mrs. Klahn.

We visited Vostarek and our other graves, and I kept up a steady banter.

"He promised me a picture of me!" said Erna.

The memorial light I had brought for Vostarek flickered on the granite tombstone, in the middle of a chiseled cross which looked even more granite-like than the rest of the stone, and the dimple at the bottom of the wick glistened like a tear. Erna, all in black, beautiful Erna said: "I'll bring him a chrysanthemum, he has no flowers." As she went off to her father's grave, I glanced at Mrs. Klahn. Her eyes were moist, and I felt close to tears myself. She looked so lovely and sad, trying to conceal her tears by looking off into the distance (like the explorer Amundsen gazing at the misty polar horizon). I turned away toward the trees lining the cemetery road, they were mainly oaks, I stared at them intently because I was afraid I might break down and cry (even though I was no longer Alice's little boy; I was a head taller than Alice). Erna came plodding through the leaves carrying a white chrysanthemum, she put it alongside my light on the chiseled word *Vincent*, which claimed to be the true name of the deceased. Good Lord, for me— and for everybody in Cepin—he had always been the brewmaster or Mr. Vostarek, never Vincent! Reflections from the cellophane surrounding the chrysanthemum added more light to my memorial jar. I heaved a deep sigh and felt that I could finally talk without a catch in my voice.

"I'll paint anything you like, Mrs. Klahn, and I'll do a picture of Erna, too. The trouble is, I don't see enough of her."

Erna turned to her mother. "I'd better give him a snapshot, for a model."

Mrs. Klahn agreed, and asked why *he* no longer came to see us (i.e., he = Jan Chrysostom), now that he was a grown man.

I felt like answering: because I am not loved. But I kept quiet.

We walked along the cemetery wall, with Chlumec down below. Behind the wall appeared a square of light. It was the old mortuary chapel. The glistening letters above the portal read

THE SAINTS IN THEIR HEAVENLY ABODE
REJOICE IN YOUR DELIVERANCE

The inside of this way station for coffins was lit up, the red-and-blue flower in the Gothic window bloomed with color. Halfway to town, in the middle of the birch-lined road, Erna stopped, turned toward the glimmering cemetery, and sighed: "How beautiful it all is."

I turned, too. The scene looked like a painting of the Resurrection.

"It's a good thing they turned off the current in Chlumec," I said. "If Chlumec was lit up, the cemetery wouldn't stand out like this."

The town below was dark, lost in the late-afternoon November dusk. The lights were going to be turned on much later because the factories needed electric current to fulfill their quotas and had priority on electricity. And so, just about the only lights to be seen were a few floodlights over the shipping yard of Bonek's chocolate factory and warning signals blinking atop the star on his smokestack. Otherwise, all was in gloom, darkness upon darkness, and even though there may have been more candles inside people's houses than in the whole cemetery, their flicker did not pass through the shuttered windows. I was not bothered by the darkness, of course. On the contrary, it went along well with being in love. I was listening (again!) to my own voice, and the two Klahnesses were listening to me, too. Actually, I wouldn't have minded if the lights never went on at all, because I knew that my words-in-the-dark were persuasive.

But at that moment Erna, probably sensing my power, commanded: Let there be light!

We had already reached the corner of River Street. Erna's command was obeyed, and even the window of the First Mutual Czech Insurance Company lit up.

As the bulbs sputtered with the sudden influx of current, a big picture of Mrs. Hatus flickered into view in the window. The inscription over it read: WEASELS IN OUR MIDST. The unretouched photo was suspended over a bag of peas. Loose peas lay scattered around, dry and shrunken as goat turds. HER HOARDING DAYS ARE OVER, said another poster, portraying a clenched fist in the act of crushing bags full of money, as well as the weasel (lady weasel) squatting on top of them. Out of the other bags and sacks arranged in the window trickled flour, grain, and sugar. The tableau was supposed to suggest that everything had been stashed away in a secret hoard. Bars of Largior chocolate were scattered about, too, in their old wrappers with plump Fortuna and the horn of plenty. An actual horn had been stuck at the source of the cornucopia—a hole in the planks surrounding the weasel's den. The face of Mrs. Hatus, sixtyish and wrinkled around the mouth, looked terrified. They had shot her from dead center, the way they photograph criminals, and she had probably stared at the man behind the camera as the shutter was being snapped.

·   ·   ·

Butterfly! (an exclamation)

I had no time to be sad about such things. Across from
the insurance company, in the Town Hall on the other
side of the little park, I was about to dance again. With
Maestro Bazika, not as a butterfly, and not to swing
music (which was prohibited), but at least to the waltz
and the tango. I already knew some basic steps, after all
I had danced with Erna to the tune of "Nine Canaries"
and with Alice (this year) to the phonograph record of
"Kiss, Madonna, My Burning Lips." But I needed the
courage to try it with other women, too. I often examined
myself in the mirror, and sometimes I looked very handsome. Ah, Comr. Pavlenda, in those days I was much
more confident of my good looks. It must be clear to you,
from the upper left-hand corner marked *Photograph*, that
I am no Adonis. No plug-ugly either, of course. From
Edvin, in terms of appearance, I inherited only his color-
ing and dimple. The rest is merely acceptable, inoffensive,
without Edvinian charm. It is as if you took a freshly
painted picture of my dad and soaked it in water. If it
wasn't for my eyelashes and dimple, my face would never
stand out, but because I have that magic triangle it
sometimes happens that it lights up on me and I give
the girls their due. The girls, the givers, are thus outwitted, and that's beautiful, Comr. Pavlenda, because at
such moments *I* become the orchid!

May the good Lord bless Edvin for that!

Whereas from Alice I inherited my plain outspoken
self. She passed on to me this mouth, to speak plainly
when there is something to be said.

Item: I was finishing the portrait of Erna. Modeled
after a photo, but with the gosling and her hair much
longer. Since I had been painting her, I fell in love with
her all over again. I wanted to go dancing with her at
Bazika's. But she had to travel to Hradek every day to
school and it was hard to see much of her (they wouldn't

let her enroll in any of the Chlumec schools). I saw her
on weekends when both of the Klahn women were home;
one arrived from the north and the other from the south;
they met at the Cepin station and from there they walked
to the storeroom in back of the Silver Poplar to see if
any spare potatoes or other things had been left around
for the taking, but every spud was guarded as if it were
a treasure. Astor II had been replaced by another dog
(who shall remain anonymous because he snarled at me).
The dog chased Erna and Mirena, but they always walked
faster when they saw him. That animal really was a
loudmouth and a bully. And so they would pass the
malt house and arrive home. Mrs. Klahn playing the
clavier and Erna sprinkling the wash—that's how I
always visualized them, no matter what they were actually
doing. And as for visualizing myself—I saw myself bringing them the painting.

"Where is mine?" Mirena would ask. Her picture was
taking me longer.

"It's not finished yet. I haven't done the Cepin tower
yet, because nobody seems to know what it really looked
like."

"Let's go and take a look at it," Erna would say.

And I told myself I ought to kiss her again, but this
time like Errol Flynn in *Robin Hood*. She was not
eighteen yet, but that didn't matter, she'd catch up. I
took her in my arms, felt her mouth. And look: she had
put on lipstick, a very thin, barely visible coat. But she
was using makeup for my sake, to make up for the years
she fell short of eighteen. It reminded me of the numbers
on her daddy's adding machine: he'd press a lever and
the right number would appear in red on the strip of
paper that popped out, as if the machine were sticking
out its tongue. My lips touched hers, and Erna held still.
She *held still*, Comr. Pavlenda—that's terrific when a girl
lets things happen like that! That's fantastic!

I didn't need the adding machine (it was called Felix) to figure out that Erna and I would dance again, as we had danced before when I was still a butterfly (a long time ago!). Maestro Bazika planted himself in the middle of the hall, clapped his hands, and called out: "Promenade, gentlemen, promenade!" Aunt looked him over and said: "A shrimp, but he's got balls!"

And so my dancing life began. Ludmila Vlaciha was there with Mrs. Klahn, and of course—Erna. Since Olin had been sent away "mining" (Aunt never referred to him as a prisoner), she was always looking for places to go so she wouldn't have to stay home alone.

I half closed my eyes, I wanted to see the invisible. But it was real.

In my pocket I had a bunch of hearts cut out of colored paper. Alice had sewn a red border around them. I pinned them all on my chest and admired myself in the mirror—I looked like some Russky generalissimo. Alice walked in, laughed, took off all my hearts (but one). Whereupon: I danced with her.

"Maestro is a shrimp, but he's got balls," I said to my first partner. She looked at me, gave me a heart, and, without saying anything, stared over my shoulder. Dumb goose. I paid her back for that snotty look by pressing my palm against the small of her back, leaving a sweaty stain on her taffeta dress. Get lost, I said to myself (meaning her), I'll catch somebody else. And to the next girl I said again: "Maestro Bazika is a shrimp, but he's got balls." This girl was no dumb high-school student, she knew what balls were all about. And she knew that I was just playing a little harmless word game, so she picked it up.

"He's really oscillating," she said.

"Oscillating? What's that?"

"Look it up in the dictionary," she said, and lifted her eyes, but in a completely different way from the ninny before. I gathered that my approach was working. And of course I had no thought of staining this one's dress. I pulled out my handkerchief and wiped my hands. But as I put it back, it passed close to the girl's nose and gave her a whiff of my aroma (it had soaked up my underarm perspiration during intermission, when I had taken off my damp shirt and wiped myself off).

The girl took a sniff. Maestro Bazika called "Promenade, gentlemen, promenade!" And so I took her (the scentress) by the arm. She seemed to soften, and as if drawn by my odor, she followed obediently by my side. I noticed Mirena in the arcade under the balcony and she looked so beautiful that I would have loved to give her a sniff, too. But she was leaning on Erna, examining the gilded heel of her pump. Mrs. Klahn was still wearing black, but she looked happier. Her dress had a décolleté, and a black ribbon with a cameo was tied around her long, bare neck. A velvet dog collar. Her narrow sleeves reached to the back of her hand, where they opened wide like the jaws of a gargoyle. Erna fluttered at me like a flag. She was dressed in light blue muslin, so delicate that for a moment I feared the Klahns might have been guilty of hoarding.

At this point, the scentress asked what I was doing on Sunday.

I answered: "Sunday? Oh, that's so far away . . . that's tomorrow. I don't know yet."

I jacked up my price, because I knew I smelled good to her.

With Erna it was the other way around. I asked: "What are you doing Sunday?"

We were dancing a permissible waltz, played by the comrade musicians from the chocolate plant, but in the old days this same band was known as the Melody Boys, and the music still had traces of forbidden zip.

"Sunday I'll be dancing with you," she said.

"How come?"

"Sunday is today! It's after midnight!"

I tried to hold Erna close, to keep her from wiggling away. I wanted to give her a whiff, the way I did her predecessor.

"They're watching us!"

"Let 'em. You have very pretty . . ."

She looked up. "What?"

"Well . . . hips." I behaved myself. But then I started up again. "And you also have a very pretty booz . . . booz . . ."

"Please, Jan!"

"I know" (i.e., I floundered between embarrassment and excitement). "Bosom is a stupid word. But breasts isn't any better."

She dug her nail so hard into my little finger that tears came to my eyes. Through those tears I said: "Breast is worse. Like chicken breast. Or bust—that sounds like a statue. What is it actually called? I know one word, but that's indecent."

She hissed at me to be quiet.

"I'll bet you know it, too."

She stamped her little gilded hoof right on top of the old scar from my sandal strap.

"Ouch," I said. "I love you. You'll love it too, I am sure."

"What?"

"Well . . . it!"

Now she drew me close, but only to stop up my mouth with her nearness. I breathed on her: "You know what I'm talking about, just say the word!"

We danced on, no—we pushed the floor with our feet but kept standing in one place while the floor moved this way and that. We were alone in the center. The others gave us room, withdrew to the sides of the dancefloor, and gaped. I saw Mrs. Klahn, she kept bobbing up in front of my eyes and the black ribbon drew a circle around her neck as if to indicate a dotted line where her head was to be cut off. My aunt's smile swayed in the distance, too. And I urged Erna: "Come on, for God's sake, say it!"

She clenched her lips, and spun me harder and harder so that I'd be too busy turning to have time for talk. The hall whirled behind her head, my hold on her was loosening. I had to get it out of her. "Say the word, do you hear me?"

I felt that it was already on the tip of her tongue when she suddenly tore herself away (typical move, Comr. Pavlenda!). Actually, the only thing that tore was her heel, the little hoof flew off, and as she stumbled, I fell, too.

It's awful the way we kept falling, first one and then the other, always at the most inopportune time (inopportune for me, Comr. Pavlenda).

Once again I *almost* found myself on top of her, again I wanted to help her up, I made a move, and she whispered: "Enough!"

As sternly as the sorcerer's apprentice to the overflowing pot.

.   .   .

Bayer's Piano School (preparation)
Item: He (Jan Chrysostom—I am using the third person so that I don't speak about myself all the time, which I am forced to do by those questions of yours, Comr. Pavlenda. Also, I want to indicate that I had become someone else, a different J.Ch.K.), well then, *he* was drowning in tears; i.e., he reasoned thus: if everything that has to do with this fiery flower, this *Masdevallia*, affects *bodies*, then why didn't I stick to scentresses who wanted me? And if it happens *beyond* bodies, in that beyond where I send my prayers asking God for forgiveness (not because of my fear of punishment but because

of my love for Him, my Lord), why must that *Masdevallia* always intrude and ruin everything? And why am I feeling so unbutterflyish?

(The expression "drowning in tears" seems overblown —most probably J.Ch. simply bawled. But if the term "drowning" implies that he was constantly submerged in tears and that they filled his eyes at every emotion-filled moment, then it is rather accurate.)

E.g., the weather was freezing (it was getting close to Christmas), Erna and J.Ch. went to the movies, where the latter bought the former a bar of Dianthus chocolate as a present, but he didn't dare give it to her until they reached the Administration Building of Cepin National Farm State Cooperative (formerly the Amdas villa, and before that, the Vohryzek villa). He reached into his breast pocket to prepare Erna's after-kiss gift, but the chocolate bar had turned—freezing weather notwith-standing—into a shapeless warm pancake which folded in his hand. He repeated this attempt with a scentress, with the same brand of chocolate and in the same freezing temperature: the bar remained stiff. In both cases, tears.

And on top of that, when Alice asked about the brown spot on his shirt, right over J.Ch.'s heart, he said: "That's Bonek's shit!" Oddly enough, she agreed.

.   .   .

J.Ch. painted a picture depicting the "Destruction of Chlumec." The town was shrouded in a veil of leaves. Only the roofs of the houses stuck out, and the steeple of St. Barbora, on the tip of which sat a grackle (*graculus*), the sole living creature. The trees on the surrounding hills had the look of briars; on the thorns hung pieces of meat which the bird had gathered. The eye of the bird shone, whereas the light of the sun seemed frozen in a sphere of ice.

Another time, J.Ch. took a scentress to the Pleasure

Park, to the statue of Hercules with the sleeping lion at his feet, and there in the cold he put his hands on her breasts and inside her lap. That was beautiful. *Item*: He decided to take piano lessons from Mrs. Klahn so as to have a chance to be close to Erna, touching-close.

And again, tears: at Midnight Mass in St. Barbora's, when he saw Mrs. Klahn kneel on the stone floor during the elevation of the Host, and Erna after some hesitation kneeling too, both bareheaded, their black hair reflecting the candlelight, no—he had to look to the right and examine the baptismal font to hide his emotion.

Snow was on the ground. J.Ch. accompanied the two Klahnesses to Cepin, his eyelashes covered with frost. "I'd like to take lessons with you, Mrs. Klahn," he said. "I'll study hard. We have a small piano at home."

She objected that he might be a bit too old to start, but in the end she agreed. Erna said: "Buy yourself a Bayer book."

They were just passing the former brewery, and there was furious barking by the new dog, guardian of the potato bin.

The Bayer book = *Bayer's Introductory Method for the Piano*, Comr. Pavlenda. J.Ch. found it, dog-eared and torn, among Alice's old piano music. He asked Alice to negotiate with Mrs. Klahn about the cost of lessons. "You're a nuisance to her; she'll refuse to take your money and she could use the time for another pupil!" "I'll bring her the pictures I promised her," he said, and finished the Cepin tower using a different tower as a model. At the foot of the castle he left only the brewery and the tavern. The window of the room with the piano was open. The linden was just a tiny sapling then.

With the finished picture he ran past the full-grown tree, epaulettes of snow on his coat.

"Coffee?" asked Mrs. Klahn.

"Please don't treat me like a guest," he said.

"To warm you up. A *pianist* with frozen fingers—that's no good."

He waited for the swan-necked Rosenthal teapot + swan-necked Mrs. Klahn + those cups with the gilded edges. He took the Bayer book out of his bag and put the Cepin picture on top of it.

Spoons clinked as they chatted. It seemed as if the lesson would never start. He noticed once again how closely Mrs. Klahn resembled Astrid Zorska. The mica windows glowed in the American stove. The stool in front of the Bösendorfer remained vacant. He almost wished she would sit down at the clavier and play the Trout.

> *Ein Fischer mit der Rute*
> *Wohl an dem Ufer stand . . .*

The afternoon train whistled by, a train that was *not* bringing Erna. Since the beginning of the year she had been renting a room in Hradek and stayed there during the week. But J.Ch. was not flustered by this bit of news. He acted as if he hadn't heard. The train started for Chlumec. Black steed . . . Mirena placed her hand on the keyboard and said: "You have to relax all the way from the shoulder!" The lesson began. "It's important to sit up straight." She demonstrated. It was getting dark; she turned on the little light on the music stand, but so gracefully, with a delicate flick of the finger, as if the switch, too, could respond with a musical sound. Her hand returned to the keyboard; her fingers spanned an octave of white keys. "The thumb," she said, "is a clumsy finger. We have to give it special training."

At last the time came for J.Ch. to take Mrs. Klahn's place on the stool while she brought over the one standing near the window, upholstered in black velvet, with gold tassels at the corners. She sat down, lower than J.Ch., her face beside his shoulder. "That's good," she praised him. "A firm curve of the index finger and pinky. You'll always get excellent attack on the keys that way." She stretched out her hand to the piano hand of J.Ch., and at her bidding J.Ch. "smartly" lifted finger No. 2 (one), let it drop (two), and struck the key (three).

The sounding board sighed a middle C—and J.Ch. discovered Vostarek's color piano! ! !

That middle C was purple, and right behind it came orange and yellow. He loved the last one the best. That one brought Mrs. Klahn closer to him.

J.Ch. felt that she got the scent of his body just like the scentress at the dance, and that she was going out to him through the dark of night toward the yellow landscape created by J.Ch.'s fourth piano finger.

Whereupon: The Bösendorfer made a dissonant sound.

In terms of color, this meant the hues of an oil slick, the eye of a peacock feather, and that vibration which flowed into J.Ch. from the hand of Mirena Klahn lying on his own.

J.Ch. did not deny his awareness of the contact. He responded with his own vibrations. He sent them to Astrid Zorska, blindly. He closed his eyes to keep out the burning light. So that he could dare to rise. He actually longed to pull away (for a moment, a brief moment), but this brought her even closer. He leaned against her and felt that she was pressing against him, too. That enabled him to look. He opened his eyes and saw himself in the Venetian mirror. A mistletoe branch was stuck in a corner of the frame, and under its red berries he saw a face, flushed and astonished. J.Ch. smiled at it.

. . .

Personal Testimony of J.Ch.

I disappeared inside her without really seeing where. Afterwards she was terrified, shaking all over. "God," she kept saying, "I'm awful, just awful." But she kept petting me, and got angry when I addressed her in the polite form. I had to promise her over and over that I wouldn't tell anyone about it (not a word, you hear?). She didn't trust me.

As for me, I didn't believe that what I had experienced was the real thing. It seemed to have been over too quickly, compared to the eternity I had been waiting, and the angle didn't seem right for the real thing, either.

I left when she started crying. Or did she start crying when I left? I don't remember. She took a big portfolio off the chest in the veranda and handed it to me as a gift. She told me I was not to open it until I got home. By the way it was wrapped I could tell she had wanted to give it to me from the very beginning.

I set out, the streetlight across from the Silver Poplar was lit, the wind leaned into my portfolio as if it were a sail. I carried it against my chest and it slowly became covered with snow. From past experience I expected an explosion of barking, but the new non-Astor stood leaning against the fence on his front paws, snowflakes stuck to his protruding tongue, and he just stood there, jaws surrounded by a ring of condensed moisture, his eyes fixed on me. He knew, the filthy beast! I waved my arm in his face, but even this gesture, which normally provoked him to a frenzy, produced no response. He calmly jumped down and ambled behind me to the end of the fence. There he again raised himself on his front paws and stared after me.

I jogged to the train. I was wearing ordinary shoes, and I didn't feel like walking all the way to Chlumec through the fresh snow. I caught the local. A big coal stove heated up the car. The conductor was just shoveling in more coal. He was all alone in the car. I warmed my soles against the stove. He asked me what I was carrying.

I said: "This," so I wouldn't have to admit I didn't know what was inside.

I untied the portfolio.

"Did you paint that?" he asked.

"No, a friend."

"It's a beautiful job."

The portfolio contained Mr. Vostarek's moth pictures. The first one was *dendrolinus*.

.　　.　　.

To Monsignor Rosin, Historian of Chlumec
Reverend Father,

Please accept this missive of mine, even though my writing to you is a concealment with respect to the Questionnaire and a false statement with respect to the *Erklärung*. You see, I should be writing to Comr. Pavlenda, yet I intend to keep silent, at least on this particular matter; I intend to keep some things to myself despite his wanting to know everything, including those things which are only for the good Lord to know. (He wants to make sure there is nothing I direct to the good Lord at all.)

Where am I? At the point where I am beginning to awake? At the point where my words are not yet directed at Pavlenda, even though I have honestly aimed them that way? Then let it be you who hears my confession, Reverend Father. I have sinned. I have been sailing against my time-stream. I have been sailing on an ice floe while the rest of the ice passed me by in the original direction of the current. On my floe stood a clavier, the wind turned the pages of *Vierhändige Klavierstücke*, a dog licked my bare feet, my hand froze somewhere between E and B, sounds began to emerge from the clavier, yellow sounds which hurt my half-frozen eyes. I was playing for Mrs. Klahn, she was there, under the cover of the clavier, as if lying in a coffin. We sailed upstream,

not like sinners but like wretches. Today I am old enough
to confess it, Reverend Father. I will pass from this
baptismal font, where you pronounced: *Efeta!* over me,
to this screen behind which I now sense your presence.
I beg you, judge the condition of my soul. Ah, I *do* have
a soul, a butterfly cocooned by Chlumec. I will rise if
your absolving blessing bids me, I will rise like an imago.

And forgive me her tears, Mirena's tears, for I learned
of them from within her inmost self. While I was inside
her I knew that she was weeping. When she began to
weep, it was *I* who lay under the wing of the clavier, and
she was the one standing on the floe, her bare feet licked
by a dog. Letters arrived in my coffin: "Janek," she
wrote (she wanted to be the only one who called me by
that nickname but I didn't like it; it made me nervous),
"don't tell anyone about us, I am very unhappy, don't
come to our house any more." Or she wrote: "You are
not guilty, I am the strange one: half of me wears a star,
the other a cross, like a Christmas-tree apple. Don't hate
me, don't think badly of me. I am a bad mother, don't
be a bad son—say a prayer for me."

Reverend, I prayed for her, but not in the way she
wished, not in that sense; I was simply sorry that she
drove me out (out of her inside, where I had wished to
settle). I was an unhappy creature like her, but my
unhappiness was beautiful, in Mirena I passed close to
what I had long considered beyond reach, i.e., Erna!
When I thought about that I began to tremble with
excitement, and even though it was *bitter* grief it didn't
fill me with disgust but with wonder. I soared—icily; I
floated on ice. (But those are today's words, not words
of that time.)

And so I ran back through time, time before Erna,
time even before myself; I slipped under my own existence and passed beyond my horizon until I saw the
time axis of the stream immersing all living things, and

I saw that those whom I had passed in the other direction (like Erna or the scentress) were simply at different points in this same spiral flow, and the nearer they were to the point of submersion the brighter they shone and the more self-illuminating they became, like my own self—the more chrysoberyl the more self-illuminating and self-consuming too. I was afraid of that consuming consummation, I was afraid of that chasm, though my fear was really caused by my leaning too far, my staring into the enormous opening left by the nail in Christ's hand . . . I felt that passing through that opening could be a kind of caress, too.

But this still was not my greatest transgression, this sinful spying into divine matters (I saw their existence but I was ignorant of their cause); I sinned through pride. It seemed to me that the ability to see ahead was my own special gift, and that I could deride all those whom I had passed because they were destined to stumble just as I had known they would.

Perhaps I am full of pride still, because I am turning to you as my confessor and yet I catch myself talking to you as if you were my historian, in the hope of leaving a *written* record (at least in the *History of Chlumec!*).

Don't laugh at me until you've heard how I treated Erna.

I stopped playing the piano, but I did not stop making love to her mother.

She kept resisting, but whenever she scented my body we were soon doing it again. In the birches behind the cemetery, for instance. She trembled all over. After she got up she saw the mortuary chapel with the inscription THE SAINTS IN THEIR HEAVENLY ABODE REJOICE IN YOUR DELIVERANCE, and also Klahn's grave, but the latter she probably saw only in her mind's eye. And in the Pleasure Park, behind the riding school. I watched her fingers clutching the earth, her nails buried cuticle-deep in the

soil among the newly sown stalks of wheat. She lifted her
face toward me and waves of color splashed over her
cheeks with each of my spurts; I stiffened and arched
like a branch on fire, my eyes teared, but I was able to
catch each one of her tremors. I asked her whether she
had felt my seed going in. She said that she hadn't, so
probably she sensed it only at the surface. On our way
back we passed the memorial stone pillars (erected to
your memory, too, Monsignor Rosin); Bonek had the
original cross with the crown of thorns torn down and in
its place now stood a metal dish designed to hold a flame,
as if this were the site of some Olympic ceremony. We
walked down the alley from the bandstand to the
Capousek inn. From the balcony of one of the villas some
bitch with a head full of curlers shouted: "Hey Romeo,
something's sticking out of your pants!" Mirena blushed
and her eyes filled with tears. It was true, my shirttail
was sticking out. I shoved it back in, angrily, because
Mirena's embarrassment was sure to widen the gap between this bout of lovemaking and our next, and I was
sure to get more letters ending with "Burn this!" or "Not
a word!" or "Never again!"

I was impatient, I wanted her to catch my scent, I
wanted her to take me inside her body (even though I
was never allowed to see the place; I had not yet kissed
her where I had kissed Erna). And I kept using the polite
form of address with her, and she said that I wasn't
good-looking but that I smelled good. I tried to assert
myself, started sporting a fancy hat; I told her it was
because I didn't want to be recognized, but in reality I
wore it to make me look more mature. When I came
home thus appareled (I did not merely wear it, I
appareled myself with it), Alice remarked: "My dear
fellow, you should watch yourself."

"Why, Mom?"

"So you don't become ridiculous."

That upset me; furthermore, Mirena talked to me the same way. In *these* things she humiliated me. But I wasn't powerless, and because I suffered from the unpredictability of our affair (always unsure whether there would be a next time or a time after that), I wanted her to suffer, too, to make her powerless while I was inside her. But ever since that bitch in curlers had shouted at us I hadn't gotten so much as a postcard from Mirena. As if she finally understood that all her goodbye letters were just another way of continuing the affair, she decided to stop writing altogether. I waited. Since there always had been a problem with getting letters through to me, I maintained a certain amount of patience. Finally, I went to see Aunt Ludmila in the hope that she might suggest we visit the Klahns together. However, Aunt informed me that Mrs. Klahn was in Hradek, with Erna! Good God, she had done that on purpose!

Item: I waited for her in front of the music school. She quickly walked by me, hardly answering my greeting. She rushed, hurried, to prevent me from keeping up with her, i.e., to make it clear—in case I managed to draw near—that I was being an awful nuisance.

I hated her far better than I loved her.

She came back on the 20th of May, Whitsunday, the liturgical color of which is red—the color of fire and love. I knew that I would find both Klahn women in St. Barbora's. Mirena stood all the way in the back, behind the benches (ever since our affair had started she hadn't dared approach closer to the altar). She was holding a hymn book, a red bookmark under her thumb, and sang in that alto voice of hers which always made me listen in silent wonder. "The Cherubims' Song of Glory." During the Sanctus I stepped close to her shoulder; Erna stood on her left, distracted, her eyes roving, so that she was the one to see me first and she smiled, but I wanted to get closer to Mirena, I breathed into her hair, and as

I did so, her voice faltered; i.e., she smelled my presence.
I had again scented my handkerchief in the inside breast
pocket of my suit. I had done so in order to make it
alluring to her, to keep her from escaping after she
herself had captured me. Don't run away from your
victim, that poor, living, smellable victim, warm him and
cool him with your magic juices—that was my message
to her. In the church. Although she hadn't looked up yet,
by that break in her alto I guessed that she had picked
up my scent, inhaled my essence. She knelt down on the
stone floor, on the granite slab, she beat my breasts (hers,
but they really belonged to me!). "Let's do it tonight,"
I commanded. "I will come to Cepin tonight, by the
evening train."

I glanced meaningfully in Erna's direction. Fidgety,
irreverent, she smiled at me once again, interpreting my
look as a message repayable by a smile. But my glance
was intended to ask her mother what she was going to
do with Erna that night, with this girl, this forfeit that
she held in her hand.

I suddenly realized what I had been doing—trying to
induce Mirena into sending her daughter away, while
that same daughter was smiling at me as a reward—and
I felt a pang of remorse. But at that point we were already
leaving the church.

Erna said: "Actually, it might be better if I left tonight. The morning train is always late and my whole day
is messed up anyway."

Mirena said: "Suit yourself, Erna."

She almost whispered it, and lowered her eyes.

I lowered my eyes, too, to keep from inflaming Mirena
even further.

I told them that Alice had invited them to lunch.
Mirena turned it down. She spoke for both of them, but
Erna felt like coming. And so I stayed with Erna, who
munched on the rabbit in such a listless way that Edvin

asked her if there was anything wrong. He didn't realize that she was eating politely, like a lady, and that was why she seemed bemused. She drank her tea the same way, politely. She held the cup with her pinky soaring out from the handle like the wing of Hermes. I caught myself making fun of her; i.e., aping her. I held my cup in the same idiotic fashion. Alas, while I'd been involved with her mother, she'd been riding a different ice floe. We were like the puppets on my little stage; Bellengardo trips over Don Mucho, their strings tangle, and suddenly the play is ridiculous. In relation to Erna I was the older one, at least now I had a weight on my shoulders. I wanted to be reasonable and understanding, I wanted to forgive . . . and it seemed to me I had something to forgive her for: her refusal to put out for me. But I wasn't able to forgive.

I couldn't bring myself to forget her refusal to put out. She hadn't opened up to me, and now it was too late for any carnivorous ideas; now she could wave her tentacles and snap and wiggle, and she'd get nothing shoved up there but my fist.

This was the fourth time that afternoon we strolled from Town Hall to the savings bank and back. It was the fourth time we passed people promenading along the same route to show off their partners or themselves. Corsairs of the corso. This was one institution my uncle had not yet abolished. He probably would have if he knew how to go about it.

Erna said: "I thought maybe you were sick or something."

"Why?"

"Well, because you haven't come by in such a long time."

"I seem to have lost interest in everything."

"Really?"

"Yes. And I have a lot of work."

"Today, too?"

"No, today I'm free. But only until eight."

"Even if *I* had more time?"

"But you're leaving."

"I could leave later."

I smiled and told her the truth: "I'm meeting someone."

But she answered: "I know."

I tensed, until she added: "You're expecting Olin. They've decided to let him go. Mom said that somebody had mentioned it in a letter."

I smiled again, vaguely, to let her interpret it any way she chose.

She asked: "But if it wasn't for Olin, would you stay with me until a later train?"

I felt sorry for her, I felt a knot in my throat. All the same, I answered (like a stab): "No, Erna, I wouldn't."

She didn't flare up, but asked softly: "Why?"

"You don't love me."

She was sad, she was mine. But I was talking to her in a different language than our old love language.

"You know . . . I like you a lot, Janek!"

"If you really liked me you wouldn't be aping that silly name. Don't call me by that name. It disgusts me."

"You've had enough of me, is that it?"

"Enough? What do you mean? I haven't had *any* of you."

"I didn't express myself correctly, Jan."

Oh God, why was she humbling herself? I slapped her face and now I'd have to hate her for it besides.

"You expressed yourself precisely—precisely opposite to the truth, because it is you who are tired of me, Erna, I know it."

She preferred not to understand. "There is something wrong with you. You are strange."

"Yes, I am."

"I mean lately. Only lately. Something has happened to you, Jan."

I sneered. It was supposed to be a tragic sneer, but it seemed to lack the necessary detachment and so I wiped it off.

"Erna," I said, "I have to confess something to you. But not here."

"Let's go to the Pleasure Park," she said. She must have been very upset to suggest such an obvious (and doubtless commented on) withdrawal from the arena. As soon as we left the corso, I took her by the hand. She was waiting for it, I felt that; in fact, it obviously gave her pleasure. When we reached the pavilion I made her sit down on a bench. I myself remained standing (somewhat guiltily), in silence.

"Is it bad?" she asked.

"What?"

"This thing that happened to you."

"Depends on whom you mean . . . very bad for me, and for you—maybe. It won't be so bad if you take it the right way when I tell you about it. And if you forgive me."

She blinked a few times, like a flickering candle. "You can trust me with anything." And then, after a quick swallow: "You know that I like you very much."

"Erna," I pleaded, "you'll forgive me, won't you."

"Yes," she said. (Quite seriously, in an honest voice. Why did she have to be so decent, Reverend Father! And why was I making those idiotic grimaces?)

"Erna," I sobbed, "I must get married!"

"Married? To whom? ? ?"

She disappointed me a bit. I had expected that my words would leave her speechless.

"I can't tell you that, Erna. Not that I don't want to.

I simply can't. Although . . . I suppose . . . if you promised not to tell anybody . . . not a living soul!"

"You know me!"

"But this is an enormous secret, you understand? She is . . ."

"Already married?"

"Something like that."

"Christ!"

"I'm a swine, you're right. It's awful!"

"Maybe it was just an accident. Nobody can force you into anything if you . . ."

"If I don't love her? Of course I don't love her, but she can make a lot of trouble for me."

"She's blackmailing you!"

"Erna," I murmured, bending close to her ear, "this must *really* go no further. If you like me just the teeniest bit, promise me you'll never breathe a word to anybody!"

She nodded.

"It could be called blackmail, except that it's mainly my own stupid fault."

"But still, you don't have to put up with it!"

"I have to."

"How come?"

"She's got me in the palm of her hand."

"Christ, how is that possible? How did it happen?"

"Some people are just plain unlucky. She took a liking to me, I probably fitted in with her degenerate ideas."

"What?"

"Oh sure, she's degenerate. And she sensed some kind of crack in me. Such types always home in on one another."

"How old is she?" (The concreteness of that question!)

"Thirty-four."

"Do I know her?"

"You probably do. Actually, everybody does. She is quite well known."

"You're not involved with that Rohanova woman? Good God, Jan!"

I sat down next to her, stroked her hair. I was moved, too. That absurd notion of hers made me sad all over again—and yet I almost laughed out loud. Slavka Rohanova was an actress from the district theater company that occasionally visited Chlumec. She had once performed *La Dame aux Camélias*, in Town Hall, coughing herself to death in that butterfly dance hall of ours. It was so ridiculous that I gave Erna a long account of it. But Rohanova and me—no, that killed me! Erna, my love, that was quite a blow, poor darling, bride of Jan Chrysostom the gold-mouthed one. A liaison with Rohanova—that nefarious woman, seducer (so they say) of little boys! I couldn't imagine such a thing in my cock-surest dreams! Poor Erna, how highly you value your own charms if you compare yourself with a knock-out like Rohanova! And now I had to pretend that this was indeed so, I had to let my shoulders droop to signify assent or anything else she wished to read into it.

"So you're going around with actresses!"

I repeated my gesture of resignation. "I cannot help it. But as God is my witness, how I long to get out of it. Erna, if only you could learn to love me, if only you could forgive me!"

Erna said: "I forgive you."

Yes, that's what she said, Reverend, and her voice—for the first time—had an alto sound. Perhaps if it had not been for that alto, I would have stopped right there, you see, I would not have gone on with this conversation.

But I did say: "So you forgive me? Really?"

And she (child-like, simple): "But you have to leave her."

"Whom?" I said, delighted.

"Well . . . her, that woman."

"I already told you that isn't possible. Not just on my account, but for other reasons."

She looked at me and it was hard to tell whether she was only feeling sorry for me or whether her pity was slowly turning to contempt. She was trying to make up her mind. I watched her hesitation with special satisfaction. Then I dug in my spurs.

"I don't love her and therefore it's just as if there was nothing between us. If you care for me at all, this shouldn't bother you. You and I can get together again. You could be like . . . like my real love. With that other one I would only do whatever I had to."

"Really? That's all?"

"It's a fact. In every other way there'd be only you. You understand . . . *making love* . . . there'd be only you."

She shook her head. "No. That's no good. I couldn't do that."

"Even though I love you? Even though this other thing is just meaningless nonsense? What difference could it make to us? We could love each other all the same. We could get together every week, at least twice. Thursdays, Mondays . . ."

"No," she said.

"I was right. You don't love me."

"I do, but I couldn't share you with anybody else. Least of all with that woman."

I guffawed. "Share! That's rich! You don't even know whether I'm a boy or a girl. Only by the color of my little pants. Blue for boy."

She got up, smoothed her skirt.

I said: "I'll walk you to the train."

She stepped close to me, embraced me, pressed against me, down below too, with that *Masdevallia* of hers. But it meant she was going to take it along with her on the train and sell it somewhere else.

She got on the train. I waved, waited for the train to start moving, then jumped onto the last car. We were on our way, she to Hradek and I just that one stop to Cepin. When I got off, I waited for the train to disappear, then crossed the track to the platform of the Cepin station, where Mirena was waiting, under the stairs, at the end of the railing. God help me, Reverend, to become a better human being.

.   .   .

Apple Tree (words without music)
She stood there in her blue buttoned-up dress, her hair pulled back to make her look more severe. But she couldn't scare me, anyway. She said she was waiting for Erna. I told her that if Erna had gotten off the train, I would have kept going.

In a more sincere tone, she said: "Why are we doing this?"

I answered: "Why didn't I hear from you, Mrs. Klahn?"

She: "I was afraid."

I touched her hand: "Of me?"

"Of myself."

We walked along the path by the railroad tracks, all the way to the bridge. The trees were in bloom, the Cepin slope looked whitish in the darkness, the telegraph wires hummed during the pauses in our conversation.

"Mirena," I said, "what can I do to make you happier?"

She stroked me. "Be nice."

"That's not my department. I'll jump off the bridge for you."

I took off my shoes and pulled myself up the riveted arch. Then, with hands outstretched like a tightrope walker, I slowly climbed to the jumping-off place. Mirena crossed over on the wooden footbridge, carrying my shoes. She shouted at me that I was out of my mind. But

I was already poised at the top of the arch with outstretched arms, my lungs filled with May, I saw the trees lit up; one crab-apple tree was burning white at the end of the bridge and Mirena walked toward it with such fervor that I was sure she was going to turn the tree dark with a single gesture of her hand or else make it glow even brighter with a single stroke of middle C; the sound of locomotive whistles was coming from the Chlumec yards and I felt that the bridge and I were riding through space together and also that if I were to plunge after Alice today I would not plummet to earth but soar upward like that brewer Vostarek, that butterfly. I scampered off the bridge, ran to Mirena, she hugged me and led me to the tree, covered me with her body, a breeze blew and the petals from the trees snowed down on us. I lay underneath her as the bridge trembled and light from car windows passed over her rear and thighs; I saw her in that light just as I had once seen Erna. I slid down the embankment to place my lips against those other lips; I felt Mirena's hands pressing me to that place, stroking my hair, for eternity.

It was for eternity. I realized it, first, by the way she kissed me, as if I were an amulet; she sucked me from top to bottom in order to possess me totally. But the final realization came later, when she went back over the footbridge and I stood alone facing Chlumec. Another train passed, blocking my view of her; sparks dropped into the water and when they died I no longer saw her. She must have run down the meadow.

I reentered Chlumec at 22:35 hours.

Note: In addition to those finger exercises from the Bayer book, I know one piano piece by heart: after having watched Alice so many times, I picked up one minuet. That's all I retained from my education, as far as the piano is concerned.

15. A NIGHT IN THE KENNEL

At the precise hour when I was entering the town of Chlumec (22:35), the train which rained sparks and concealed Mirena from me was bringing a thirty-eight-year-old man in shabby clothes and extremely rumpled trousers to Chlumec. In his right hand he carried a deep, broad-rimmed hat and in his left a package consisting of a rolled-up military raincoat covered with newspaper and tied with string. That's all he had with him. We met at the end of the Cepin path, the one running along the right of way, at the very moment I was about to leave the path and he was setting out on it in the opposite direction.

We let each other pass. I was fooled by his angular face and sunken cheeks; for his part, he was fooled by my age—I had grown so much older and taller. But something made me stop nevertheless, he heard me and turned.

"Olin!" I said. "Aren't you Olin?"

He said: "What? Is it really you?"

I ran toward him . . . by now it was obvious to him that I was indeed Jan Chrysostom.

He was Flying Officer Olin, subverter of nationalization and interpreter of dreams (mine).

．　　．　　．

The first dream which he interpreted for me was the following:

The sleeping dreamer is lying naked, his arms crossed on his chest like a corpse. His body is white and his eyes stare upward. Mourners, absent and yet somehow present too, lament over him; they don't realize that he is carefully observing them. They pretend not to notice that in place of a sexual organ a tree is growing out of the deceased, a blooming apple tree full of bees. The dead man is surprised at their blindness and determines to remain dead until they take notice.

Whereupon Olin said: "Show me what you are painting nowadays."

I brought him the picture of Chlumec covered with leaves ("The Destruction of Chlumec"), and Erna with Gosling.

"But that's not her."

"No," I replied.

"Don't sleep with that *other one* any more," he said.

"I won't."

I asked what else he saw in the dream.

"Keep painting, my boy. That's the best thing for you. If you ever acted the way you paint, you'd turn into quite a bastard."

"That was what I dreamed?"

"Yes."

.   .   .

At home we were happy: I, Alice, and Edvin. We were trying to find a set of teeth for Olin so that he could chew with us on the meat of murdered rabbits. The blue sign extolling the well-known lager was now overgrown by shrubs, but you, Olin, had a bite of chopped rabbit meat with cranberry sauce, soon Alice and Ludmila would bring you a set of dentures from a Prague specialist and then you'd smile at my father Edvin to show him that your dental equipment was as good as his (except for that *dens caninus*—no dentist could match such an unusual phenomenon), and then interpret for me . . . not a dream, but a WOMAN! Interpret why that woman left me! She didn't want to live in Cepin any longer, she sold the clavier and the Venetian window through which I had looked into her room. All that was left of it was a dark rectangle in the paint (and a shadow on my lungs?).

I wrote a poem in the style of Astrid Zorska (it's in the family):

> *On my lips . . . a butterfly!*
> *I'm reeling and struck dumb*
> *A butterfly lit on my lips*
> *I hear, my death, your drum.*
>
> *On my lids . . . a shooting star!*
> *It blazes on my lashes*
> *A shooting star lit on my eyes*
> *And burns my days to ashes.*

(Don't laugh at me, Olin! First of all, your smile might fall out of your mouth with your dentures, and besides: I am a better painter than poet.)

But Erna was in Hradek and Mirena was in Hradek, everything was in Hradek; in other words, all fucked up. That's how things turned out even when I tried to be serious and not ironic in the least. And I swear, a butterfly did land on my lips, a soul landed there, not mine: the soul of souls. Am I guilty?

"You sure are," maintained Olin (with a smile, because all he knew was my dream, I didn't tell him anything else).

"No," I replied, also with the help of a certain smile. "I fell, Olin, but I didn't jump of my own free will."

"But you enjoyed your fall. You were excited by that open chute through which everything came pouring down after you."

"Upward," I said. "I fell upward."

My eyes were pleading. But Olin took out his dentures, those fledgling teeth, and examined a spot that hurt his gums.

．　　　．　　　．

To Comr. Pavlenda (c/o GRANIT*)*

Why was Cepin all fucked up? Well, because the
Klahn women had left for Hradek, and not even Olin was
allowed to follow them—in fact, Olin was not even
allowed to cross the brewery yard, they told him that
way he wouldn't miss his old Cepin beer, i.e., even Aunt
Ludmila now moved to Chlumec (River Street, No. 16),
she cooked for Olin, washed his clothes, and again told
people that he was "mining," though this time he was
mining wood! He and Edvin were lumberjacking in the
Moran woods; their territory extended from Svetlice all
the way to the robbers' crosses. In the middle of this
tract of land was the Zdar game warden's lodge and the
stone quarry. When they finished with wood they could
start on the stones. Nobody was going to take that away
from them, because they were careful and locked the
woods behind them: Unauthorized Persons Keep Out.

Perhaps this was the same kind of incantation we used
to recite with Erna and Mr. Vostarek when we hunted
moths and butterflies while helping ourselves to blue-
berries. As we left the forest, we would always declaim
in unison:

> *We're closing the latch*
> *On this blueberry patch.*

That was to make sure nobody cleaned out our favorite
spots. If Edvin and Olin had used the same foresight
they would have been all right. However—and it's important to point this out—one reason Olin followed Edvin
had to do with the name of the game warden's lodge:
Zdar. As soon as Olin got his new teeth he began to
search for the true Zdar. First he took a trip to the Zdar
which was the birthplace of the bandleader killed over
the English Channel. Olin searched through the village

to find a cat with hazel eyes and yellow fur. The Zdar breed! People remembered those "rusty yellows," but no living specimen was left. Somebody told Olin that all the animals were long dead, killed by the dogcatcher because of their disease—their "rusty yellowness." Olin thought this over and after some meditation said to Edvin: Why not try this Zdar place nearby (the Moranian one, Comr. Pavlenda).

Item: He set out with my father to cut trees.

Occasionally I went out to see them, all the way to the crosses. September was beautiful. Olin told me stories about Fatima and I told him about the apple tree growing out of my loins. Or he told me about the crow shot by the French, and also about the English girl from the house called The Fires (I reciprocated by keeping silent about Mrs. Klahn).

Uncle Bonek helped us to celebrate a gorgeous September day by sending up his last salvo of smoke from the chocolate-plant smokestack, for on the following day he was slated to become Chairman of Chlumec, he was about to enter a new, more significant career, but as for us—even on election day we sat at the edge of the locked woods and looked down on the smoke coming from the right (smokestack of United Chocolate Works) and from the left (smokestack of the former Vlaciha & Klahn brewery) and we felt good.

Olin said: "Tomorrow is payday. If it's another nice day we'll wet our whistle at Chiang Kai-shek's (that's in the Anchor Tavern on Jost Square, Comr. Pavlenda, and they serve good wine).

And at Chiang Kai-shek's he continued: "I didn't want to spoil things yesterday. You were gazing into the valley with such mooney eyes, and it was a fine day . . . but things don't look too good for you, my friend."

"The chronoscope?" I asked, for in addition to

numerology Olin knew a lot about astrology and prepared charts. I had printed some sheets for him with a zodiac I copied from an ornamental brass plate.

"That's right," he said. "I see an ox of a pig trying to muscle into your constellation."

I tried to think whether I knew anyone of that description in Chlumec, but Olin said it was someone from far away.

Then I went into the army and met Lieutenant Mikit.

• • •

Lieut. Mikit (testimony)

He was waiting for me in the same place from where Olin had just returned. Not that he wanted me to mine ore. There was no ore left, anyway. He wanted me to become a soldier, and in those barracks ringed by barbed wire (but cut here and there) I was to learn this trade.

It was no longer a camp but a receiving unit, that was its official name, because it received us at one end, sucked us in, and spat us out at the other end, shorn of hair and unhappy.

As soon as I could, I wrote to Olin: "You did that on purpose, mon cousin, you dug up everything of value and now I am supposed to cover up for you!"

Olin answered: "Circumspection, brother, circumspection! Everything has not yet been dug up, far from it!"

And so I picked out a flower growing on a pile of slag partly covered with grass, and when Corporal Klenot prodded me up the slope I kept thinking of that flower, that yellow cinquefoil, and I pretended that it bloomed there to commemorate the soul-expiration of Bighead (if you recall, Comr. Pavlenda, the horse that worked in the mine was called Bighead). But actually I was not as sentimental as all that; concentrating on the flower merely made it possible for me to control myself and keep from hitting Corp. Klenot over the head with the shovel that kept slapping my thigh so insistently as I kept juggling and stumbling. Every once in a while he ordered me to drop and I took a dive into the grass or whatever else happened to be underfoot. And I suffered. Or more precisely: I learned that this was how one started to suffer if one was to be long-suffering. The last spot where I flopped on my stomach had subversive power. It enticed me, pulled me down, and tried to seduce me into killing Corp. Klenot. Not on your life, I said to myself, invoking the cinquefoil: avaunt, lures and snares! Begone elves and goblins! I would paint Red Army heroes according to the wishes of Comr. Lieutenant, who had asked at morning drill for volunteer artists.

Whereupon: I stopped squeezing the handle of the shovel in paroxysms of rage, and said to Corp. Klenot, who was just lighting a cigarette: "Comrade, I will give it a try!"

He blinked. "What are you talking about?"

"The painting. I'll paint a Red Army man side by side with one of our Partyzans, gazing into a distant valley while the sun of freedom rises over the horizon."

"Yeah?"

"Or it could rise behind the mountains like it does on a fifty-crown bill."

"You serious or you just shooting off your mouth?"

"I am serious. I'd like to take a crack at it."

"You've got to know *how*. Without know-how, you can't do it no-how." He laughed.

"Well, I do know how."

He looked me over quizzically. "Yeah? . . . And would you know how to paint *me*, for instance? I'm talking about painting in real oils, on parachute cloth."

"Paint you, Comrade Corporal? That wouldn't be easy . . . you have unusually chiseled features. But I guess I could bring it off."

He offered me a cigarette (he was younger than I). "I mean *me*, holding a rifle. No . . . an automatic, and looking into the distance at a girl."

"Why not."

He ordered me to get up. "I'll try you out, Kepka."

Item: I painted Corporal Klenot in oils on a piece of parachute cloth. It was not so much a matter of facial expression as of rendering the uniform, insignia of rank, and an acceptable face. The girl, too, was only vaguely reminiscent of her model, but she looked beautiful; i.e., she had the kind of looks that Corp. Klenot would find beautiful.

"Kepka, that's great!" he exclaimed after examining the work. "You're a crackerjack! Her tits bulge out too much, she might get pissed off about that. Though in reality, Kepka, in *reality* her boobs are twice as big. This big!"

He modeled their outline by cupping his hands into the shape of a huge spoon.

"Liza's tits just fit my mitts," he said.

Her name was Alzbeta (Liza) Hladka, and the painted cloth was dedicated to her in Gothic letters. And when I added, for good measure, a complicated acrostic on her name, Corporal Klenot went to see Lieutenant Mikit, Officer for Political Affairs (hereafter referred to as O.P.A.) and highly recommended my services.

. . .

Portrait of Lieut. Mikit

Sunken-eyed like a gastritis patient, cheeks somewhat hollow as if constantly sucking on a piece of candy, plenty of hair but low forehead, almost good-looking but small in stature, vest-pocket-size man forty-two years old. And of course slender, at ease in his uniform, which made him what he was (lieutenant). I would not have found him displeasing if it hadn't been for his eyes, i.e., if they didn't sink so far into the sockets that they were practically gone. And on those occasions when he did manage to squeeze them to the surface they turned to water like two puddles of piss.

I painted a picture for him 2.5 x 4 meters in size, to fit into the lower section of the no-longer-mining mining tower. It was visible from afar and the inscription at the bottom could be read all the way from the state highway beyond the woods. The dawn was dawning, its glow glowed in the faces of my heroic heroes who marched forward with rifle and automatic, the Red Army man most fearsome of all because his weapon had the greatest firepower. It was all very picturesque and soldieresque. They gazed at the rising disk which gave their eyes an orange glint. Lieut. Mikit was especially pleased by this aspect of the painting. "You're a devil with a brush, Kepka," he said. And I replied: "I do my best." He asked me what I thought of a slogan he had thought up, to go with the picture: "Hand in hand—now and forever!" You're a devil with words, Mikit, was at the tip of my tongue but I actually said: "We ought to print it in gold letters on a red background," and he praised my graphic solution.

That was how I transferred Bonek's idea for a new wrapper of Dianthus chocolates (formerly Largior) into the region at the foot of the Hard Mountains.

In an expansive gesture, Lieut. Mikit pointed toward one of the mountains looming up in the distance (direction Trojmezi) and promised to provide me with ample space for my next effort, space which equalled in area the garden behind the Cepin brewery (i.e., 1.4 acres). My heart sank, but I smiled and followed Lieut. Mikit into a jeep, which took us to the NON-ASTORS.

·   ·   ·

The Non-Astors (elucidation)

It now appeared that my life would continue to be concerned with dogs.

In the past I had known only Astors. Astor No. 1, who in spite of all of Bonek's attempts at training remained a mere astor; Astor No. 2, the dog that pulled my cart, *Canis chlumecensis* (who never suffered as a result of this service, for whenever he got tired of hauling me I put *him* in the cart and pulled him to give him a ride, too, and during the time of my weddings to Erna I would climb into the cart only after we had reached the outskirts of Cepin, so that I could make my entrance by dog-and-carriage, to give the impression that I had ridden like that all the way from Chlumec, and it should be noted that Astor No. 2 saw the point and never tried to ridicule me in front of the girl), and only after Astor had been sold on me because as a Vlaciha dog he could no longer be kept at the brewery and we didn't have enough rabbit meat to feed him and ourselves—it was only then that I made my acquaintance with the first non-Astor. He guarded the potatoes stored in the bin and barked at me as if I were a stranger. Once, instead of barking, he kept examining me with curiosity as I had reported earlier; i.e., I had the impression the dog was following me because of what had transpired between Mrs. Klahn and myself; but now I tend to think that I was under investigation by a whole gang of non-Astors and he had merely been sent out by them to check on me. Non-Astors are *super-dogs*, and here in Blatno there were thirty-six of them.

They lived in kennels, twelve occupants in each, and sometimes I was given the job of feeding them. Or else Lieut. Mikit called me and sent me out to paint pictures. I went around to the various units and painted "Comrades in Arms," "Struggle for Peace," "The Liberators," and "Mutual Friendship." On my return I would sprinkle the kennel floors to keep down the dust, rinse off super-dog piss with a hose (so that soaked-in urine didn't irritate their paws), or else I was entrusted with the task of

Political Instruction (P.I.) of the canine-unit staff. But this happened only rarely, when easy problems were to be discussed or the material called for pictorial illustration (e.g., when our forces were surrounded by members of hostile military pacts on some Pacific Island, etc.). I used colored chalk, Comr. Pavlenda—and I had a ball!

But sometimes I wrote to Olin (with more circumspection than before): "Olin, perhaps I should have h.K.o.t.h.w.m.s. after all" (hit Klenot over the head with my shovel), but Olin answered: "Take it easy, Bighead!"

In other words, he called me by the name of that horse, if you recall, Comr. Pavlenda. And so it seemed that animals were destined to play a bigger part in my life than I had imagined.

For example, I penetrated into the Blatno oak forest to a depth of approximately 150 feet in approved military fashion, zigzagging and then cutting across a meadow. In the woods I lay down on my back and napped for a few minutes, i.e., until non-astor Flash from Kennel No. 3, stall No. 4, began sniffing me. He frightened me because he snarled in my face and because I had already witnessed his ability to work people over.

"Kepka, you're goldbricking," I heard Lieut. Mikit's voice.

"I'm working," I replied into the dog's snout. "I have an idea for a new picture."

Flash bared his teeth. He had a touch of the wolf in him, and was an excellent tracker.

Mikit said: "An inspiration?"

"That's right, Comr. Lieutenant."

"And what is it about?"

"Peace," I said. An expression of approval came over Mikit's face. Hmmm, peace . . . he waved his arm, abracadabra, at Flash, who immediately returned to his master. The lieutenant cast another magic spell in front of the animal's eyes, his left hand motioning backward and downward, and the dog at once sat down on his haunches.

I got up and walked a few steps toward the officer. "He's marvelously trained," I said (meaning the dog).

"He's a good dog," said the lieutenant, "but don't try to change the subject. *How* did you visualize peace?"

"As a soldier holding a sword in his right hand and an infant in his left."

"That's clever. I'll send you to Mestec." (That was the location of the unit where I was to paint the picture, Comr. Pavlenda.)

"But you know, *I* would approach that subject differently."

"For example . . ." I said.

"For example, as a woman. Then everybody would realize that peace is a beautiful thing . . . everybody would feel it *concretely*. You understand what I want to say?"

"I'm trying, Comr. Lieutenant."

"Of course, no nakedness or crude stuff, but yet in such a way that it makes you feel like a regular man. You are a regular man, aren't you, Kepka?"

"I'm trying, Comr. Lieutenant."

I couldn't leave well enough alone, and started telling him about my experiences with scentresses. He didn't believe that girls would do such a thing, and he told me rather casually that a dog was more sensitive to smells: for example, dogs could tell when the dogcatcher had eaten some canine meat and they could recognize the smell of dead comrades on him. At last he shifted the conversation to another track altogether. Out of the blue, he asked me whether I knew how things stood with man.

"Which man, Comr. Lieutenant?"

"Man in general. Mankind. You understand?"

"I see."

"At first man was not even man."

I struggled to find the aim of this communication.

"He was nothing," said Mikit, rolling up Flash's long leash. "You understand? Just a part of a savage band."

"Yes." I sighed with relief, because it was evident that I was going to be treated to an educational lecture.

"But you can't stop progress," he said.

"No."

"Progress in the upward direction! Even though it's often painful, Kepka."

Mikit tossed the rolled-up leash into the air and it uncoiled like a paper streamer, or like the spiral of progress under discussion.

"Progress keeps going on and on. Spiraling upward. Toward us. Toward me, toward you. Understand?"

"Directly at us, Comr. Lieutenant?"

"Yes, you could put it that way, Kepka."

He started to wind the leash once again. "Everything must be seen *concretely*."

"By concrete examples," I said.

Again, that look of approval. "Would you know how to continue?"

"What do you mean?"

"I mean—do you know what happened next?"

"Well, after the first primitive society came the slave society . . ." etc. etc., I recited the whole story for him, leaving nothing out, until at last I came to *our order* of society, which included the two of us (the three of us, counting Flash) seated in the woods behind the Blatno barracks. As I was talking, it became more and more evident that progress unfolded in a systematic manner and that from the very beginning it had been aiming at this particular clearing in the woods and our three figures as its culmination.

He enjoyed my dissertation and as we were about to take leave of each other he said to me confidentially, like an old swordsman entrusting a deadly parry to a prize pupil under an oath of utmost secrecy: "You want to know something very strange?"

"? ? ?"

"This is extremely interesting: all the older orders of society already carried the seeds of future orders in their womb, whereas ours had to be created from scratch, out of nothing."

"Without any seeds"

"That's right."

He wanted me to remember that carefully; a task had been entrusted to me! Lieut. Mikit was about to leave for district headquarters and I was to explain to the dog-handlers in a P.I. lecture what I had learned in the woods.

I thanked the lieutenant. He said: "Now tell me about that handkerchief. Just exactly where did you place it?"

Taken aback, I said: "Under my armpit, Comrade Lieutenant."

"Exactly where?"

"Here, I'll show you."

The lieutenant once more motioned magically with his left arm (he stretched it out and then quickly lowered it noiselessly to his side), Flash rose and trotted alongside Mikit as we walked back to the barracks.

Next morning the lieutenant left for the district capital, his briefcase stuffed with papers. I gave a lecture to the dog-handlers, explaining the seeds of progress in the womb. I illustrated the idea further by means of eggs, out of which emerged various figures in historical costumes. Through the window of the lecture hall I had a view of the gate and I prepared a smile of welcome for the Comrade Lieutenant when I saw his car drive through and stop in front of headquarters.

But he did not return my smile, he strode into his office, eyes blazing.

The driver told me that he had waited two hours in front of the district courthouse. Then Mrs. Lieutenant came running out, followed by Lieut. Mikit, who however had not been given a chance to catch up to her. They called him by name and rank, they sent the porter after him, but when the name Mikit rang out, his wife answered in a loud voice: "You can go lick it!" and rushed off. He shook with anger but there was nothing he could do, he was as helpless as when they yelled the same rhyme at him in the barracks ("Mikit" from one barracks, and "lick it" from another, while he raged in the middle, i.e., in between those buildings, running furiously back and forth). But here the perpetrators were obvious.

Item: After his fury subsided, the lieutenant remained standing on the sidewalk and stared at the ground, his briefcase still under his arm, until the driver led him into the car and drove off with him.

When he arrived back at his office, he locked himself in and in spite of the fact that he was Officer of the Day he refused to talk to anyone and didn't eat a bite. Finally, at 1:32 a.m., he came out and announced that the whole battalion was to take part in a drill. Eight hundred men, thirty-six dogs, arms and equipment left at top speed for an encampment seven miles away in the deep woods. Mikit remained all alone in the barracks. He went back to his office, locked himself in, and cogitated.

Fellow officers arriving for duty just before 6 a.m. were so astounded by what they saw that they waited in front of the gate for Capt. Dzim to decide whether to enter the area (now the camp became an "area" for them, too, just as it was designated on the signs warning civilians to keep out), or whether to check first with divisional headquarters.

Capt. Dzim ordered them to enter the camp. Lieut. Mikit continued to maintain his silence, refused to respond to knocks on the door, shouts and questions; e.g., "Are you all right?" "Where are the troops?"

They began to have their doubts whether anyone was

in the office at all. Captain Dzim therefore ordered one of the junior officers to give him a boost and peered into Mikit's office through the side window. He saw the lieutenant's ashen face, which stared back at him without the slightest sign of recognition.

"Mikit!" screamed the captain.

And the lieutenant, in a voice that seemed to come from an enormous distance and yet all the more distinctly, responded with an invitation involving his ass. The human ladder holding up Dzim collapsed in consternation. In the meantime, we soldiers sent patrols out of the woods to have our commanders brought back to us.

We searched for them and they for us until we met. That day they were kind to us, ordered me to continue my political instruction until a substitute was found for the *ill* Lieutenant Mikit. They also gave me the keys to his office so that I could get the lecture material I needed out of his cabinet. The doors of the cabinet were held shut by a thick red-white-and-blue plastic band, and from the way the books, papers, and posters lay scattered around inside, it was plain that Lieutenant Mikit had not done much studying. I soon found several brochures about progress, but there were many more about the training of dogs. I also tried to open a desk drawer. It was stuck and the statuette of Comr. Lenin twitched and began to shake & tremble faster and faster as its round base tried to reestablish itself on the desk; I became scared, for Comr. Lenin's arm was stretched out in an imperious gesture, i.e., pointing to the door, which looked as if he were expelling me and guarding Mikit's drawer. I therefore grasped him by his fur cap and turned him toward the window; now he pointed to the kennels, and to the Blatno camp beyond. I pulled the drawer out of the no longer defended desk.

Comr. Pavlenda, I really don't know what got into me. I had no special reason to open the drawer or to read

Mikit's private notes. I did it absentmindedly, without curiosity or excitement, but I read! In the book headed *Basic Orientation for Members of Security Units*, in the "Remarks" column, Mikit had written in his angular handwriting: "No, this is not based on the truth!" A little farther down, as if he had been about to start a letter but changed his mind: "It is not true that before the plaintiff's arrival I always scrubbed the floor in order to provoke her. I did it only for the sake of cleanliness." He tried to describe some of the things that bothered him, but he was unable to finish a sentence. He began over and over with the contention that "the plaintiff" lied, did not tell the truth, was mistaken, wronged him, and he interspersed these assertions with various reproaches, complaints about "having left our common household," and finally addressed the plaintiff directly: "Hanna dear," he exhorted her, "how could you say such a thing, how could you say that my washing your lingerie disgusted you! I only did it so that you'd have nice clean things to put on . . ."

I closed the book, dropped it back in the drawer, I dropped it like a coffin next to a typed document headed *Request for Legal Action* (in triplicate), containing in Part II (evidence) a statement to the effect that *disharmony* was constantly getting sharper and sharper, that the plaintiff was *especially disgusted* when the defendant forced her several times daily to change her underwear, insisting on helping her personally to do so, "with an exaggerated thoroughness that made me extremely nervous."

I tried to imagine Lieut. Mikit occupied in this manner, but this image did not please me and so I let myself be evicted from the office; i.e., I turned the statuette to face the door and when it pointed the way out with its upraised right arm I obediently complied.

That night I slept in the kennel, not actually with the

dogs but very close to them, on the bench of the dog-handler's annex, near the stove and underneath the bulletin board with orders for the rations to be fed to the animals and information to be fed to the men the following day.

The rations were to include fish meal (253 cal per 100 gm), and as to the information, it was to be "The Proper Handling of Anger."

I slept peacefully, except for a dream I had in the early morning hours. I dreamed about a letter I wrote to

ASTOR THE SECOND
c/o The Heavens over Cepin

but on awakening I couldn't recall the content of the letter.

As I walked out of the kennel I got a strong whiff of canine odor. It was seven-thirty, and I determined that henceforth I would try to sleep there as often as possible, because in the other barracks reveille was at 6 a.m.

Then I noticed a civilian on the other side of the wire, nodding at me furiously. I looked closer and recognized Mikit. His civilian clothes had confused me; he looked like an underexposed photograph.

"Kepka," he chortled (trying to shout and whisper at the same time), "come here."

"Comrade Lieutenant!"

"Shush," he hissed through the rhomboid cunts of the wire fence, "I am no lieutenant any more."

"Then what are you?"

"A ruined man," he said, and there were red blotches on his cheeks. "But I'll put an end to it soon, you'll see."

I asked him how he planned to do it and he replied that he was going to grab that filthy bitch by the neck like this and strangle the living daylights out of her.

He frightened me, the motions of his hands were so

realistic, down to the final twist. I preferred to laugh it off. And he joined me. The super-dogs, watching us and sniffing in our direction, were also getting ready to smile, some of them starting to raise their upper lip for a canine grimace.

"But now let's get serious," he said. "Where did you put that handkerchief?"

"What?"

"Show me where you placed that handkerchief. The seductive one."

"Here," I said, and again showed him the spot.

He said: "You're lying. I tried it and it doesn't work."

"Everybody is different," I protested.

"You're lying."

"Why should I lie? You're a mature man."

"A ruined man. I'll hang myself."

"Then you'll really be out of it."

"I know what. I'll borrow your handkerchief."

"You don't borrow things like that."

He barked: "Give it to me!" and fumbled for my blouse.

"Christ, Comrade Lieutenant, you can't be serious!"

He stuck the fingers of his left hand through the wire cunts, grabbed my blouse, his face again flushed with those red spots, while his right hand fished in the pocket of his civilian jacket for his service revolver, caliber 7.45 mm.

The dogs started barking when they heard my shouts and saw me holding Mikit. I had stuck my own hands through the wire to hold the lieutenant close and keep him from pulling out his pistol.

While the two of us were thus entangled and enmeshed, the guards came running and arrested Mikit.

At that moment I recalled my letter to Astor II, my cart dog.

The letter said:

> *My faithful buried dog*
> *pick up Camila in heaven*
> *put her in my cart and pull her*
> *over the spot where I am now*
> *and let her strew forget-me-nots*
> *on this carpet of piss-spotted asphalt*
> *and on my face*
> *or I will go mad.*

It started to rain; i.e., my plea had been heard.

. . .

During the rain, in the dog-handler's hut, I talked to Capt. Dzim. He was drunk because all the battalion officers had been drinking to the memory of Lieut. Mikit. They were happy to be rid of him and they were also happy to have seen him in such a fury—he had tried to shake off his handcuffs till blood ran down his hands. (Handcuffs of that type get tighter and tighter with each movement, Comr. Pavlenda, you can rub your hands raw.) Capt. Dzim was overflowing with happiness, and with liquor, and so they put him in the dog-handler's hut until a civilian car came to pick him up. I was guarding him in the meantime. He told me to get him something to drink. Rum. I answered that I was supposed to stand guard over him.

"Guard me, Kepka," he said, "but get me a bottle."

I said I couldn't.

He told me that his request was a categoric apéritif and that I should be grateful he was being so lenient with me.

"You're glad to be alive, aren't you, Kepka."

"I am, Comr. Captain."

"Then shake your ass and get that bottle on the double!"

I went to get it. In the meanwhile he sat down under

the bulletin board, next to a pail of old eggs intended as canine-feed supplement, and before I returned he had thrown almost half of them at the poster *Courage in Hand-to-Hand Combat*, a subject scheduled for discussion the following week. He laughed and hiccuped, after each throw exclaiming: "Screw combat! Screw your seeds! Screw your womb!" As each egg splattered over the poster and dribbled down the wall, he kept blabbing on about Lieut. Mikit. The pail contained 86 eggs, i.e., 160 cal per 130 gm (I recorded it in the loss column); in other words, the damage was substantial.

Then he turned to me. "You can trust me."

"Yes," I agreed.

"And confide in me."

Again, I agreed.

"Confide in me about *everything*. You understand?"

"No," I said.

"I see. You hesitate. But a pass . . . you'd like a pass, wouldn't you?"

"I would, Comr. Captain."

"Then you'll help me?"

"Help you? How?"

"Look. One favor deserves another. Tell me who was the one screwing her behind his back, and you'll have your pass."

"Who . . . what . . . behind whose back?"

"Mikit's missus."

"Oh, I see. In other words . . . who was the man . . . like . . . is that what you mean?"

"Exactly," he said.

I disappointed him. "Actually, I know nothing about that."

"You're scared to tell me, aren't you."

"No, it isn't that."

"You're scared," repeated Dzim.

"I just don't know."

"Too bad."

"Anyway," I said. "He was a poor devil. I almost feel sorry for him."

"For Mikit? You idiot!" roared Dzim. Then he whispered: "Listen!" He put his finger to his lips, an index finger dripping with jelly-like, primal egg stuff, and said in a hushed voice: "He was a hangman. A *hangman*!"

Item: I learned that the person in question, Comr. Pavlenda, had contracted to perform the aforementioned function, i.e., that he had signed contracts for each individual performance of this task, and that only after the class struggle had somewhat subsided had he changed occupations, i.e., he had himself transferred to instructional duties, much to the distaste of his new colleagues (insofar as they knew about his past).

16. LYING IN THE GLADE

"And if Mikit hanged himself," I asked Olin, "would that be considered an act of suicide or an execution?"

But Olin, even though sitting next to me, had drifted off to a house approximately 70 miles from London (Southend-on-Sea, Essex).

He had been doing that quite often lately, going off on trips, back to where he had already been and also forward to where he would be someday. He traveled forward by means of a chronoscope and sometimes took me along.

We were again sitting on a hill overlooking Chlumec, the spot where the woods were opened and shut, I was no longer soldiering in Blatno but learning from Uncle how to travel by the stars. His ephemeris was good to the year 2222. By then I would probably be dead (but so will you, Comr. Pavlenda!). Sometimes I ran forward to the date of my death and looked things over. Not that I was eager for that day, but I am as mortal as other mortals. Until recently (almost until Blatno) I was so full of life that I had no inner intuition of a death date, whereas recently whenever I took a deep breath I immediately crossed myself in the holy Catholic manner.

. . .

Then I saw the day quite clearly: Friday, right after Three Kings, A.D. 1614, and I testify against you, Comr. Pavlenda! You slipped something into my bread, you poisoned me, I've been out of my head for a year and I cannot be rid of you, I keep hearing your voice urging me to write!

And you say: "Jan Chrysostom, you will have me on your conscience!"

But I reply: "Good my friends, I utter the truth. He has in his possession the arm of a hanged man and the severed member of another man, and a bloody tunic."

You retort: "Thou art a lying villain!"

But I cite the month and the day, and I tell how you made people's bodies rot by means of sorcery and how you wiped horses with the flesh of unbaptized infants to make them barren.

And you shout: "Miscreant, hellhound! Thou liest most abominably!"

Item: I point to the spot where we are now standing, and circle it with my finger.

They take you away to have your head chopped off. The executioner raises his arm and you ask: "Why the delay?"

He smiles, puts away the sword, and speaks to your head: "Nothing, sir, nothing. Pray, look. It is all over."

It is Jan Jatro the Younger, the executioner with the lightest touch in the annals of Chlumec.

·   ·   ·

Or I run forward in the ephemeris to A.D. 2222, the day of Jan Chrysostom, the golden-mouthed bishop, that is my name day, which comes toward the end of January, and I am again inside Alice, yet Alice is there, too!

And naturally so are Olin and Edvin, Mother is frying potato pancakes, buttering them with a goose feather, and we (Erna, Mirena, Mr. Vostarek, and others) stand in line at the stove, waiting our turn. And as soon as a pancake is done we take it and juggle it from hand to hand to cool it, and mine goes flying off into the sky over Chlumec like the sun of freedom on a fifty-crown note. But it is not shining on a Partyzan or a Red Army man, they are no longer in Chlumec, it is dimly lighting up the snow-filled January sky. This dim winter light illuminates the face of Father Marik, lying deathly ill in the chapel under the portrait of Pater Stach, the painted eyes almost livelier than those of Marik, sacristans and almoners crowd around the dying cleric—begging, thank God, has returned to Chlumec. The forest has expanded into the ravine, wolves prowl the winter fields as far as the swamp and the Pleasure Park. One of them is especially vicious and Father Marik implores him in a weak voice: "Brother wolf, in Christ's name I order you to desist from harming anyone. Let there be peace between you and the human race!"

How fortunate that this is my name day. I watch the scene around the stove and I feel Astor pressing against my legs, Astor the draft dog, begging for a piece of pancake. "Brother dog," I say, "here, this is for you!"

I pluck the disk out of the sky and the snow starts falling again over Chlumec.

·   ·   ·

Then Olin turned toward me (another of Olin's turnings) and said: "If Mikit hung himself, it would be murder."

"How come?"

"Because he would be killing himself with the intent of depriving us of a public figure."

I didn't contradict him because I was glad he had come back from Southend and could help me make a choice of profession. Ever since my return from Blatno I had been under pressure to choose my future occupation (*viz.*, Question 14).

Olin concluded from my chronoscope that my occupation should contain an element of vagueness; i.e., that I was best suited to become a policeman, photographer, lifeguard, or doorman in a bordello. That was revealed by the configuration of my tenth house, *Honores*.

But none of the above appealed to me.

"All right then, how about gardening," Olin offered as a compromise.

"That's better," I said. But I kept pressing him further until he dreamed up landscape architecture for me.

And so I became a landscape architect.

. . .

Bonek found out about it and sent me a message asking whether I could transmute the Pleasure Park into the Garden of Friendship and Peace. Bonek wanted Chlumec to become beautiful. He bought a sprinkler truck for the town, also a hearse and the kind of sanitation truck that has a long snout on the side for sniffing the sidewalk and sucking up dirt. Bonek had changed. He started to be kind to us, too.

Alice said: "I think it's because of all those sweets he's been eating at the Hatus place. He's lost his teeth."

Olin said: "I think it's because he's bitten off plenty and now he needs to chew on it."

But the truth of the matter was, Comr. Pavlenda, that Bonek Kepka, Chairman of the National Committee, Chlumec, had a set of dentures, oddly enough made by the same specialist as Olin's, so that the sole *dens caninus* left in the Kepka family glistened in Edvin's mouth and Edvin smiled and bared it at me when I asked him whether he'd mind my making some money working for Bonek.

"Our town doesn't need any more fucking up," said Father.

"Too bad. It could have been a nice windfall."

And so Bonek turned to other experts and together they built a Ceremonial Hall, a glass structure next to the mortuary at the edge of the cemetery, a transparent hall, all glass and steel, a waiting room for corpses, intended to reduce the number of Popist funerals (Bonek was always trying to reduce something or other, or else to increase it). It was a depot for dead Comrades. When a Comrade died, he was picked up by the newly purchased hearse of the Funeral Service (formerly Hajek & Pelikan), a hearse without angels or gilt. (The plumed horses were beyond pleasure and pain, in heaven with Bighead.) In contrast to the sanitation truck, the hearse did its sucking through its rear rather than its front. Actually, the back was like the mouth of a hippo; when the rear doors of the hearse opened to devour the coffin, the rear end resembled the gaping jaws of a hippo. It waited for its morsel right at the ramp behind the Ceremonial Hall— then, plop! and it was off to Hradek, to the crematorium.

All this fascinated me so much that I started painting it. I envisioned Bonek's United Funerary Enterprises (Boneks Funusfabrik!). When my uncle reached his full stride, this establishment could spread over the entire valley, and include rows of wreatheries, ribboneries, crematories, sorrow banks, etc., all sorts of ancillary enterprises, everything bedecked with stars (to please Bonek) and clustered around the star on the Hatus smokestack and on the Ceremonial Hall on the hill.

When this was finished, I painted Bonek himself, Leader of Chlumec, cutting the umbilical cord in the form of a ceremonial ribbon and pinning a decoration on my chest for "that excellent piece of work" but at the same time whispering in my ear: "Didn't you underscale it somewhat, Jan Chrysostom?" And a balloon coming out of my mouth replied: "Not at all. The problem might be the opposite, an undersupply of corpses." "Jan," said my uncle with all the gravity of which he was capable on such occasions, "the planned quota must be fulfilled!" He put on his leather coat, stuck a Turkish-delight cleaver in his pocket, and we were off to fulfill the quota.

.   .   .

Item: Olin turned to me (still another Olin turning) and said: "The power of that sniffer of yours is almost frightening!"

"What do you mean?"

"You were absolutely right about that cleaver! Bonek will soon have need of it!"

"For doing what?"

"For chopping off his own head. His turn has come," said Olin. He opened Uncle's horoscope (we had his also, Comr. Pavlenda) and pointed to the eighth house, where Sun and Saturn were on the verge of total opposition, 180 degrees.

But Bonek sensed nothing, went to City Hall, to his office, to his desk inherited from the late Mr. Hatus. The sundial indicated high noon, the dial supported by Saturn holding a vintner's knife, and underneath were the inscribed lines of Lady Ursula, wife of Jost of Chlumec:

> TIMES GOE BY TURNES
>
> THINE END IS NIGH
>
> THOU CANST SHOUGH DEATH
>
> LIKE A SUMMER FLYE

Such was the message Lady Ursula had commissioned for the City Hall in A.D. 1541, simultaneously with a sarcophagus for Sir Jost. When the sarcophagus was being put in place over the grave, Ursula uttered a curse against all potential disturbers of her husband's peace. The sarcophagus was of white marble and Jost had lain there peacefully, hands crossed over his sword, for 424 years. Then Bonek heard about the discovery made by Comr. Kuruc on the playing field right in front of our windows.

They were excavating the foundations of a new stadium and as the shovel of the tractor scooped up the ground it gradually turned the lawn into a graveyard.

Alice watched from the window and she said the scene reminded her of the fairy tale about a water sprite: a row of pots, a row of souls.

To me it looked more like rows of gray mushrooms growing in the grass.

The tractor driver ran to find an educated person, and somebody told him to get Kuruc, the school principal.

Kuruc came, reached into one of the pits, and picked up an old war ax. A photographer appeared and took a picture for the *Chlumec News*. A fresh copy of this paper was daily on Bonek's desk. He looked this one over, then put his coffee cup on the photo of the excavated ax and began his dying. (From this instant, the movement of Saturn with respect to the Sun was inexorably that of opposition.)

Comr. Director of the School District entered and Bonek asked him what could be gained from the excavation scientifically; for example, archaeologically. He lifted the saucer off the picture of Kuruc to show what he was talking about.

"We could study *Elephus primigenius*, said Comr. Director.

"What's that?"

"A mammoth, Comr. Chairman. Similar bones have been found elsewhere."

"I don't want animals," said Bonek, as a preface to his death.

"Graves, then," said the director. "We could study graves."

Bonek liked that much better, because in the catacombs under the church were buried many Franciscan monks, and he had heard they were simply lying on boards and were well preserved.

"Of course, there is old Jost," Comr. Director recalled. "Nobody's ever opened his crypt."

"Then we'll do it," said Bonek, and for the first time

since my christening he entered the Church of St. Barbora and went right to the spot on which his candle had dripped during the Christening ceremony.

Bonek was followed by several workers, who pried at the white Silesian marble with crowbars, lifted the sarcophagus, and deposited it on a wooden platform near the sacristy.

Now Jost was looking straight at Bonek. Bonek was wearing a tweed jacket; Jost, short trousers, a round Spanish collar, and on the right side, above the collar, a crest showing a griffin with a nut in its beak. But Bonek noticed only Jost's nose. "Who knocked it off?" he asked.

Jost answered: "It crumbled away through the years." But Bonek, feeling an itchy dampness at the root of his own nose, sneezed and failed to hear Jost's voice. Bonek began to feel chilly.

One of the workers pointed into the crypt and insisted that it contained still another stone slab. Another worker recalled the legend about Lady Ursula's curse and they all declared that they were too terrified to continue.

Bonek was angry, asked someone to fetch his warm overcoat, and sent for the Director of Manual Labor. The director in turn summoned eight gypsies, who were known to be illiterate and had only recently arrived in Chlumec.

These, after dusk, lifted the second slab.

Bonek was pleased. He ordered searchlights to be turned on, and aimed one of them at the hole in the crypt.

The beam was swallowed up in darkness.

It seemed there was water down there.

Bonek didn't believe it.

They stepped aside to let him see for himself.

"We should lower a rope ladder," they said. "Who knows how far this thing goes."

"And who knows whether Jost isn't lying somewhere else altogether?"

Bonek glanced around, stared into the hole, and said: "This is a well! I can hear the water!"

Then he noticed a lead tablet with a Latin *maledictio*. But he mentioned nothing about it, went back to the bench, and rested his feet, which felt like ice. He was shaking with cold, in spite of his overcoat.

"We'll continue tomorrow," he said to the gypsies and left the church, hoping to walk off the numbness in his feet. And look: he is in Franciscan Street and Marta Vohryzek is coming toward him with a bagful of bones from the butcher.

Bonek thinks: "She is taking a big chance to go shopping at this time of day and not during the pre-scribed hours!" Bonek turns away, pulls out his handker-chief, and blows his nose so that he won't have to greet Marta, so that he won't have to look in her eyes.

That's better. Now I won't have to report her! He blows into the handkerchief and his head pounds as if the Jew Vohryzek was pounding marrow bones in his brain.

Bonek looks around. His eyes search for a firm point, to stop the ground from swaying.

Item: He sees Marta. The very person he wanted to avoid.

She is so close he cannot pretend not to see her.

He has to greet her.

"Good evening," he says.

"Good evening," says Marta, smiling.

But as she smiles, her teeth reveal to Uncle that she is Death.

.   .   .

Bonek began to make full preparations for his demise (*das Vollsterben?*). He put all his papers in order, notes, bills, reports, statements. He also prepared a very detailed list of people who were to receive notice of his death. Although he had tried very hard to be different from his father Edvin, he resembled him at least in this—his closest and dearest constituted two whores from Hradek. In Chlumec he had kept his nose clean. That's why he sent them a message from his deathbed not to come to Ceremonial Hall but to wait at home or possibly at the crematorium, so that they could take one last look at him before the coffin was finally hammered shut. We were the only other relatives he had. He wrote to us, too, and we sent our condolences "in the name of the entire family."

He had also invited many other people to his funeral, including the Klahn women.

They came. Erna, all in black. And Mirena.

As they were leaving the Chlumec station I went out to meet them and saw that Erna was leading a little Erna, i.e., a little girl created by someone else's member, i.e., she had given her flower to somebody in Hradek and not to me.

I asked little Erna what her name was, and it turned out to be Katerina ———ova, the dash being the name of the member's owner.

I, too, was in black. I looked at Mirena. She was not in mourning clothes, she wore a pinkish dress—and she looked *old*. Floating on a different ice floe. She, too. I could no longer get inside her or sport in her or sail in her. Everything had come to an end. When I thought about it the needle pointed north, toward the robbers' crosses. But it was only now that I really loved Mirena; when she was no longer moist.

Times goe by turnes . . .

.   .   .

At our house (No. 1278) we dressed Katya in mourning.

She said: "I have *never* worn this dress before."

Erna said: "Of course you have. Last fall, when Grandpa Karel died" (a non-Klahn fore-member, member that begot that other member).

Katya said: "So this is a dress for fall?"

I said: "You bet it is. We'll go out and have a big fall, won't that be fun?"

I took Katya by the hand and together we climbed up the hill to the Chlumec cemetery and Ceremonial Hall. The butterflies came fluttering up from the valley, too, the yellowish *Papilio machanon*—"one of our most common butterflies"—I always thought of Vostarek's description in the swallowtail's file—"faithful denizens of our fields, meadows, and gardens." Another type of faithful denizen got out of the car, rushed straight to Erna, and squeezed her hand. "My deepest sympathy, Comrade Erna. They don't make them like him any more."

He was referring to Bonek.

But why was he saying it to Erna? Probably because she was the loveliest mourner among us.

Katya called out: "Uncle!"

Alas, Comr. Pavlenda, as far as she was concerned, I was an uncle = a middle-aged, settled person!

"Uncle, do policemen have children?"

"Why not, Katya. They are people like us."

She thought it over. "And what are their children called?"

I named various names.

"But doesn't it seem *strange*?" asked Katya, and I agreed, because oddly enough I began to see it that way, too.

I kept looking at the world through Katya's eyes for a while longer. And that was great fun. For instance, the funeral official turned into an illusionist. The Great Bellachini! First time in Chlumec! Magic of all kinds! Makes things and people vanish and materialize at will!

He motioned for me to step forward to check Bonek's medals.

Why me? I turned to see if I could find anyone more suitable, but I was stuck.

Bellachini tapped the little medal boxes with his long finger; they opened, one after another, and the contents glistened.

Then he tapped three times and the plush cushions which were to receive the medals stepped forward and stuck out their chests while the Comrades carrying them held them up to be decorated. Bellachini, Master Illusionist, ordered the first cushion: front and center! Comrade First Secretary of Chlumec inspected the ranks until he reached us, the bereaved family members. "They don't make Comrades like him any more," he said to Edvin and Alice, and to everyone else to whom he extended his hand in sympathy. Even to me, Comr. Pavlenda! Only Katya was left out.

But she screamed: "Me too, me too!" And she grabbed the Secretary by the hand and shook it herself.

While this was going on, they turned on the music. "The March of the Fallen Revolutionaries," for as I found out our Bonek had *fallen.*

The Master Illusionist hitched up his trousers under the jacket of his ceremonial uniform and gave instructions to the pallbearers standing at the door of the hall.

"Comrades," he said to them, "move slowly, with dignity. Watch me! When I move my cap from right to left, you take half a step forward, and when I move it the other way you separate and let the family pass through. Ladies first. Clear?"

"Yes," said one of them, carrying a decoration *for outstanding work.* "But we should have rehearsed it first, Comrade, there should have been a rehearsal."

I closed my eyes. I skipped this ephemeris, and picked

out another one, the one relating to my own death (no date):

I am inside the rabbit hutch. Somebody, probably Edvin, puts his lantern down on the cardboard roof and reaches out his grasping hand toward us.

I start squealing, it is my turn.

Now I realized how one knows the time has come, Comr. Pavlenda: you simply feel a hand passing right down your spine.

Somebody sobbed. It wasn't I. It was Katya.

Eyes wide open once again, I whispered: "What's the matter?"

"I'm sad."

"Why?"

"They are playing such sad music, aren't they."

I covered her mouth with my hand. My left hand. With the right I stroked her hair, her Erna-like hair.

It was a beautiful May day, May 13, Thursday. Through the smoky glass of the wall, smoky light was falling on Bonek.

We rose. Comrade Secretary bowed to the coffin and said to Erna (again, to her!): "Bereaved Comrade, Comrade family members, we have lost a Comrade!"

Here let me cite, Comr. Pavlenda, the sterling qualities of Bonek which we were told would live forever:

(a) His exemplary modesty
(b) The power of his logical mind
(c) His uncompromising strength of character
(d) His faith in the masses

Finally (point *e*), Comr. Secretary turned directly to Uncle with the words: "Bonek, those goals to which you have dedicated your life will not die, for we will faithfully strive to achieve them. This is our solemn promise to you."

Then Kuruc spoke, "for the people's organizations," and said: "Permit me to cite the words of the poet:

"We are self-created law, we are life undaunted,
and unconquerable quest!"

And he went on to recite practically the entire poem. Then he said: "Let us rise, Comrades, and observe a minute of silence in honor of an unforgettable Comrade and a fine human being."

During that minute an airplane flew toward Frankfurt, a Boeing, we could hear and see it through the smoked-glass wall.

Katya whispered: "Uncle, Uncle!"

I tried to silence her, but standing at attention as we were, it was difficult to find her mouth with my hand.

"Uncle, I want to recite something, too. May I?"

"Shush!"

"A little poem. Very sad. About a rooster:

"He's lying in the glade
His feet point at the sky
I fear me he will die."

Somebody sobbed.

Yes, Comr. Pavlenda, it was I. Loudly, pathetically, even Comr. Secretary looked up in surprise to see who it was. If I had applied for a job as mourner, I could have looked forward to quite a career in Chlumec.

. . .

The next thing on the program was the following: three trombonists, the only live musicians present, stepped up before the catafalque, together with the bearers of cushions and the pallbearers. The trombonists lifted their instruments to their lips, the pallbearers reached for Bonek. The "Hymn to Labor" resounded through the hall. They worked hard, Bonek was heavy, during the last years he had gained a lot of weight.

The sliding wall gradually parted, revealing the open-mouthed hearse (purchased by Bonek).

The ceremony was clearly at an end.

As soon as he passed the gate the driver shifted into high gear and hustled Bonek off to Hradek, to the crematorium. One thing Bonek hadn't quite been able to manage was to purchase an oven for Chlumec, and so the ceremonies generally went like this, Comr. Pavlenda: the sliding wall opens, the guests follow the coffin, which is either carried by hired bearers (funerals, 1st class) or they carry it themselves (2nd class), together with the wreaths and flowers, not everything of course, but only as much as fits into the window of the hearse, then the pallbearers slide the deceased into the hearse and pile flowers around him (1st class), the doors are closed and the hearse crawls mournfully along—but only as far as the gate. At that point the driver always steps on the gas as if the deceased had suddenly gotten tired of all that shit, took to his heels, and left the living to fend for themselves.

To show that it was all over, Bellachini stopped at the gate and put on his cap with the black visor. For a few moments he looked sadly after the vanishing hearse, direction Hradek, and then he nodded at me.

I followed him to the office.

"Sign here," he said.

Why me? I looked around, but again there was nobody else.

I reached for the pen, and in return for my signature they gave me all of Bonek's medals and decorations.

Two boxes didn't open. Bellachini excused himself, he must have bent the catch.

I said: "That's all right, Mr. Belohlavek, we'll put everything in order when we get home."

I stuck a few of the loose medals in my pocket.

Item: As I hurried to catch up with my family, who had gone ahead to the cemetery, I jingled on my way.

Olin placed blue lilacs on the grave of his former partner. The lilacs came from the garden, the side of the rabbit hutch with the Vlaciha & Klahn sign.

Olin snickered: "When I die, bury me alongside my partner. You can put the ashes of that jerk Bonek by our feet, and instead of a memorial tablet you can use the sign from the rabbit hutch. That would make a great epitaph:

Here lie
Vlaciha & Klahn
celebrated, well-aged pair of lagers
available only in the finest establishments.

And where will I end up? (Note in explanation to possible question of Comr. Pavlenda). Well, I suppose in the same place. My name will be added to that pair of lagers. Or else I, the time traveler, will become a P.S. to Vostarek; the space traveler.

Now Mirena started sobbing.

She put a yellow narcissus on her husband's grave. And how she wept! It made my heart ache. But I couldn't put my hand to my heart, because a box with a medal *For Victory* was in the way.

As for my epitaph: Chrysostom, Chrononaut.

.   .   .

The next thing that happened that Thursday, May 13th: in the afternoon, Mirena looked at the egger-moth picture over the piano in my room. She went to get some nonmourning clothes for Katya, glanced up at the picture —and departed.

She wanted Erna to come with her, too, but their bodies had already become too separate, Erna was no longer as dirigible as before. "Bye, Grandma!" she said to Mirena. "Bye, Grandma," repeated Katya.

But I was silent. *Grandma* bothered me more than *Uncle*!

"Bye, Klahn woman," I said at last. "Uncle will go and sort some medals." In the words of the slogan—forever and ever, and never more.

.   .   .

Item: I played with Katya.

After we had decorated each other a few times with medals, we sorted the medals according to size and put them away in their cushioned boxes in the cupboard, next to the rose-hip wine. The little girl said: "Why does Bonek need so many cushies? To sleep better?"

(A cushie, Comr. Pavlenda . . . do I have to explain?)

"Sure," I said. "They'll put one under his behind and he'll sleep in comfort."

"But mine is more better," she said. She led me to the room with the piano, where she and Erna were to sleep. At the head of the bed was a small cushion decorated with a duckling cut out of yellow felt. "It's called Janie," she said, lay down, rested her right cheek on it, stuck her thumb in her mouth, and by the time I started stroking her hair she was sound asleep.

I determined that if at all possible I would try to sleep in the same room. Quietly I set up a cot under the window and returned to the kitchen.

There we held a private wake for Vostarek, for Klahn, even for Bonek—but mainly for ourselves, because we were going to die. First we drank some Zernoseky wine, then some awful red brew from Oran, and when that disappeared (Thursdays the Anchor Tavern happens to be closed), Alice brought out last year's rose-hip/dandelion wine. Edvin kept praising it and praising it until it looked as if ammonia alcohol was next. At that point I got up and disappeared in order to make last-minute plans for the sleeping arrangements.

By the light of the street lamp, as it passed through

the partly raised curtain—in that dim, fluctuating light
I saw that the veins on my arms were swollen. From all
that alcohol? No! It was from excitement. With my hands
touching the damask, I counted the rate of my breathing,
I tried to slow down, concentrate my breaths so that in
their almost imperceptible rhythm I could hear another
breath, another sound, the lapping of the tide on which
I was floating, a voyager through time and space, tiny
in all that immensity, a frightened Chrysostom clutching
at the billowing sail to keep the boat from capsizing.
How feverishly I clutched the damask curtain, veins
pounding, waiting for Erna!

At last she came. She did not want to wake me. She
got undressed, and through half-closed lids I photographed her into my soul. She kissed Katya and lay down
next to her, on the couch.

I whispered: "Is that you?"

"Did I wake you? I am sorry."

"I wasn't sleeping, Erna."

"You should be ashamed!"

"Why? You're beautiful. You're the onliest, beautiful-
est girl I've ever had."

"Had?" she corrected.

"I didn't mean it like that."

"How did you mean it?"

"The way it used to be."

"What?"

"The way it used to be between us."

"I don't remember," she whispered almost aloud, and
stretched out her arm alongside Katerina's face on the
pillow with the bird of yellow felt.

"You remember?" I said. "The gosling!"

"*Duckling*. You're talking nonsense!"

I crossed over from the cot to the couch and knelt
alongside Erna. "You won't believe me, but I *really*
wanted only you. It's a fact! Cross my heart!"

"You'll wake Katya!"

"Let me lift you up."

"I'll scream!"

She threatened me with this rhetorical, antiphonal threat, but she would resist only if I faltered. I bent over her to see her more clearly, and my more agile hand, the right, darted under the quilt and touched the entrance (*introitus vaginae*, Comr. Pavlenda). It was already damp, i.e., I felt that beautiful curve inside, arching like a graceful cuff of a dress shirt, and in response to my touch it quivered with the first throb, still faint and distant, but eloquent and mine: here, everywhere, in all women inhabited by me.

Up above, I kissed a mouth, also half parted, also arched. It had to happen, and at last it would.

.   .   .

However,

Oldrich Vlaciha burst in, poked around the room in an alcoholic stupor, stumbled, collapsed on my cot, reeking of ammonia.

My hand, still under the quilt, quickly disengaged. My heart sank. And there was no place for me to put my hand except to my heart. I was furious. I thought of the acrostic which I had once composed for Corporal Klenot's girl Alzbeta:

> *Although your heart may be aching*
> *Love of mine, remember how*
> *Zealously I guard your mem'ry*
> *Bound by our solemn vow.*
> *Evening shifts will soon be over*
> *Time for loving's coming near—*
> *And for joyous mating, dear.*

.   .   .

At just about the same time, our Bonek was dancing. The crematorium in Hradek was old, built to run on coke. A cart would roll up from the incinerator door to the gate of the oven. From the other side, coke dropped down a metal chute, gradually fell through five grates, one after another, until the heat became searing, and then the real dance would begin. At least an hour and a half was needed per kilogram and a half of ashes.

The whores who were supposed to take their last farewell of Bonek didn't come. He had promised to show himself to them, and now it was all over. So the last person to see Uncle was to be the cremator. But he only watched out of habit. He peered through the peephole to see how the oven was doing. Through a disk of dark glass, like the smoked glass used for watching eclipses of the sun, he took a peek at Bonek. And lo: Bonek was dancing. He was writhing to beat the devil. On the next coffin (non-oak) the attendant had placed a bag with a piece of grilled chicken wrapped in foil. Later, when he got hungry, he would warm it up against the oven door. In the meantime he busied himself by sealing a few tins of swept-up bones with a soldering iron.

The tins made a rattling noise.

It was six-thirty in the morning.

Olin was snoring. I could hear him all the way from the kitchen.

17. CLOUDCASTLE

In recalling the poem for Corp. Klenot, I thought of the original uncensored version. You see, Comr. Pavlenda, before Klenot presented the poem to Alzbeta he changed "joyous mating" to "our two souls mating."

I recalled it in the morning, while Erna was having breakfast. Our two souls had mated, but that was all.

She gulped down her food, most likely so that she wouldn't have to talk. I could tell that she was thinking about her train connections to Hradek. I spread some rabbit paté on my bread and said: "Eleven thirty-five."

"Thanks," she gulped. That's how we parted. Forever and ever. And never more.

I waved Katya goodbye. I was standing in the garden. The sun was going down.

The family was trying to wake up Olin. "Olin, get up, the Anchor is all lit up already!" He was rumpled, tousled, sunset-red. He turned to me in one of his turnings: "Jan Chrysostom!"

That's how he always addressed me when he wanted me to pay special attention. An ironic quotation mark.

I answered, in the same vein: "Yes, Uncle dear?"

He said: "Miserable swine!"

And I retorted: "I am innocent."

"You lie! How many times have I told you that you should paint instead. You understand? Next time you get another of your swinish ideas, pick up your brush and you'll become a great artist."

"Thank you, Uncle," I replied, to get his goat, but he

pushed me so hard that I flew into the lilacs, and landed under the Vlaciha & Klahn sign. The branches closed over me, I had trouble getting up.

Thus cornered, I said: "Very well, Olin. I will become an artist, if you insist."

He helped me get free. With his left arm he pushed the foliage out of the way, with his right he helped me to my feet, and we made peace.

· · ·

This shove cleared my head so effectively that henceforth I no longer had any need of a human body to travel through time, but used exclusively Olin's ephemeris or else my own vision, which had become exceptionally keen.

Olin calculated the so-called crumble point of Cepin; in other words, the moment when the atmosphere would finally crumble the Cepin rock completely flat. His calculation was based on the premise that every one hundred years the Vazoom lost 10 cubic meters of rock to erosion. I took part in the calculations, but I lacked Olin's ability to think so far ahead. "Olin, this isn't for me!" I said. He retorted that there was no doubt about it: if no new mountains were formed in the next fifty million years, Chlumec would become as flat as a pancake.

For me, Comr. Pavlenda, the concept of a crumbled Cepin was useless. It would have necessitated the conclusion that Mr. Vostarek had not really flown over it! No, I would not want to live in such a Chlumec.

And so I showed Olin the snapshot that would appear in the *Chlumec News*. I was going to have my picture published in a newspaper, just like Kuruc with the old battleax. Some fellow had taken the shot in A.D. 1530, for the *Spectaculum Mundi*, and I was just sticking my head through the vault of the sky when he snapped it.

I am attaching the photo because it gives an excellent

idea of my approach as a chrononaut: just a quick peek, that's my speed, and not an iota more than needed!

The town in back of me, Comr. Pavlenda, right behind my shoes, is Chlumec. Brother Sol and Sister Luna need no explanation. But the tree in the middle—that's the tree that grew out of my loins during my dream.

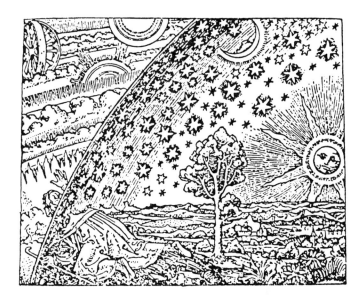

Or I visualized (and painted a picture of it) how those whores came to see Bonek, after all: They hop over just before daybreak, knock on the lid, tap, tap. "Bonek dear, open up, it's us, your little lambs!" "You're wolves," replies Bonek. "My little Melanie and Sofie had far softer voices!" The whores start crying and he recognizes them by their sobs and moans. Joyfully, he opens up. "So you've come after all, girls! You've made me very happy! Now I can die in peace." He puts his head down on the pillow, smiles, lets death bake that smile permanently on his face, and while it is being baked the whores ask him a riddle:

"In her flower bed
A maiden blushes red.
For a lump of coal
She will warm your soul."

"Can you guess the riddle?"

But when he doesn't answer, they shove him in the oven, cover him with a lid like a goose, and baste him with their tears. "Bye-bye, Bonek," they shout. "You'll make a feast for the devil!" One of them turns him over, to make sure he is done on both sides, then she peers through the peephole and lo: Bonek is dancing! "Melanie," Sofie calls to her colleague, "come take a look. My, what a lovely sight!" And the two of them push and shove to get a good look at Bonek.

· · ·

Surely, Comr. Pavlenda, you must have guessed the riddle by now! No? The blushing maiden is fire! *Fire!*

· · ·

Bastis

Fire appeared to me also, in a dream. It burned clear and steady, without anything shriveling or writhing à la Bonek. According to Olin's interpretation, this meant happiness. Actually, *harmony*, to stay with the terminology used by my sole remaining uncle, who did not assign any particular value to the happiness/unhappiness configuration but concerned himself only with harmonic or discordant elements. I follow Olin's lead in this, although privately I continue to believe in happiness.

I have the feeling that at certain times I have indeed been happy, Comr. Pavlenda, and I beg you to include this piece of information under Question No. 8, *State of Health.*

I was coming back from Hradek (not from seeing Erna, that had ended long before), no, it was just a business trip, in the early spring, they were still using stoves to heat the cars just as they had done years before when I used to go by train to my piano lessons. Smoke was coming out of the chimney that stuck through the roof of the car. In Jiven a fellow got on, sat down next to me, placed a big candy box on his knees, a three-tiered box of Dianthus candy made in Chlumec (we are now exporting it to the whole world, Bonek would be proud!). The box had holes in the lid and through these holes I could see a pair of blinking hazel eyes. I asked him what it was, and he replied: "A kitten." "For whom?" "For anybody who wants it." "Would you give to me?" "I will give it to the first person who asks for it.'

I said that I was the first.

He untied the box, and discarnationed the lid. The kitten inside was yellow, just the color I had imagined Fatima to be. I lifted my head, and the fellow was gone. Vanished . . .

He must have gotten off. The train started up and the people who had gotten off were on the other side of the track. I could not see them, could give no further information. I stroked the kitten. It meowed and undulated under my hand. And then it left its bed of fluffy flannel at the bottom of the box and scrambled out of its Dianthus home.

.   .   .

Item: I returned to Chlumec with the kitten next to my heart. It peered out of my coat, out of my breast pocket. Its behind warmed me. I felt the warmth and smiled, and then I felt dampness but I continued to smile.

"De-stink yourself," said Olin, and examined my find. He asked what the fellow in the train looked like. But I was quite unable to describe him.

"That fits," he said.

I didn't know what fitted with what, Comr. Pavlenda; i.e., I busied myself arranging a den for the kitten. I dug up a photo-developer can to serve as a mini-toilet.

Then we went overboard, Olin & I. Olin wanted us to go into the cat-breeding business and to found a breeding station to be known as *Bastis* (at Mr. Vlaciha's old place, in Chlumec). We were just being silly.

But the kitten was doing fine. We named it Ma Fille, but we actually called it Mafia or Mafinka.

It kept climbing up on Alice's ficus tree, and whenever I shouted "down," Olin shushed me.

When Mafinka scrambled down, she knocked off one leaf after another; they kept falling like the leaves in my painting "The Destruction of Chlumec." I was furious, but Olin was all the more friendly to Mafinka. She snuggled up to him and he said: "You see, there's a cat for you! A cat will never make friends with an unworthy person!"

And so I, too, became trapped in pet care. I wiped the little asshole with a piece of cloth dipped in chamomile water, I worried because Mafinka seemed cross-eyed.

"Olin," I said anxiously, my finger in front of the kitten, "don't you think its eyes are crossed?"

Olin, too, placed his finger close to Mafinka's eyes. It almost seemed to me that the finger was trembling. He was nervous. A cross-eyed specimen would ruin our plan to create a new breed for the Fédération Internationale Féline d'Europe.

Olin thought the time had come to look for a tomcat. I thought that our kitten was still too young. However, Olin was convinced—and kept insisting—that one should start as early as possible, as soon as a *uter* was available. (A *uter*, Comr. Pavlenda, in the terminology of O.V., was a special type of womb; *viz.*, below).

"It seems a pity," I said.

"That's because you don't understand the essence of happiness."

"Perhaps you mean harmony," I corrected him.

"Idiot," he said. "Harmony only concerns those who have already been born. Happiness involves the *unborn!*"

"What? They already exist?"

He measured me from head to foot with contempt.

A uter, Comr. Pavlenda, thus seems to be an incubator of happiness.

.　.　.

The harmonic forces began to outweigh the dissonant ones. Olin stopped working in the woods and got a job teaching English in the language school that had just opened. After Bonek's demise, Kuruc became the new Commander of Chlumec. He liked foreign languages. And, ensconced behind Hatus's desk, he began to like people, too. One day he got together with Olin in the Anchor wine cellar (i.e., at Chiang Kai-shek's) and told Uncle that Cepin lager was an excellent brew. Soon Edvin, too, put away his ax and returned to those eight women in the wrapping department of the United Chocolate Works, and once again the conveyer belt conveyed to him not only cooling bars of chocolate but also their loving, longing glances. Oh yes, still!

.　.　.

Item: Even I realized that I should devote myself to some creative form of work (a propos my occupation: I was more of a gardener than an architect. I managed to beautify neither flowers nor spaces, and I accomplished little beyond seeing to it that flowers kept dying in stages, so that some were always in bloom). In brief, I returned to the spot where the forest was opened and shut and I decided to paint a huge canvas. But when I reached the spot and set up my equipment, I looked down into the ravine and saw that the task was beyond my strength. The ravine was actually a triangle bounding a square of woods, i.e., the landscape was like the symbol of a

squared circle and at the same time a great eye of God
staring from the sign of the Holy Trinity. How could I
paint such a vision, still haunted by Partyzan and Soldier
gazing into a sunset over my shoulder? They watched my
canvas, they wanted to know if I was still capable of the
beautiful kind of work I had done when I painted them.

And so I put away my paints and brushes and hurried
back to Chlumec to raise cats.

At home I searched for the pictures which I had
painted with my original vision: "The Destruction of
Chlumec," Erna, Cepin. And especially Vostarek's moths
and flight scenes. I asked fellow townspeople to look for
them in their closets and attics. I examined these pictures,
studied them, while wiping crust out of hazel feline eyes,
using the chamomile water I had formerly employed for
cleaning the animal's other end. I made those eyes light
up, so that I could paint them and by their reflection
light up my own.

But the cat kept making a mess. I would enter the
room where one pair of her eyes was drying on the table
near the window, and catch her walking over them and
smudging the wet paint. I clapped my hands, the frightened cat jumped on the piano and turned it into an
instrument of colors. Her paws made a harmonic progres-
sion from left to right. But her attack on the keyboard
was far more advanced than mine used to be when I
practiced the Bayer method. I shouted again. Again, she
took fright and for a change jumped on the curtain. She
caught hold of it with her colored paws and climbed to
the top of the curtain rod. There I could not reach her,
I merely shot angry glances at her from below.

"Alice," I called to Mother. "Come and tell me whether
I'm seeing things!"

Mother wrung her hands. "What do you mean? The
mess?"

"No," I said. "Look at that black dot up there" (up

near the ceiling, Comr. Pavlenda). "Doesn't it seem to you that she has balls?"

"Yes, it looks that way," said Mother.

"Well, that's quite a blow," I laughed, and shouted: "Olin, Olin, come and see what's happened to your uter!"

That afternoon Olin told me: "Yes, she's a tomcat. Can't be helped. We have a Mafius. He'll be a sire."

"But what about happiness," I asked. "Where is it now?"

"Up shit creek," said Olin darkly.

·   ·   ·

Item: Olin slinked off to Chiang Kai-shek's, full of sorrow. He lifted his head and saw Kuruc who was drinking at another table.

"What's the matter, Mr. Vlaciha?" asked Kuruc.

"Ah, shit!" replied Uncle.

"You're sad," said the Commander of Chlumec.

"No, I am not," answered Olin.

"Yes, you are; that's one thing I can always tell."

But Olin said: "Between us linguists" (i.e., between a French teacher and an English teacher, Comr. Pavlenda), "what the fuck business is it of yours? *Merde!*"

And the Commander of Chlumec retorted without getting upset, for these were strange times: "Just between us—you can't see as far as the tip of your nose."

Olin crossed his eyes.

Kuruc said: "You know, you could easily establish your innocence."

Olin shifted his eyes from the tip of his nose back to Kuruc: "What do you mean?"

"You just sign a piece of paper claiming damages."

"And then?"

"You'll pick up a nice piece of change. And you'll be able to brew your beer again."

Olin was dubious.

"Not privately. But almost. In *association* with other breweries," the commander explained. "Locally, here in Cepin. You understand?"

Olin tried to concentrate. He was drunk.

Kuruc smiled in encouragement.

Olin said: "No, I won't buy that, Kuruc. You'd have me locked up again."

Their eyes met over the little table in the dark wine cellar. Then Kuruc said: "*I*, Mr. Vlaciha? What sort of person do you take me for?"

And Olin repeated his suspicion once again, and they kept drinking until both of them turned very, very sad.

. . .

Item: I did two other things. While Olin was out drinking, I obtained my divorce and wrote to small-animal breeders. "Divorce" implies that I had been married, and that's true. I had a lilac wife, who wore cute little lilac dresses. Very affectionate, had me in tears. But she was hard to stroke and kept me from more interesting adventures. Then I wrote to the breeders regarding the cat; i.e., to be exact, I wrote to J. Skurata of the Feline Commission regarding a uter for Mafius, since he had stopped being Mafinka. If we were going to found a breeding station we had to start somewhere.

Olin came back from Chiang Kai-shek's, and he, too, was about to write. It was supposed to be a memorandum about the brewing of light Cepin beer. But also about his innocence, as suggested by Kuruc.

And so Olin sat down to write.

He stroked the cat at the same time. They did everything together. The cat helped him rather than me because cats prefer writing to painting.

Maf, with his plush-soft paws (great image, don't you think, Comr. Pavlenda?), paraded around the house. But as soon as Olin reached for a pen the cat came running to him and shared all of his mental activities.

He showered Olin with hazel sparks from his deep-set eyes until he sensed Uncle's thought. Then he shot out his paw and grasped the idea in midair as if it were an ordinary housefly.

Olin understood and didn't write a single word.

But J. Skurata wrote—and I did a third thing. The letter stated that in the future I should always measure the distance between the anal opening and the sexual opening, whenever I wished to distinguish males from females.

Thus:

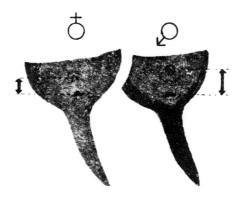

In other words, in the tomcat the distance is greater.

On the basis of Mafius's photograph Mr. Skurata concluded that he was a superb specimen and advised me that in a certain German city, at Fichtenberger St., No. 111/5, lived a certain Juta Teussner von Wolkenschloss (Wolkenschloss or Cloudcastle was the name of a breed as well), who kept an experimental file on sand-colored, short-haired cats with hazel eyes.

I got in touch with her.

But that was *not* the third thing I did—which was to request advice (again of J. Skurata) on how to organize a breeding station and what was the minimum number of members required in order for me to establish a society for the protection of cats.

Skurata answered: ten.

I knew of twelve potential candidates and went around Chlumec gathering signatures.

This is how the Feline Protection Society of Chlumec (F.P.S.C.) came into being, and this was the third thing I did.

.   .   .

Then I began to negotiate with Germany, with the help of Dr. Pleskot, librarian of the city of Chlumec and member of F.P.S.C. (member No. 4).

Allergnädigste Frau Teussner, we wrote, are you interested in Mafius of Bastis with hazel eyes?

But Germany replied:

Sehr geehrter Herr, Herr Kepka: Your letter has *beirrt* (confused) us. Our cat's name is *Fatima von Wolkenschloss*, her father is *Aristotle von Wolkenschloss* and her mother *Turandot vom krummen Turm*, so I fear we may not be able to help you.

Fortunately, the exhibition photo of Fatima also included her mistress. Long blond tresses flowed down her cablestitched sweater; her hair covered much of the face, but this gave her face even greater emphasis; Fatima von Wolkenschloss, her front paws crossed and her head nestling under the bosom of Jutta von Teussner, glowed bright yellow against the dark background of the sweater; the mistress's hand kept out of the way so as not to cast a shadow over the glistening fur; the hand with its long, pianist's fingers rested on Jutta's knee; she was seated in the winner's chair, against a copper-colored background.

I saw that she was no Brunhilde but a real Krasavitsa, a shapely beauty.

Item: I borrowed a cablestitched sweater, sat down in the grass under our apricot tree, Mafius in my lap, and sent the resulting photo to Fichtenberger St., No. 111/5.

But before sending it I scented it: I carried it for a certain period of time (precisely measured!) in my breast pocket.

"Roooaaa, roooaaa," growled Mafius, in a voice he had not used before.

"*Lieber Herr Kepka*," answered Jutta, "I've weighed the risks and I believe I could come to see you." (Following developments in Chlumec . . . most interesting . . . keeping fingers crossed.)

I smiled.

Mafius spoke again in his tone of muffled lament. He sprayed a tomcat odor, a penetrating smell emanated from his paws (the signal smell), and next to my foot he deposited a gold coin of urine.

A gold *Solidus Mafensis*.

Hard currency, Comr. Pavlenda! Even now, after so many years, whenever a cat visits my house she carefully sniffs the spot.

Then (but still in that same ephemeris) the Chairlady of F.P.S.C., Alice Kepka (member No. 1) said to me: "Here is something for that stinker of yours!" And she handed me a leash of black leather, her own handiwork. On top, it was decorated with gold thread, and the underside was felted for comfort. I attached an F.P.S.C. ribbon (my own handiwork) and strode downtown like Kaspar Trubac with his cani-balized dog.

I passed my fellow Czechs, all of them as Czech as soup ladles—healthy red noses, close-cropped noggins, yet nobody smirked or complained. Of course, all this was still happening *in ephemeris*.

Lovely day.

When I reached the Mint House I whistled to Dr. Pleskot. I wanted him to stop writing and translate for me. He shouted: Just one more sentence!

And he wrote: "Behold! A mystical unity, a realization which is partly infantile but at the same time connected with a foretaste of a golden age of identification of creator and creation: that is the PLEASURE PARK OF THE IMAGINATION which opens before our eyes."

He was preparing a new exhibit devoted to Vincent Vostarek, and this passage was for the catalogue.

Once the catalogue was completed, the good doctor planned to turn to the *History of Chlumec*, Vol. VII, and Addenda. It would contain all the material which Rosin had been unable to finish and had left in the form of notes in his file boxes. In addition, there would also be some of Dr. Pleskot's own material, of which he had already a full cabinet.

Perhaps the book would describe how we descend to the black steed's rails as twilight is settling over Chlumec, a luminescent summer twilight as lovely as if it made a special effort to show itself off. And a photo of the express train pulling into the station, and out of the car emerges a cage shaped like a model-railroad tunnel, and pasted on its side is the label: TENERO COME IL RICORDO

A tiny padlock swings to and fro and jingles against the cage as Jutta von Cloudcastle gets off the train.

All the way at the bottom of the page there would be a snapshot of Mafius, rubbing against my trouser leg, eyes half shut and tail lifted high in the air like the letter *J* turned upside down, which stands for *joy*.

. . .

More of the History of Chlumec, Vol. VIII (thesis)

We put her up at the Anchor, in Room No. 7. The key to her door was weighted with something resembling a pear or a mouth gag. The moon was full, still in that same ephemeris.

I took the cat's house and carried it to Jutta's room on the first floor, the window of which looked out on a cliff. There I said, in accordance with p. 23 of *German Self-Taught:* "*Hier ist der Schlüssel.*" And Jutta, conforming to the same lesson, replied: "*Danke.*"

The next sentence in the book was: "*Sie können auch den Lift benutzen.*" I hesitated, because the Anchor has no elevator.

Jutta kept smiling.

The cat's house rested on a luggage cot. I stepped closer. Jutta took a tiny key off her bracelet and unlocked the cage.

"*Guten Tag,*" I said (I knew that, too).

Fatima stepped out.

She stretched herself, jumped on the table, then on the floor. She wore a collar like her mistress, velvet embroidered with the initials F.v.W.

I peeked into her house. It was upholstered in green velvet. When Jutta saw that I was pleased, she reached into another suitcase and pulled out two blue Meissen plates. For the cat's food.

On the inside of the open suitcase lid hung medals, ribbons, and rosettes honoring Cloudcastle. Deutscher Edelkatzenzüchterverband, Madison Cat Club, and cat lovers of many lands united to pronounce Wolkenschloss *vorzüglich*, excellent, *meilleur*, and best in show.

Jutta *Edelkatzenzüchterin* stood proudly by. Her eyes shone dark blue. J. Skurata would classify them as Siamese, breed 13b.

Item: My interpreters arrived on the scene, namely Dr. Pleskot and Flying Officer Vlaciha. Fatima von Wolkenschloss snuggled against me, I held her in my outstretched arms and she licked the underarm of my cable-knit sweater.

Dr. Pleskot said: "*Hitz, mitz* (i.e., chi-chi-chi, Comr. Pavlenda), and then he spoke from Chapter 8, *German*

Self-Taught (Travel by Train). After that, he passed on to Chapter 11 (Food and Drink). At that point Jutta set out the two Meissen plates (*tsvoh Meisna shahlen*) and filled them with hazelnuts.

We feted Jutta with a skewered roast served on an oak plate. It was at Chiang Kai-shek's. The juice of the meat trickled into the little trough at the edge of the plate. Jutta ate with her hands; she was glad to be here.

We enjoyed being with her, too.

Dr. Pleskot explained the *History of Chlumec*, Vol. VII. Jutta nodded, *fershtay, fershtay*, but it was a difficult subject and she didn't really *fershtay* a thing.

But it was nice of her, in a way, to pretend.

That's what Olin said. He lifted his glass against the vaulted ceiling until the wine pearled his face red. He added: "For her, we're just a tribe of Hottentots."

"She's got it made," said Dr. Pleskot.

"That she has," agreed Olin.

Then they lapsed into silence and mourned over their lives.

I felt sorry for them and so I offered to explain things to Jutta: "*Kookmahl*, look here." I waved my hand in the direction of J. Carek, Jr., Doctor of Law, in the next box (he, too, was a founder of sorts, Comr. Pavlenda: he snuggled up to high-school girls and promised to decorate their rear ends with bunny tails as soon as he became Chairman of the Chlumec Playboy Club). "*Kookmahl*, Jutta, *morgan, morgan, Meisna shahlen!*"

Jutta took a swig from the wineglass. "Ja."

I saw the rivulets of wine inside the glass converge toward her mouth.

Item: I bewailed the past. "*Sheiss ist kaput.*"

She broke into guffaws.

Item: I greeted the future. "*Gehma Katzen machen!*"

And Jutta herself added: "*Hitz, mitz, alles gut! Es reimt sich!*" And she swayed back and forth the way the

Krauts do when they are drinking, and although this ziggy-zagging normally seems stupid to me, now I rocked from one half of my ass to the other and ziggy-zagged and hitzmitzed and sang at the top of my voice:

> *"Morgan Meisna shahlen*
> *Sheiss ist kaput*
> *Gehma Katzen machen*
> *Hitz, mitz, alles goot!"*

"You see"—I pointed at my interpreters, who were slowly drifting away from me—"they understand!"

. . .

By the way, Comr. Pavlenda, did you realize that all the sounds which animals make during mating are actually voices, oral sounds? In other words, it isn't music, as I used to think (*viz.*, color piano), but song. I must therefore revise some of my earlier statements regarding my achievements. Only after Fatima von Wolkenschloss rose up and allowed herself to be pursued, i.e., only after she began dancing her retreat, was Mafius allowed to bite her neck. I thus lost some of my self-admiration, even as far as the giving is concerned. Probably it is basically they who do the giving.

"Rooaaa!"

And then I said (still in the ephemeris): "Chiang, champagne! Our cat is knocked up!"

"*Shampanya*," Jutta waved her arms, because she loved the wine.

"Chimpanya," I corrected her, because it was time for monkeyshines.

But Jutta understood differently: "*Für Schimpanzen!*" She clapped her hands. "*Aus Schimpania!*"

"*Ja*," I agreed.

And Chiang Kai-shek brought it over and asked what happened to Olin and the doctor. He winked at me like a sly pig. I pointed at J. Carek, Jr., Doctor of Law, in the next booth, and said: "That old smoothie is here again. In our honor you will fire a salute and pop a champagne cork right in his eye."

Chiang took careful aim, but the cork flew off in an entirely different direction, rose from the launching pad, and soared toward some planet. Probably Venus, judging by the gravitational pull exerted on me by the smooth furry creature sitting next to me. "I'm fond of you," I said to her. "Sail your face toward me like a kite in autumn, I will put it on like a mask and look deep inside your soul."

"*Ja*," retorted Jutta.

(No matter what she said, it made sense.)

On the lip of my mask (whose lip was it?) appeared a drop of blood. I licked it off.

And then I pursued her until I was caught under the mirror in room No. 7.

Fatima von Wolkenschloss sat on a tasseled pillow, after Mafius had injected her, a full moon in each of her eyes, a third in the glass panel behind her, and the fourth —the real one—behind the open window.

That cat saw everything. She was a seeress.

But Jutta was moist, the way I love it. I love all of them when they are moist like that. I love to lie underneath them; no need to act the stronger one. To feel the contractions. To see the gooseflesh on the breasts and to stroke it. To watch the grimaces, so similar to St. Barbora's under the outthrust sword.

Tenero come il ricordo.

She rested, a pillow between her legs, catching the last waves. Perhaps she was trying to hide the scars on her belly, not wanting me to see them. But I had noticed them right at the start, and so I ran over them with my fingertips until she herself began to smile. I said to her (but in Czech): "Weren't we great together?

The way your insides moved—it was like a birth! I swear!
Even your breath smells of birth!"

.   .   .

Item: I got up and ran to Fatima's castle, that suitcase
with honors, and I decorated Jutta. For her hair, a
ribbon from the Madison Cat Club; for her breasts,
meilleur from Paris; for her belly, *best in show*; and in
her lap I placed a flag from the Deutscher Edelkatzenzüchterverband. That last word is terribly long, Comr.
Pavlenda, terribly long, and after pronouncing it I grew
stiffer and stiffer and became rooted to the spot.

And so I have remained.

"They're invading us," said O. Vlaciha, getting off his bike at Forestry Administration Hut No. 2, in the Moran forest, where some friends had wangled a room for me over the summer so that I could paint in peace.

I was just shaving. "What did you say?" I asked, holding the buzzing shaver at arm's length. "Who?"

"The Turks, who else," he replied, and I said: "You're joking!"

"Take a look!"

I pulled up the blinds and saw a row of bugs crawling down the road from Hradek and Svetlice toward Chlumec. They kept crawling, tanks and more tanks, antennae, feelers, suckers, leaving behind smelly puffs of gas, noiseless because they were so far away.

"It can't be true," I said.

And Olin said: "Shut it off."

As if it were a TV program that could be turned off.

"What are we going to do?"

He shrugged. He was worn out, having cycled up the long hill on my bike. He sat down on the edge of my bed. "Those jerks have occupied the post office. I couldn't call you."

"What's today's date?" I asked.

.   .   .

Item: O.V. gave me the coordinates of this ephemeris.

"Shit," I said. "A date to remember, isn't it."

Olin said: "The bells of St. Barbora's are ringing."

I said: "I must get dressed."

Up to that point I was naked, with a dangling member (i.e., tail) that looked strangely ahistorical.

．　．　．

Item: We descended to Chlumec, which had been conquered. Olin sat on the handlebars and we rattled down the hill. In the sky whirred a helicopter scattering leaflets over the steeple of St. Barbora's. The two bells were still ringing: Jakub and the Virgin. The former protects against storms and tempests: A FULGURE ET TEMPESTAE LIBERA NOS DOMINE MDCLXXXII. The latter against death: IANUA COELI ORA PRO NOBIS!

．　．　．

Then I reached Jost Square, and that had been conquered, too. Machine guns were set up at the foot of the Mint House, aiming in the direction of the Pleasure Park of the Imagination.

On Monday there was to have been a gala opening. The poster was my handiwork. Inside there was an exhibit of all the extant paintings of Vincent Vostarek. My puppets were also on exhibit: Bellengardo, Bonecrusher, Cutthroat, and all the rest.

Bellengardo stood behind the moat of well-fortified Slakenvald Castle, whereas Dr. Pleskot was standing unprotected in front of the Mint House, alongside those machine guns, and he was trying to explain to the machine-gunner the *History of Chlumec*, Vol. VII.

A tough assignment. The soldier nodded: *Ya znayua, znayu,* but in reality he understood nothing.

I arrived on the scene and offered my services. It was 9:45, still in the ephemeris. I said:

> *"Morgan Meisna shahlen*
> *Sheiss ist kaput*
> *Gehma Katzen machen*
> *Hitz, mitz, alles goot."*

Item: The soldier said: *"Ya znayu, da, da."*

But Dr. Pleskot lost his patience and forgot the soldier was Slavic, too. *"Hovno znayesh,* you know shit!" he burst out. The soldier lifted his automatic and said to Dr. Pleskot: *"Ty govno!"* and shoved him back into that Pleasure Park of the Imagination.

Thirty-three citizens of the town of Chlumec witnessed this scene, including three members of F.P.S.C., and six hundred days later one of them lodged an official complaint.

Now, however, all the citizens contented themselves with derisive whistling at that soldier and also at his colleagues, who were clustered around the Marian Column, drinking water from the fountain.

They were bone-weary, dirty, and they were in no mood for whistling. One of them, Crut Akim Petrovic, fired a salvo in the air, direction Town Hall, and shot the vintner's knife out of Saturn's hand.

Times goe by Turnes.

The citizens of Chlumec, as Czech as soup ladles, with healthy red Czech noses and close-cropped noggins, scattered.

I rushed to the Mint House to see Dr. Pleskot. "Shouldn't we put those pictures away in some safe place, Doctor?"

But he paid no attention to me, he kept staring out of the Renaissance window.

Bellengardo and Bonecrusher hung by his side, Vincent Vostarek was flying overhead in a balloon. The firing stopped.

I followed Pleskot's eyes. Down in the square Mrs. Kosina, F.P.S.C. member No. 7, lay motionless on the pavement.

"Dead?" I whispered.

Pleskot turned to me in an Olin-like turning, but in contrast to Olin he had tears in his eyes. He said: "No. She just stumbled."

Item: I took my Bonecrusher, Bellengardo *et al.*,

packed them in the suitcase which I had brought for this purpose, and set out for home.

A group of soldiers guarded the bridge. A tank was blocking the roadway, and the tank had a diagonal stripe to distinguish it from Czech tanks. (I still have to retouch all the pictures which I painted for Mikit, Comr. Pavlenda, because the white stripe is missing.)

A guard stopped me and asked what I was carrying.

He cut open Bonecrusher's belly to see if anything was hidden there. I reached out to get my suitcase back, but two other soldiers reached out for me first, spun me around—direction Hradek—prodded me in the back with their rifle butts to make me gasp and jump. Then they shot me dead.

They shot me full of holes. But I kept walking. Even with bullets plopping out of little holes in my body. I was light as air. Back inside Alice. I glanced at my watch to see the precise time of my death.

It was 10:57, precisely as per ephemeris.

How did you figure that, Olin? My death was in a totally different place! All the way *over there*! I pointed to it. Cunning as he is, he didn't answer me.

.   .   .

Item: I looked down at Chlumec from the air and saw myself standing on the Red Army bridge, minus suitcase but alive and scared.

Eventually I calmed down. Then a car with a white stripe drove up to the Forestry House, disgorged a captain and two sergeants, who walked through the hut and the little room with the lowered blind. They pulled up the blind and saw that the house was located in a strategic spot.

Then they saw my electric shaver, my Prussian blue and cadmium white and all my other equipment.

One of the corporals plugged in the shaver and the motor began to buzz.

The way they made themselves at home & set up their Cyrillic typewriter, it was clear they had come to stay.

The one looking through field glasses was Commander of Chlumec. The setting sun illuminated his face and . . . but I had already painted all that before. His field glasses swept the landscape from St. Barbora to the Hatus works, and he established curfew hours for the town—again the old *Ausnahmenzustand* (martial law).

Another Commander of Chlumec, Kuruc, sat in Town Hall behind Hatus's desk, in the room with the big windows over which Saturn's knife had once reigned, and wondered who was the real commander of the town, and where he was located.

It must have been past 2000 hours; the gnome on the sundial no longer cast a shadow. The words of the inscription were intact; the shell had demolished only Saturn's right hand.

· · ·

Item: At dusk Kuruc saw two reflector beams crossing over the Zdar forestry headquarters in the form of a great X in the sky. He took that as a signal. So that's where they are, he said to himself, left Town Hall by the rear entrance, crossed the square, and walked into the Mint House. There, in the hall, stood the bicycle which Olin and I had been riding a short while back. He confiscated it and pedaled out to the army encampment.

He was wearing a white tablecloth from the coffee table in his office; i.e., a white flag of truth. It was wrapped around his body, concealed under his jacket. He had varicose veins and groaned as he pedaled. He panted up the hill, panted up to the guard propped against a tree, asleep, wrapped in a shabby overcoat.

"*Tovarish*," said Shorty, the linguist. He coughed. and

when even that failed to rouse the soldier he rang two short rings on my four-leaf-clover bell.

The guard awoke and, startled out of sleep, fired half the load of his automatic into Shorty.

Times goe by Turnes.

The guard had no sooner opened fire than the other soldiers began shooting too, salvos and individual shots and rockets, and it was a great show.

Out of sheer habit my dad ran to the rabbit hutch, and only when he got there did he realize that it was now a cat-breeding hutch. He turned on his flashlight to see what Mafius von Bastis was doing, but the cat had disappeared.

The captain, too, the one with field glasses, turned on his flashlight. His name was Chochlakov and he shone the beam of his light on Kuruc and on the bicycle and then back again on that flag of truce, now red, draped around the chopped meat of Kuruc. His body was lying on a slope, flat on its back, the undamaged head facing downward, toward Chlumec. His blood, too, flowed in the same direction; i.e., toward Chlumec.

The blood, too, Comr. Pavlenda!

But you know, I promised you that I would kill Kuruc someday, and now, you see, I've kept my word.

.   .   .

They buried him, still in the ephemeris. Quickly, secretly; as is done in cases of unfortunate mistakes.

Then they bought white paint and whitewashed the writing on the walls. Housecleaning everywhere. Bonek's sprinkler truck was brought up to rinse away whatever was flushable by water: ashes, potsherds, dust & St. Barbora's hair.

The sanitation truck drove down the avenue to Jost Square, circled the Marian Column, and sprinkled in the direction of the Pleasure Park of the Imagination. A poster was in the way, and so it had to come down, too. Everything was flushed down the sewer at the corner of Seminary Street.

I was headed in that direction, too, and as usual I superstitiously made a detour of the sewer and took the long way round via the Anchor, passing Chiang Kai-shek's entrance, where a flag still flew over the door. Olin was standing there, bottle in hand. He was watching all that housecleaning. He told me to get a bottle for myself, and so I walked in the Chiang (F.P.S.C. member No. 8) gave me one on the house.

At that point I notified Olin that Mafius had disappeared.

Olin stiffened and then silently pointed at injured Saturn on the Town Hall façade.

I retorted that we had miscalculated the cat's ascendent. Olin, however, stared at the cobblestones of Jost's pavement shaped like cats' heads—the only monument to Mafius in Chlumec—and said: "You idiot, he took to the hills!"

I accepted this opinion.

.   .   .

Bonek's sprinkler passed by and I felt its tiny droplets misting my nostrils.

The driver of the truck was F.P.S.C. member No. 12. Olin hailed him and invited him to take a drink. They drank, sharing the bottle, and then Olin asked him to turn on the front sprinkler heads. He laid a hundred-crown note on the orange fender of the truck. The man refused to take the money, however, saying that he would be glad to oblige a fellow F.P.S.C. member.

He climbed into the cab, pulled a lever, and the machine's perforated snout started to spray Uncle. Olin sat on the ground enjoying the shower.

He called to me to try it, too.

I agreed, sat down next to him, and in a moment I was

sopping wet, water streamed down my back, my jacket clung to my body, my pants clung to my thighs, and when I stamped my heel a geyser shot out of my shoe and splashed the back of my knee.

I turned to Olin and shouted over the din that it was a pity, all the same.

"What are you talking about?" he shouted back.

"The cat's disappearance."

"Take it easy, Vazoom," he replied, covering the neck of the bottle with his palm to keep out the water.

. . . .

Item: He drank up and I, too, leaned out of the waterfall to take a swig, and perhaps it looked as if I were crying but that was only a professional trick, like raindrops falling in one's eyes, mixing human fluids with heavenly fluids, making tears more copious or else concealing them altogether.

But Olin looked at me as if he suspected me of bawling, after all, and commanded: "Take it easy, don't shit in your pants."

I retorted that I had already taken care of that on the Red Army bridge.

And Olin said: "But you must admit it's been a lovely binge."

I asked what he was referring to.

And he replied: "Well, this . . . and everything."

I got a package. Third-class mail, but tied with a green ribbon, and I felt again the droplet of blood on my lip, memory of Room No. 7.

The package contained a letter from Jutta von Wolkenschloss, inviting me to come to see her. *Now, especially*! To make sure I found the place, she enclosed a detailed drawing of how to get to Fichtenbergerstrasse 111/5. An arrow pointed at Jutta's house, and underneath she wrote: "*Maf mit!*"

She also sent some gardening magazines which she had promised me when she learned that I was really a Gartenbautechniker and not the mere Gartenmacher I claimed to be. But on the very top of the package lay a magazine called *Friedhof*, dealing with the landscaping of cemeteries, and this startled me.

With my propensity for seeing everything as a sign, I kept hesitating, until the cage dropped and there was no way out.

The tenth house, PEREGRINATIONES, had darkened.

Well, and then I had a dream about a homunculus, about my walking into a pharmacy where a faceless woman sold *Pharmakon athanasias* in a little green bottle, and as soon as I saw it I wanted to drink it. I bought a bottle. They sold it for a song—i.e., to be precise, for three crowns sixty—and I always paid with a hundred-crown note, so that the faceless woman always took forever giving me my change, and even before I got the change I pulled out the stopper, the bottle stank of fish oil, but I closed my eyes and drank until I almost swallowed the homunculus inside, who was also J.Ch.K. but gesticulating wildly for me to spare him.

Yet at the same time I felt the fear of the homunculus, I also felt the fear of being devoured, and I awoke.

And then I went to see Oldrich Vlaciha, whose face was beginning to show liver spots but who kept on drinking all the same, and I asked O.V. over a table at Chiang's what he thought about all that.

He was my dream interpreter, etc., as I had already mentioned.

Now he believed that Chlumec was making me nervous because I was on the list of undesirable citizens. He pointed out that my outlook was not going to improve until I learned the headstand, the queen of all the asanas, and underwent a transformation to higher consciousness.

"The invisible is real," he said, "the visible is delusion."

Item: I tried that asana, that inverted yoga pose; I toppled over and injured a tendon above my heel (*tendo Achillis*), for a moment I was blinded by the pain but gradually my sight cleared and a solar city began to emerge, *civitàs solis*, non-Chlumec, and I started to paint. I also wrote a meditation on this city. Its history was characterized by the fact that its lousy historical periods balanced the good ones.

In the meantime, according to the chronoscope, I successively passed through the vocations of undertaker, lifeguard, dealer in antiquities (my own), artisan, and maker of leather jewelry—everything that Olin had calculated in order to conceal the meaning of my life and to keep it unclear.

I also became a well-driller. That was the dead end as far as Chlumec was concerned; there was nowhere else to go.

.   .   .

Item: I humbled myself and went to see Bonek, my uncle, etc., as I noted earlier, in order to have him explain to me the meaning of all this. And to give me a break.

I went to see him during his office hours (from 14:00 to 17:00, every Wednesday). He was sitting behind Mr. Hatus's old desk, somewhat gaunt-looking but otherwise quite alert.

The Prague specialist had managed to make a remarkably faithful replica of the *dens caninus* in Bonek's new dentures. He flashed this tooth at me, but not threateningly. As I came in, I noticed how he kept swallowing those choppers, how he sucked at his dentures as if he were eating them . . . and how he smiled at me with them; i.e., he was not fixing the dentures in place in order to frighten me but in order to be able to talk without lisping.

I said to him: "Bonek, I am glad to see you. What are you doing, old trooper?"

And Bonek said: "As you can see, I am always busy."

He pointed at the piles of papers and folders. I scanned the room and everything seemed exactly the same as I remembered. Except perhaps the lunch package on the radiator near the window. In the old days, while his stomach had still been in good shape, Bonek used to eat out.

I said: "Bonek, that's the hard way to get yourself a hot lunch."

Bonek answered: "I keep it there so it doesn't get cold. A chicken, wrapped in foil. That's the only thing I can stomach these days."

He went to the window, spread out the foil, broke off a piece of the breast, and offered it to me: "Would you like some roast chicken?"

I said: "It must be cold," but he retorted that it was just right.

We began to quarrel and I quite forgot the reason for my visit. I was furious with myself, and before I collected my wits, I found myself out in the hall. Perhaps Bonek wanted it that way. Perhaps he had deliberately picked a quarrel to keep me from bringing up my business.

I peeked through the keyhole to see his expression.

He was still sitting behind the Hatus desk, his teeth were out, and with that empty maw, those toothless gums, he was smiling at the chicken, while his hands held the dentures and busily ground the meat into patties.

I also have high hopes of getting a job as flag and poster designer in the enterprise Granit in the city of Prague (i.e., here and not in Chlumec), on the 19th of September.

Your blue-green eyes, Comr. Pavlenda, and your penciled remark DO NOT CROSS OUT seem promising.

I will supply flags, banners, posters, and panels, on behalf of your organization, to all enterprises, plants, and offices.

And I will prepare slogans, proclaiming who is surging ahead toward what and who is marching hand in hand with whom.

I am good at that.

You want a sample of my work and you ask whether I would be able to handle something like *this*. You unroll a poster and ask me what I think of it.

"Looks like a slightly retouched Garamond," I say, and you ask: "What's that?"

"A kind of typeface."

Item: You pointed out that you were asking about the content of the poster, not its form.

"It is a slogan," I add to my previous testimony. But you explain that it is the Sixth Commandment—no, the Sixth *Norm*, taken from *Ten Norms of Socialist Morality*.

"Of course," I say. "Guard and Protect the People's Property."

You laugh and say: "Like: Thou Shalt Not Commit Adultery."

You roar with laughter, so that I wonder whether you're not making fun of me.

Then you ask: "Would you be capable of producing something like this?"

And I answer: "Certainly."

Item: As a test assignment, you ask me to bring you a rendition of the Ninth Norm. I write it down in my notebook:

LIVE A CLEAN, ORDERLY LIFE
AND HONOR YOUR FAMILY!

.   .   .

Or else I am in Super-Alice, i.e., inside Alice, with Alice. Here I have nothing to fear, for my death is over and done with.

Mother is at the oven making potato pancakes and spreading melted butter on them with a goose feather. We are all there (HONOR YOUR FAMILY!), Edvin and Mirena & Erna, waiting in line. Mother says (in the midst of buttering, just before she slides another pancake off the spatula into my palm, so hot that I have to juggle it from one hand to the other): "Jan Chrysostom, are you cheating again? Wait your turn!"

"But theirs was thicker!" I protest.

"Never mind that. Everybody gets just one."

"But I love them more than anybody else," I say, and Alice is angry. But I soothe her feelings right away, I tell her that she is the Alicest little Alka, and I also tell her: "Give us a smile! Come on, you're my best girl!"

That disarms her completely. She picks up the next pancake (down in Chlumec, they call them "turnovers"), tosses it at me, I juggle it, and Olin says: "If you're so smart, go to town and see if the Russkies are still there."

That's just like Olin—he drags politics into everything.

To please him, I get ready to go out the gate, not the *orificio externo* described by Dr. Simsa in his *Household Medical Guide*, but the *orificio aeterno*. I am getting ready, I am almost there, when Alice says suddenly, i.e., she stops me: "Jan, they have left. *I am sure of it*. But you'd better not look!"

Erna makes fun of me, says that nosy people age faster—as if it mattered any longer.

.   .   .

At the same time, a certain cat in Fichtenbergerstrasse, No. 111/5, seeks out a quiet & protected corner, warm and free of drafts. She fetches bits of paper and cloth, tears everything into small shreds. A change can be seen in her face: it is drawn, cheekbones stick out, the eyes are big and have a painful expression, so that a sensitive person cannot help but feel sympathy.

Yet cats give birth easily.

I am preparing a poster. Norm No. 9. I am using *display* type, but with yellow lettering on a red background, the Dianthus system! I put it in a folder, and encouraged by your telephone call, Comr. Pavlenda, I feel quite natural and at ease as I prepare to climb the Granit staircase to turn my test assignment over to you personally. I have already reached the first step—both my feet are virtually there—when I hear the guard calling me back to sign in.

And so I come back to the little desk with the book NAME—AFFILIATION—TO SEE—TIME, I fill in everything with the pencil attached to a long spring. The instant I let go of the pencil it shoots out toward the guillotine-like sliding partition next to the guard. He is a type I know inside out, a professional colleague (for I, too, was a guard once).

He reaches for the log book with his hairy hand, hunches over it inside his booth, and reads my entries.

Then he snorts, scans the pigeonholes behind his back, finds an envelope (size A-4), and hands it to me.

It contains my application for employment.

I ask whether it is possible to call Comr. Pavlenda on the phone.

"He is gone," says the man.

"When is he supposed to be back?" I ask stupidly.

"Don't know," answers the man. "Try next week."

"Thanks," I say, and glance through the glass partition at the fellow in the booth, and he is looking back at me, at me, and through me, as if I were but another pane of glass.

"Thanks very much," I say. A degree louder than the first time . . . so loud that my voice resounds through the Granit spaces. But I realize at once that this was improper.

The guard looks at me with his sunken eyes (so sunken that they're actually no longer quite there), and answers in a still louder voice that I am welcome.

I walk out. Perhaps gracefully, perhaps even rather briskly, yet I feel as if my feet were made of lead, I am so tired.

And then it occurs to me that I know who that doorman is.

I take a deep breath, and I am quite certain. I am sure I recognized him: Mikit, the lieutenant.

He is on guard. Good God, good God, I whisper to my frightened self, and cross myself with a great Catholic cross; i.e., with the fingertips of my right hand I touch my forehead and then my breast and then the left shoulder and then the right.

· · ·

February 28, 1974–April 14, 1975

· · ·

> *Narraverunt mihi fabulationes, sed non ut lex tua;*
> *ego autem loquebar de testimoniis tuis*

JIŘÍ GRUŠA was born in Czechoslovakia in 1938. An acclaimed poet, he moved into fiction, writing *The Questionnaire* in 1974 and circulating it in a Samizdat edition of nineteen copies. For this act of "initiating disorder" he was arrested in 1978, imprisoned, and after three months, forced to emigrate. He is now living and writing in West Germany.

PETER KUSSI is a writer and translator who has introduced a number of contemporary Czech authors to American readers, including Milan Kundera and Josef Skvorecky. He teaches at Columbia University in New York.